CW00864196

KYAN GREEN

BATTLES THE MULTIVERSE

Books by Colm Field

Kyan Green and the Infinity Racers

Kyan Green Battles the Multiverse

KYAN GREEN
BATTLES THE MULTIVERSE

COLM FIELD
Illustrated by **DAVID WILKERSON**

BLOOMSBURY
CHILDREN'S BOOKS
LONDON OXFORD NEW YORK NEW DELHI SYDNEY

BLOOMSBURY CHILDREN'S BOOKS
Bloomsbury Publishing Plc
50 Bedford Square, London WC1B 3DP, UK
29 Earlsfort Terrace, Dublin 2, Ireland

BLOOMSBURY, BLOOMSBURY CHILDREN'S BOOKS and the Diana logo
are trademarks of Bloomsbury Publishing Plc

First published in Great Britain in 2024 by Bloomsbury Publishing Plc

Text copyright © Colm Field, 2024
Illustrations copyright © David Wilkerson, 2024

Colm Field and David Wilkerson have asserted their rights under the Copyright,
Designs and Patents Act, 1988, to be identified as Author and Illustrator of this work

All rights reserved. No part of this publication may be reproduced or transmitted
in any form or by any means, electronic or mechanical, including photocopying,
recording, or any information storage or retrieval system, without prior permission
in writing from the publishers

A catalogue record for this book is available from the British Library

ISBN: PB: 978-1-5266-4178-6; eBook: 978-1-5266-4177-9; ePDF 978-1-5266-4176-2

2 4 6 8 10 9 7 5 3 1

Typeset by RefineCatch Limited, Bungay, Suffolk

Printed and bound in Great Britain by CPI Group (UK) Ltd, Croydon CR0 4YY

To find out more about our authors and books visit www.bloomsbury.com
and sign up for our newsletters

For Mum and Dad, aka Eyelash and
Dangerous Dave, aka Blammo and Granjab

(That's what predictive text suggested for Mamo and
Grandad and I'm sticking with it)

1
The Grinster's Kitchen

My car rolled quietly across shiny blue and white squares. The sun shone above like no sun I've ever seen; flat, long and pale. Strange, white buildings zipped past; curved, shiny and smooth, without any windows or doors. Even after the many weird and wonderful worlds I had already seen, this was an alien place.

That thought made me shiver.

Without thinking I pushed my foot down, and felt the quiet pull of an electric engine *whoosh* me forwards. I hadn't thought these buggy-looking cars would be quick: they looked more like bumper cars. But they were perfect for this smooth terrain, and soon I saw more bizarre sights. A milky-white pond. Huge brown scabbly wheels

with holes in the middle, clustered together like a herd of cows. I sped up between two giant glass towers, and –

'Watch out for the sludge trap, ya great galoob!' a familiar voice hissed through the speakers, just as a slimy orange blob hurtled towards me. 'We lost three bubble-butts last week to them!'

I took my foot off the pedal, and with a gentle whistle my car came to a quick halt. I pushed a yellow button marked RADIO, and spoke.

'Uh, thanks, uh . . . Grandma?'

The voice hadn't belonged to my real grandma. Instead it was this universe's version of Kyan Green's grandma. Trouble was, I'd already found that, in a lot of universes, my Almost-Grandma wasn't actually *called* Grandma. When the voice at the end of the radio didn't answer, I worried that I had made a mistake. But then the radio crackled, and my friend Stefania replied instead.

'I don't think she can hear you,' she said, coming to a

halt alongside me, her brother Dimi just behind. 'The range on these radios isn't very strong.'

'They drive wicked though, innit,' Dimi said enthusiastically, giving his wheel a spin and rotating on the spot. '*Nuff* safe. They should have these bumpers on all cars.'

'Where's Luke?' I asked. Dimi winced, and he nodded past me. There, juddering forwards one metre at a time, came Luke. He swerved a little right, then a *lot* left, so much that I had to move forwards to avoid hitting him. Then, with a relieved smile, he paused . . .

And jerked again into the glass tower.

'Whoops, sorry!' Luke said with a laugh. 'How does it even do that?!'

'Gamma Team,' Almost-Grandma hissed angrily through my radio. 'Why aren't I seeing you already? Do you want to get eaten?'

'Did she just say eaten?' Dimi asked, his voice rising. He jabbed frantically at his radio, causing *TSS-TSS* hisses of static that set my teeth on edge. 'What did you – *TSS-TSS* – say? *What* – *TSS* – did you say?!'

'Dim,' I said soothingly. 'Dimi – *TSS* – Argh, DIMI! Remember what we said after Jet Ski Snooker? We play it cool, until we know what's happening.'

'Shut up, you lot,' Stef said (that's Stefania for 'Listen to me please'). 'I know what this place is.'

She drove around the shivering orange sludge, up to a shiny metal sculpture. It was long, flat and thin; except for the end, which was curved into a big bowl. In the bowl was more orange sludge.

'That's a giant spoon,' Stefania said, 'That's a spoon and this . . . this is marmalade.'

Suddenly the air felt very still.

'Nah,' Luke said eventually. 'No way that's marmalade. Who puts marmalade on a spoon?'

'People that *eat* people,' Dimi moaned.

'Ky, would *you* do it? Would *you* put marmalade on a spoon?'

'I do *not* eat marmalade,' I said.

'What?! Marmalade's bash!' (Side Note: Luke's recently started making up his own slang. I don't know if he knows it's made up, or if he's just misheard real slang.)

'Don't trust it,' I said. 'All those bits.'

'That's peel! That's bits of orange peel, how can you—'

'*Who cares, you lot?!*' Stefania exploded. 'If that's the size of the spoon, how big is the mouth it goes in? This is a kitchen table. This is a giant's breakfast.' She twisted in her chair, pointing around at all the weird things we'd passed.

'Those smooth, windowless houses? They aren't houses, they're jugs. That milky pond over there? It's actual milk. And that big flat sun above us? That's the kitchen light.'

'And those huge brown wheels aren't wheels,' I realised with a gasp. 'They're . . . they're *Clumped Wheat-Os*!'

'Eh?' Luke said. 'Wait – you mean Cheerios?'

'Eesh, Ky.' Dimi sighed. 'We don't get the brands neither, but the cereals your dad buys always sound so *grim*—'

WHOOMPH! A gigantic meaty hand SLAMMED down from above and picked up the metal marmalade spoon like it weighed *nothing*. Boulder-sized crumbs of toast tumbled from its fingertips as it did, crashing down – BOOM-BOOM-BOOM! – around us.

'RUN!' I screamed, and sped for the shelter of a dinner plate, Stef and Dimi close behind. I reached the shaded area beneath the plate's rim, spun around . . . and my heart sank.

'Luke!' I shouted. 'Over here!'

But it wouldn't be that simple. Luke really hadn't got to grips with his car. Somehow he'd driven right into the middle of the Cheerios herd, bashing into one then another as he tried to escape.

'Stupid – *oof!* – cars!' he hissed. 'I – *urff!* – can't get the – *oof!* – steering right!'

'You're turning too much,' Stefania said. 'Turning too much and – slow down!'

'Yeah I *get* that,' Luke hissed back. 'It isn't—'

'Still too far,' said Stef, not noticing my and Dimi's glares to stop. She doesn't mean to be, but she's kinda harsh when we make mistakes. 'You can speed up though, hurry up! More than that! Nope, too – too far!'

'Just pretend you're on the dodgems, Luke,' Dimi said encouragingly. 'Except instead of a buzzer going off when the ride's over, there's a mad giant who'll rip off all our heads.'

As if that were all he needed to hear, Luke finally sped out between the Cheerios. But he still wasn't in control. He veered right around in a circle, and *just* as that gigantic hand THUDDED the marmalade spoon back down on the table, Luke's back wheels drifted into the sweet orange sludge clinging to the back of it . . . and was stuck fast.

'Wheelspin it!' Dimi shouted. 'You've got to break free!'

But Luke was frozen. His eyes wide, his mouth open, he stared up in terror as a titanic shadow loomed across the table like a total eclipse. I edged forwards, and saw it too; the biggest, grumpiest, *butters-est* face I have ever seen.

'It's Mr Stringer,' I said faintly. 'The Giant Grinster is Mr Stringer.'

Back in my universe, Mr Stringer was our landlord, the greedy grasper who'd pulled every trick in the book in order to kick us out of our home – until the Infinite Race helped me to uncover his illegal lies. He'd been my enemy in *every* universe, in fact: the Sparks Raider who'd almost destroyed an entire ecosystem; the out-of-control copper who'd tried to run us off the road; even the arrogant, spoilt Racer desperate to cheat me out of first place in the most brutal Demolition Derby in the Multiverse. So far I'd won every battle we'd had. However, there was one *teensy* difference between those worlds and this one.

Never, in all the worlds I'd travelled to, had Mr Stringer ever been *this* big, and never had I been *this* small.

'What's he doing?' Dimi asked. 'Why's he in slo-mo?'

Dimi was right. The Grinster was taking ages, craning his neck to peer at my terrified, marmalade-stuck friend. I felt a soft current of air being sucked up through those hairy blocked *clackalacka-clackalacka* nostrils, and as the Grinster's mouth began to open, his lips pulled slowly apart like some spit-glued ziplock bag.

'He's gigantic,' Stef said in wonder. 'Everything takes longer to reach his brain. Or everything is taking less time to reach our brain. This must be how ants see us.'

The Grinster's mouth gaped open wider, revealing tea-

stained, cereal-bunged teeth, His hairy nose sniffed and snorted, and a whole *orchestra* of pigs echoed around us.

'Speak for yourself,' I said. But when the Grinster spoke, he sounded more disgusted than I did.

'UUUURRRRRRRRRRRGHHHHHHHHHH!' he roared, and picked up the teaspoon with Luke still attached. As I cried out with dismay, the Grinster flailed the spoon about, until Luke's car broke free of the marmalade, and was flung high across the table, falling out of sight.

'NO!' I shouted, and looked desperately around at Stefania and Dimi. 'No! He can't . . . Please say he's survived that.'

'We've got to find out,' Stef said determinedly, though through her windscreen her face looked pale. 'Let's go and find hi—'

As if things couldn't get any worse, General Grandma's voice crackled through the radio.

'You've done it, Race Team One – the Grinster is fetching the bug spray. Now *get outta there!*'

'Er . . . what's bug spray?' I asked. And before anyone could answer, the Grinster loomed over the table again. He held a spray canister in his hand, and as it grew closer I saw writing on it which scared me more than anything I'd seen already.

9

**BROUGHT TO YOU BY THE HAPPY
CORPORATION!**

PURGE-AWAY!!!

**ERADICATE THOSE PESKY TINIES, SAFELY
AND HUMANELY!**

'The Happy Corporation,' I said faintly. 'This is going to be
evil.'

It was. With a deafening SSSSSSSS, the Giant Grinster's
finger pressed the trigger, and a jet-black plume cannoned
out like silly string. It floated there for a moment, before
separating into five blobs. These blobs drifted apart, and as
they did they grew, expanding like odd-shaped water
balloons, until each one was the size of a tent. Then,
suddenly, they began to shake. Quietly at first, then *violently* jerking and stretching.

'There's something inside them,' Dimi whispered.
'Something that's trying to escape.'

And something did.

An evil-looking blade the colour of shiny obsidian
punctured one of the sacs. The blade began to bulge as it
sliced down, pulsing, growing, until by the time it had
reached the bottom it looked less like a blade and more
like a . . .

'Stinger,' Dimi breathed. 'La naiba, that's a stinger!'

The sac began to crinkle, sagging like a bag of thick dead skin. A long, thin, mandible-like mouth poked out from the opening the stinger had made, twitching like it was sniffing for food. It suckered at the sagging sac skin, paused . . . and in one, brutal motion, hoovered it all up to reveal a curled-up giant insect, as big as my car back home. The insect's wings opened, and with a long, angry buzzing sound, they began to beat.

'Oh. My. Days,' Dimi murmured faintly. 'Hornet drones.'

'How do you know they're called that?' I said.

'What else could they be called?'

Like an old-fashioned aerial, two long metallic antennas extended from each of the five hornet drones' heads. Slowly they rotated in mid-air, like searching satellites. One of them came to a sudden halt, facing away from us towards the city of cereal boxes. Then, as it shot away at a *startling* speed, the other four kept revolving, until they came to a stop in front of us.

'I'm detecting bug signals, Team One,' my Almost-Grandma warned through the radio. 'Now. *Get. Out.*'

'Listen,' Stefania said, her voice tight with fear. 'Luke's got to be where that other hornet went, past the big cereal boxes. We split up, but *not out of radio range*. We each figure out a way to escape *those* things. Then we join up, save Luke, and get the *fried eggs* outta here.'

Like I said, Stefania's harsh, but nobody beats her when it comes to strategy.

bzzzzzzzzzzzZZZZZZZZZZZZZZZZZZZZZZZZZ!

The hornet drones *fired* towards us with blistering pace. Stefania sped left beneath the toast rack, Dimi roared straight for the sauce bottles, and me? I drove around to the right, keeping beneath that thick white dinner plate.

'I haven't been followed!' Stefania shouted through the radio. 'Who's got my drone?' Still pursued by that violent buzzing sound, it was suddenly joined by a deafening *PLING!* that sent tremors through the thick porcelain above me. Fear in my throat, I moved to the outside of the plate, looked through my side mirror . . . and my heart stopped.

'I've got two on me!' I shouted. With Hornet One *ripping* after me, Hornet Two was *smashing* into my dinner plate shelter from above. I gasped, hit the brakes . . . and spun around as Hornet One tore past me, whipping around at such speed that its stinger carved sparks from the side of my car before *wedging* deep into the porcelain dish.

'*NOOOOOOOOOOOOOO!!!!!*' the Giant Grinster bellowed somewhere far above. Flooring it back around the dish the same way I'd come, I wondered what he was moaning about. Then, with a loud, splintering CRACK, long, thin veins began to spread across the plate, shaking deeper and wider with every vicious *PLING!* from Hornet Two above. This shelter wouldn't be safe for long; this whole dish was fracturing into pieces!

'KYA...I...YO...' Dimi shouted, his words crowded out by static. Cursing these rubbish radios, and suddenly panicked that I'd strayed away from my friends, I sped up. But these bubble-butts weren't fast enough to win in a sprint against these drones, and I knew it. When I heard that *zzZZ!* creeping closer behind me, I *knew* that Hornet One had freed itself and was gaining on me. Somehow I had to escape both these drones.

'Dimi!' I shouted. 'Stefania! Still being chased, can you hear me?'

For a moment there was nothing but static. I heard an explosion in the distance and plunged into despair. Was this the mission too far? Were we really going to let our cosmic twins down today? Then, as I kept speeding around the curve, feedback crackled through my radio and Dimi's excited voice broke through.

'REPEAT: THEY DON'T LIKE WET! THEY DON'T LIKE WET!'

They don't like wet! Daring to veer to the outside of my shelter for a brief moment, I looked ahead and saw egg yolk dripping in a waterfall – a yolkfall? – from the plate's edge. A plan formed in my mind. A crazy idea.

Taking a deep breath, I took my foot off the accelerator, and came to a stop just before the yolkfall. Within moments, the buzzing of Hornet One slashed through the air towards me, and the frenetic Hornet Two – *PLING! PLING! PLING!* – smashed into the plate directly above me. A huge chunk of porcelain began to shake free from the rest, big enough to crush me if it dropped. Still I waited. I'd only get one shot at this.

'*Three, two, one . . .*'

zzzzzzzzzzzzzzZZZ!

'Now!'

And three things happened at once. Hornet Two's stinger punctured the plate above; Hornet One whipped around the plate towards me, stinger-first; and I *slammed* my foot down, my hands whirling the steering wheel left then right to zip forwards *around* the stream of egg yolk, not daring to look back till I'd reached the teacup.

'Yes!' I exhaled shakily. My plan had worked. Hornet

One had plunged through the yolkfall – only to be impaled by the Hornet Two's deadly stinger. Now, as Hornet Two buzzed frantically to break free, the thick, oozing egg yolk was short-circuiting blue sparks across Hornet One's entire metal frame, and it was starting to shake violently. I looked up at that demented Hornet Two, saw something like fear in its frantic movements, and grinned my *toughest* grin.

'Smell ya later, punk,' I said ... and that's when the porcelain plate shattered into pieces, setting the murderous drone free. My voice died in my throat. Hornet Two turned to me with a deadly, emotionless triumph ...

And Hornet One exploded with a *KABOOM*, engulfing them both in a ball of fire!

'YES!' I whooped with relief. 'Dim, you legend, you were right! Where are you guys?'

'Follow the destruction to the cereal boxes,' Stefania replied. She wasn't lying either. The shiny road was littered with crumbs and spatters, and huge, wasp-shaped holes punched through every piece of toast in the rack. The sauce bottles were toppled like ancient glass ruins, and two husks of twisted metal sat smoking in the milk pond. As I heard a gigantic roar of rage far above me, I couldn't help but smirk with satisfaction.

'*AWWWWWWWWW, NOOOOOOOO!!!!*'

'Ha! I bet the Grinster didn't expect his bug spray to smash up his kitchen,' I chuckled. But there was no time to celebrate.

'Kyan, Stef, come look at this!' said Dimi, his voice quiet and urgent. 'I'm at the corner of Bran Flakes and Porridge. I've found Luke.'

I raced forwards, around the grid-like city of humongous cereal boxes, until I saw Dimi. The two boxes opened up into a clearing, and as I pulled up alongside Dimi, he pointed and I saw him.

'Luke!'

Our friend was trapped beneath an upside-down glass with a thin, curved handle. The glass was *right* on the corner of the table, and Luke was shouting and waving at us frantically, driving repeatedly into the glass walls. But his voice didn't come through the radio, and the glass didn't budge. Stood on the base of the glass above him, watching us silently, was the final hornet drone.

'What's he pointing at?' I asked. 'And why is that drone just sitting there?' Then a horrible thought dawned on me. 'Where's the Grinster?'

It came out of nowhere, a rolled-up magazine the size of ten trees, swooping down so fast that the draught of air

16

it created sent me spinning, smashing the cereal boxes over like dominoes. Me and Stef raced beneath the boxes as they fell, our headlights lighting up a shrinking tunnel. But Dimi was fearless in these bubble-butts, and I broke through to the other side of the cereal box just in time to see him WALLOP into Luke's glass at full speed before bouncing off and . . . the glass barely moved.

But the hornet drone did. With the Grinster's crazed laughter booming around us, it suddenly darted for Dimi's car, its stinger stabbing through the metal roof and through the passenger seat just *inches* from Dimi.

'AAAARGH!' Dimi screamed, slammed on the accelerator and whirled the steering wheel around, dough-nutting wildly across the tabletop. Breaking free, the hornet soared back up into the air, turned with a deadly grace, and plunged *straight* back down, this time aiming right for Dimi's skull.

'Dimi, NO!' I screamed – just as the Grinster's rolled-up magazine swooped across the table and smashed the hornet into the Porridge Oats box.

'*AWWWWWW NOOOOOOOOO!!!*'

'Oh my gosh, did you see that?!' I laughed. 'He took out his own bug!'

For a moment, Stef's face was deathly pale. Then,

instead of saying something kind about her brother's narrow escape, she looked tersely across to the upside-down glass still holding Luke.

'What do we do about Luke though?' she said.

Just then, a net was fired out across the clearing. It wrapped around the hornet drone lying prone by the Porridge Oats, and as I looked to see who'd fired it . . . I felt a *huge relief*. A mean, blue-and-white-chequered tank was rolling towards us. Poking out from the top of the turret was my Almost-Grandma's head, half hidden behind the telescopic sight of her harpoon gun. She looked like a military officer in this universe, and sure enough, as she chewed the cigar sticking out of her mouth, she nodded with unsmiling satisfaction, and ducked back down.

'General Loretta Price, come to save the greenhorns,' she bellowed. 'Yer up, Gunnery Officer Celestine!'

'Gunnery Officer *who* was that?' I asked.

'GET OUT THE WAY OF THE HEAVY MOB, BUBBLE-BUTTS!' another familiar voice shouted through my radio. It was my kid sister – not my *almost*-sister, but my actual sister, Celestine. She was there when we found the Infinite Racetrack, and although we argue a lot, I recently learned that she is way smarter and tougher than I've ever given her credit for.

But even so, I wouldn't *ever* give her a tank gun.

'Tines,' I said. 'Tines, is that a good idea? 'Tines? Tines, NO!'

BLASTTT!!! Celestine fired, and a flaming shell burst out of the tank's turret. At first the shot looked wide, and my heart sank – but I wasn't giving my sister enough credit. The shell smashed into the ornate handle, tearing it off and sending both flying off the table. The glass itself was sent spinning around violently, circling wider and wider along its thin, delicate rim . . . before at last it toppled over, leaving Luke free to escape!

'Woohoo!' Luke whooped, swerving left and bouncing off a sugar pot. We all raced forwards to join him (and I'm not gonna lie: to make sure he didn't somehow drive into another disaster). Then, before we could speak, the Grinster let out a groan of *pure* agony.

'*NOOO, NOOOOOOOOO!!!*'

'He must've liked that glass,' Dimi quipped.

'Great job, team!' Almost-Grandma shouted. 'We've captured ourselves a hornet drone, and if I have to tell you to drive down that table leg one more time, *I'll squish you like the Grinster couldn't!*'

Well, that threat was enough; we had to get off this table. Following my Almost-Grandma's directions, we raced towards the corner of the table, the Grinster still wailing about his precious glass above us. But as the table's edge came closer, I looked at the floor miles below and began to worry.

'Wait, Stef!' I asked. 'Won't we just fall?'

'I don't think so,' Stef said. 'So long as we keep moving, we'll have more force sticking us to the leg than the gravity trying to pull us off it.'

'OK,' I said, took a breath . . . and raced for the corner like everyone else. Everyone except for Luke, that is.

'I just can't – urgh! – get the hang of this!' he shouted, careening the wrong way past me, even as the shadow of the Grinster's titanic magazine loomed over us again.

Well, no *way* was I leaving him. I spun the wheel, screeching into a spin that smashed into his bubble-butt car and drove us *both* over the table's edge. As the magazine smashed down behind us, as our spinning wheels flew off the table and somehow *clung* to the table leg *still driving*, Luke screamed – then laughed with glee.

'You did it, Kyan!' he shouted through the radio. 'You're the best!'

That's Luke. That's my best friend.

The trouble was, I wasn't sure if he should be on this team.

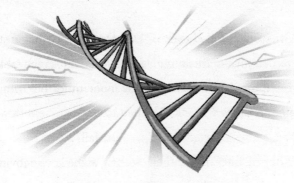

2
A New Mystery

'Aaaaaaaaaaaaaaaaaaaaaaaaaaaaaaaaaaaaaaaaaaaaaaaaaaaaaaaaaaaaaaaaaaaaaaaaaaaaaaaaaaaaaaaaaaaaaaaaaaaaaaaaaahhhhhhhh—'

THUD!

'No banging about!' Dad shouted from the kitchen, and kept cooking.

To leave a universe in the Infinite Race and return home, all you have to do is get out of the car/horse/jet ski. You'll fall through wondrous dimensions, reality will dissolve into trillions of strings you've never seen the likes of before . . . and you'll slam down *hard* on your bedroom floor. To avoid this, we'd made a thick, comfortable landing pad out of cushions carefully arranged around the racetrack. I'd slammed down right next to these cushions, on the hard wooden laminate.

Groaning, I rolled over, right in front of . . . a hologram of me, dealing out cards to my friends. Then I remembered the one thing I had to check – the most important thing I wanted to know was OK. I leaped to my feet, bent down, and . . .

'They're fine,' I breathed with a sigh of relief, and squeezed my brand-new trainers. 'It's OK, they're fine!'

'I don't know why you wear them on the racetrack, Ky,' Stefania said, struggling to her feet. She stood, right between holograms of Dimi and herself. They were laughing at a joke I couldn't hear from inside the holographic projector. 'The Metamorphic Headphones change our clothes anyway.'

'Yeah,' I said, 'but I still know I'm wearing them.' Lovingly I looked down again at my pristine white trainers, the line of silver sparkling in the light. 'Mod Sevens,' I added, 'may you never get old.'

See, I *never* get good trainers. Once every four months my dad measures our feet, then picks a new pair up from the supermarket, along with beans and rice and Clumped Wheat-Os. But six weeks ago, I *saved* our home and stopped the mean old landlord Mr Stringer from evicting us. As a thank you, and because Mr Stringer had been forced to lower the rent *and* give them some money, my parents got me a present – the smartest pair of shining trainers the world has ever seen.

OK, so if they'd known what exactly I'd been through to save this flat, I would've probably got more than just a pair of new shoes. But Mum and Dad just thought I'd seen through the lies Mr Stringer was telling to try to evict us. They didn't know I'd had to battle through other dimensions.

It was all thanks to the Infinite Race. This shabby-looking toy racetrack me and my sister found in the loft had turned out to be something called a 'Multiverse Transporter', rocketing me to adventures in other universes. Oh, and if I'd told my parents about any of them, the track would be confiscated quicker than you could say 'driving licence'. Much better that I just use the Infinite Racetrack to help the Multiverse with my friends, and enjoy my smart new trainers as a well-deserved well done.

'Kyan!' Stef said again, and I stopped checking on the trainers.

'Wassup?'

'Did we level up or not?!'

'Oh, snap!' I said. 'Wait – check the coast is clear.'

Luke, who'd landed closest to the door, hurried over and peered out, leaning over a hologram of himself that was staring down at some Top Trumps cards. After a moment, he gave the thumbs up, and I lifted the lid off the *Infinite Race X* box. Just like that, the Holographic Distraction Field disappeared, leaving just our real selves in the room.

We hadn't always had the Holographic Distraction Field. It activates along with the racetrack, so anyone looking into the room *won't* see us hopping across dimensions, but will instead see us playing cards, or drawing, or whatever else doesn't get you grounded. We'd *won* the Distraction Field, completing missions and solving codes until we reached Level 3 in the Infinite Race. Level 3 felt like a big achievement at the time, but that was weeks ago, and even though we'd hopped inside the racetrack several times since then – completing each and every mission we'd been given, from the exciting ('Jet Ski Snooker'!) to the dull ('The Luscious Lawn-Mowing Contest'. Seriously) – we hadn't levelled up since.

'I wonder how it comes up with the different holograms?' Dimi said. 'Us playing cards, and writing sorry letters, and playing dominoes and stuff. You sure you don't change anything, Ky?'

'Nothing,' I said. 'It just seems to be different every time I set up the track.'

'You could check the instructions,' Luke said quietly. I'd almost forgotten Luke was there. He'd been subdued ever since we saved him from the Giant Grinster. Hoping for some good news to cheer him up, I took a folded piece of paper out of my pocket, but . . .

'Guys,' I said, my voice trembling. 'Something's happening to the Instructions!'

Like everything else about the Infinite Race, the Instructions page is more special than it looks at first. The paper *never* creases or tears, even when I've had it crumpled up in my pocket. It's often written in code – mind-scrambling codes that take all my (grandma's) brain power to work out. And, unlike the paper that comes with our other second-hand games – like Guess Who? or Hungry Hungry Hippos or Smash the Potato in Your Face! (don't ask) – the words on these Instructions change, telling us what level we've reached. Now I watched in awe as they changed right in front of me, letters literally dropping off the page and dissolving into the air.

Prepare for the Ride of Your Lives
You are now at Level...

3

Le l 3 In in ty Racer   a e upgr   ed to The I
finity Rac   X, w   re   hey enj y the privacy gr
 nted by a Hol gra hic D straction Fie d, a d
2% q   cker Hoppi

v   o   v

                n

                       l

                          p

                                  !

'Have we done it?' Dimi asked excitedly, 'Have we made it up to Level Four?'

'I don't know,' I said. Soon, all the letters and numbers on the page had dissolved away, until there was nothing but 'Prepare for the Ride of Your Lives' left. Then something even *weirder* happened. 'It's *buzzing*,' I gasped.

'Like a bee?!' said Luke.

'Nnnnnope!' I yelped through chattering teeth. 'Buzzzzzzzzing like electricity!'

It was like holding one of those electric-shock machines at the arcades. The Instructions vibrated in my hands, and as it did, all new letters seemed to tremble out of the paper, forming new words.

D N LA UE (CL)

'What does it say?!' Dimi demanded. I was too busy shaking about with these juddering instructions to answer, but slowly, these new words formed whole sentences . . .

DANNY LA RUE (CLUE):

1. WITHOUT ANT AND DECS, LEVEL 4 WILL CAUSE YOU BUNNY EARS SOON AS ANY ALMOST FRIENDS BUTCHER'S HOOK AT YOU.

2. WITH BINS ON? HAVE A BUBBLE BATH EVERYWHERE AND YOUR GARDEN GATES WILL ADAM AND EVE IT'S YOU.

. . . Which made *no* flipping sense whatsoever.

'Another code?!' I moaned. 'How do we work this one out?!'

'Gizzit here,' Stef said, taking out a pen to make notes on the page. That's the other thing about this instruction manual: you can draw all over it and not worry – the ink will just disappear by the next time you need it. Stef's been the quickest out of all of us at deciphering the Infinite Race codes, but after ten minutes of crossing out, swearing and telling us to 'Shut up yelling things I've already tried!' she was stumped.

'Argh!' she snarled, and slammed the pen down on the page, 'We need Spider Ace! You looked online for her or what, Ky?'

'Yep,' I said, 'and no luck. I can't find any mentions of Spider Ace or Edie Scrap online.'

Spider Ace was a mysterious Racer I'd encountered in my first race. She'd been driving a sports car with the roof down, balancing a shotgun in her arm and drinking a flask of tea. Since that terrifying first meeting, Spider Ace hadn't got any less scary; she actually chucked Luke into a deadly ocean on one of Jupiter's moons as a 'test' for us at one point. But she *had* helped us, and had promised to tell us more about the Infinite Race soon. And since then I hadn't seen her, or her (very unaware) cosmic twin Edie Scrap for ages.

'What if . . .' Luke said slowly. We all leaned in, eagerly waiting for this big idea. 'What if we just play that dice game I found at the charity shop? You know. Proton Wars!'

We all stared back at Luke in silence. To be honest, I felt a stab of annoyance. Luke likes these role-playing games – like D&D and Magic: The Gathering – and last week he'd turned up raving about this new one he'd found: Proton Wars. It was a science-fiction strategy game, with dice and characters' stats and all sorts . . . and it looked dead boring, but that's not what was bothering me. No, what was annoying was that he was comparing the Infinite Race with some dumb game, like it *hadn't* saved my home, like it *didn't* stop horrible Mr Stringers from doing horrible things to people across the Multiverse.

'Is that the one with all the dice?' Dimi said, looking unhappy. 'And the protons?'

'Yeah, and I think there's a war in there too, Dimbag,' Stef said sarcastically. 'I'd actually be *well* up for some dice rolling, Luke, but it's too late now. Mum wants us back early before school starts tomorrow.'

Before school starts. After a long summer holiday spent hopping from universe to universe, those words were hard to hear. It felt like I'd got out of jail, only for someone to say there'd been a mistake and I had to go back inside.

'I don't really wanna go back, you know,' Dimi said, and I nodded along with him. But Stefania and Luke looked at us like we were crazy.

'You guys *like* school! Besides, we'll be the rulers of it! We're practically running the place by now!' Stefania said.

'Yeah, and we can spend whole days together!' Luke said. 'Not just hopping!'

'Not just . . .' I said in disbelief. 'Luke, hopping universes is *mega*. School is *lame*.'

Luke blinked. Suddenly he looked a bit crestfallen.

'Yeah,' he said, 'I guess it is lame.'

It was only after they'd all left that I remembered something odd about the Distraction Field. Luke's hologram had been sitting alone, separate from the rest of us.

3
The Last Meal

'Kyan, you're barely eating!' Grandma said from across the table. 'Come on, your dad's chicken isn't dry at all this time.'

'"This time"', Dad said, shaking his head as he scooped up another helping of greens. 'Why'd'you have to put it like that?'

'Looking forward to tomorrow?' Mum said. 'Back to school!'

'Yep!' Celestine said, and slid her new glasses to the end of her nose like some kinda boss. 'Can't wait to show off these, *Oh yeah, oh yeah, my new glasses, my glasses . . .*'

As Celestine clicked her fingers and did her New Glasses Dance for the seventieth time, Mum turned to me.

'Looking forward to school, Ky?'

'Meh,' I said. 'I don't really want to go.'

'What do you mean, you don't want to go?!' Grandma said. 'It's your education! You take what you get till you get what you want!' (She says this often enough for me to mime it.)

'I hated school,' Dad said grimly, a frown creasing his face. 'Couldn't wait till it ended every day.' There was a pause, then Mum and Grandma both turned to give him

the full laser beam. 'Only on some days though,' he added quickly. 'And you've got to go, it's the law! Get what you take till you want what you get, in't it, Loretta?!'

Before my grandma could finish pouring extra gravy on her rice and peas *and* tell off my dad, the doorbell rang.

'Ooh let me get it!' Celestine said. She's still excited that she's allowed to open the door now, and dashed off, with both my mum and dad shouting, '*Ask who it is first!*' after her.

'Oh, and before I forget,' Grandma said, 'I saw Christine's cousin's husband yesterday outside George's Shop.'

'Oh yeah, Grandma?' I said with a grin. '*George's* Shop?' George's Shop is a local convenience shop near my school, and Mum reckons the owner – called George, innit – fancies Grandma. She clearly knew that's what I was getting at, because she scowled back at me.

'Hush and listen, you,' she said, and dropped her voice down to a whisper. '*It's about your landlord, Kenneth Stringer.*'

At this, I shut up and leaned closer. Mr Stringer owns our flat – and is my arch-enemy. He's tried to blast, smash, and evict me in ten different universes already.

'What about him?' I said, my eyes narrowing.

'Well,' Grandma continued. 'You know how badly he

treated you all? Since we fought back, a lot of other tenants have made complaints about his bullying behaviour. He's in a lot of trouble and—'

And then, as if by magic, a complaining voice came floating up the stairs of our flat. It was so snide and snobby we all knew who it was right away.

'. . . the walls are still dirty. Just because I let your family *temporarily* pay less in rent doesn't mean I don't expect my tenants to care for *my* properties.'

Mr Stringer was here! We all looked to each other in dismay. As his footsteps strode up the hall towards us I felt a stab of anger. Why was our landlord here, bothering us during a family meal?

'Good afternoon, Padraig, Cynthia,' Mr Stringer said stiffly, as he walked into the kitchen and looked around at the steaming bowls of food across the table. 'Quite the spread.' He said it like we were being greedy somehow, even though all the leftovers get frozen to last us until spring, like we're bears.

'You didn't arrange to come here, Kenneth,' Mum said sharply. 'That wasn't our agreement.'

Kenneth Stringer clearly couldn't care less about our agreement. He sneered down at us . . . but he didn't look quite so smug as he used to. His expensive suit looked grubby, and while he always had a lot of gel in his hair, today it was messy: thick, congealed strands jutting out at all angles like slimy stalagmites. Even as my blood boiled at him ruining *our* Sunday dinner, the moment his eyes clocked mine, I felt a glimmer of satisfaction. *He* looked even angrier than *me*.

We're beating you, I thought. *In every universe we're winning, and you don't like it.*

'What is it then, Kenneth?' my dad said impatiently. It was a big change from how he used to sound talking to Mr Stringer: scared and apologetic, even though he'd done nothing wrong.

'Well, I think, Loretta . . . *Ms* Price –' Mr Stringer hastily corrected himself at the look on my grandma's face – 'I think you have already started to spread the gossip about me, and I wanted to come here and tell you the full truth about what is happening. Given the current market conditions, and with several new business plans underway, I have sold several of my properties, and have received an offer to sell more.'

'That's not what Christine's cousin's husband told me,' Grandma said sharply. '*She* said that your other tenants had complained as well. *She* said you'd had to sell all your other flats and were getting another job so you could keep this one.'

'Good!' I said with a grin. 'Why do we get stuck with him still then?'

'Kyan!' Both my parents snapped that at the same time. I know what it means when they do: *Just because WE don't like Mr Stringer doesn't mean YOU can be rude.* I bit my tongue and looked down, and not just because I didn't want to be in trouble. I didn't like the fact that both Mum and Dad looked more worried than triumphant.

'What does that mean for us?' my dad asked, more quietly than before.

'Well whatever "Christine's cousin's ferret's cat" might have told you, Ms Price,' Mr Stringer said, and my grandma made a furious noise, 'while I *am* currently exploring other possible avenues of income, that doesn't mean I'm finished yet. However, knowing the full details of my situation, it might not be wise to push for lowered rent or further compensation at present.'

'What does that mean?' Celestine whispered to me – and Mr Stringer flinched at the noise.

'It means that we shouldn't try to get the money we're owed for all the hurt Mr Stringer caused us,' Mum said icily, 'because otherwise he'll sell our home.'

We all stared in silence at this. Mr Stringer smiled a

thin, sly smile, and it was *everything* I could do not to scream at him. As much as we'd won, as much as we'd beaten him, he was still holding our own home over us.

'What job?' my grandma said suddenly. 'You said "avenues of income" – what jobs are you looking for?'

At this, Mr Stringer's smile faltered, and he flushed slightly.

'I don't have to share that with you,' he snapped. 'You should be grateful that I've had the courtesy to tell you this much. I'll let you enjoy the rest of your . . . meal.'

At that, Mr Stringer turned around sharply and left. As we heard the front door close, the mood was grim.

'That's something at least,' she mused. 'Whatever job he's going for, he's not getting to do what he wants. That's what Christine's sister's husband said outside George's Shop. Kenneth Stringer's the kind of man who probably assumed he could waltz into any "avenue of income" he likes.'

'That's true,' Mum said, brightening. 'No matter what he made it sound like, that whole visit told me one thing. He's having to get his hands dirty for once.'

That was a comforting thought. I thought of the Infinite Race and felt more hope. *We're beating Mr Stringer in every universe*, I thought. *If we can win out there, we can . . .*

Right at that moment, a dirty robot *creature* crept out from its home under the shelves, rolled up to my feet, nudged at my pristine Mod Seven trainers, and *sucked up the laces*!

'Urgh!' I shouted, and pushed it away. 'Urgh, *no*! Dad, that stupid thing's escaped again!'

'Don't kick it, don't kick it!' Dad bellowed, hurrying to the thing and crouching over it with an accusing look for me.

I should explain. You know that money Mr Stringer had to give my parents? Well, most of it went on bills, but we were all allowed to get something. I got my Mod Sevens, my sister got glasses and tickets to *Frozen on Ice*, my Mum got a caravan holiday for all of us, and my dad . . .

My dad got a robot vacuum cleaner. Only, being my dad, he *blatantly* bought it second-hand, because it's a *nightmare*. Its front wheel has already fallen off, and it sets itself off whenever it likes, rolling around the flat in search of every shoelace, controller lead and bedroom rug it can find, before getting wedged in a corner somewhere. My dad doesn't care though. *He* calls it 'Robot Pattinson', 'Robbie' for short, and since he's bought it he's treated it like his favourite child, even though he has to spend more

time fixing it than it
spends cleaning the
floor.

'That's right,
Robbie,' he said now
in a gentle voice I
swear he *never* uses
for us. 'That's it, home you go!'

'That thing should be kept outside!' I exclaimed, checking the laces on my shoes for any sign of damage. 'It nearly
chewed them up!'

'The shoes aren't supposed to be on inside anyway, Ky,'
Mum warned back, although she was looking with dismay
at my dad crouched over Robot Pattinson. 'It's only
because they're so clean – go and take them off.'

OK, so it was a travesty, my beautiful shoes being
punished for Dad's hateful dustminator. But even though
my family all laughed at the careful way I stepped out of
the room so as not to damage the Mods, I was still smiling.
We'd spent the summer battling Mr Stringer in over a
dozen universes, against impossible odds. And finally,
thanks to Christine's sister's husband's cousin's ferret's cat,
I'd found out that it *had* mattered, that we were *winning*.
Happier still, Mr Stringer could threaten us all he wanted,

but according to my grandma, and according to everything I saw in other universes, he was *losing control*! I continued on down the hall, and a slow smile spread across my face.

'Is it true George fancies you, Grandma?' I heard Celestine say, and as my family began to laugh, I couldn't help but join in.

4
Back at School

Going into Year 6 was weird. I felt eighteen! Everything at school seemed too low down and small, from the tables to the whiteboards to the Year 3 kids divving about like a herd of cats. Us older kids had all apparently decided on the fist-bump hello over summer, so as we all filed into the school hall for assembly, I paused several times to give a solemn "S'up?' to my other classmates, giving a tough nod with it. Then, when I spotted Mrs French, our no-nonsense Year 6 teacher, getting *seriously* tired of us all bumping fists and winking and nodding, I sat down on the benches that loomed over the floor-sitting, cross-legged nits from the *lower* years, and reassured her with a look that said: *I am Kyan. I am old and wise. You don't need to worry, Mrs French.*

'You lot are idiots,' Stefania muttered as I sat down.

'*You're* idiots,' I said. '. . . What lot?'

'You boys. What, have you started a business together? Are you all gangsters? We're only in Year Six.'

'*KYAN!*'

The hiss came from further down the row, but a hush was already falling as our headteacher, Mr Wimpole, walked up to deliver the same jokes he makes every year.

'Not you again!' he said, and Years 3 to 5 fell about laughing while we rolled our eyes. Then that hiss came again, louder than ever.

'*KYAN!!!*'

Mrs French was scowling now, looking towards the back to see who was daring to talk. Mr Wimpole's a bit clueless, to be honest; you could skip out of his assembly and come back with a cheeseburger meal and he wouldn't notice. But there's still days when I wonder if Mrs French used to be a prison guard.

'KYAN!' There was nothing for it. I recognised that voice, and I couldn't just leave him hanging. I leaned forwards, and saw Luke, beaming at me while pointing at the door to the sports stores.

'WE CAN PLAY DODGEBALL!' he hissed, and gave a thumbs up. I swear he'd been taking whispering lessons off my sister, but it wasn't even just that. The whole thing was just . . . *childish*.

'. . . So?' I said.

I really didn't mean to make that sound harsh, I *really* didn't. But the snickers passed down the line, even from Alex Bridges, and he drank a beer once! Luke looked bemused; not even annoyed or upset, but *baffled*, like something had changed that he just didn't understand,

and because he's my bestie, I suddenly wanted to do anything to get him out of this mess.

'Just kidding, mate,' I said with a smile. 'Dodgeball will be—'

'KYAN GREEN, YOU HAVE THE NERVE TO TALK DURING ASSEMBLY! HAVE YOU NOT LEARNED A THING FROM SIX YEARS AT THIS SCHOOL?!'

Mrs French, Man. It's more like I wonder who she was guarding.

The assembly was nearly finished when Mrs French handed Mr Wimpole a note.

'Ah, yes,' he said. 'Thanks, Mrs French! Now, it is my pleasure to announce that our school librarian Mrs Cadwaller broke her leg.'

There was a *very* confused pause at this, until Mrs French coughed pointedly.

'Wait, no!' Mr Wimpole said. '*That's* bad. What's *good* is that to cover while Mrs Cadwaller recovers, we have a special new *mobile* library ... which *also* solves the problem of the school library's structural issues! Marvellous! So without any further ado, let me introduce you to Miss ... er ... Where is she?'

We all looked around the hall now for our mysterious

new teacher. But there was nobody new around.

'You don't suppose she has the wrong date for start of school, Mrs French?' Mr Wimpole said, then looked horrified. 'Or maybe we do!'

'All of us?' Mrs French asked. I knew then I was getting too old for this school, as I was starting to feel a bit of sympathy for her. They all kept looking around for a moment more, and then, from the end of the row, Luke pointed to the big windows along the side of the hall – the ones that look out to the schoolyard – and shouted out:

'Someone's driving!'

'*Someone's driving!*' Alex mimicked, and there were a few snickers. But Luke kept looking intently out until suddenly there was the approaching roar of a *huge* engine, a noise so deep and deafening that the hall windows began to actually *rattle*. Blasting out alongside the rumbling engine was music, every bit as loud as the beats at Carnival, except this music was heavy metal: the drums *smashing*, the electric guitars *fast and furious*, and somebody *screaming* their head off like they were in *terrible* pain.

'You don't think it's *her*, do you?' I murmured to Stef, but before she could answer, her gob fell open.

'Oh, sweet mercy,' Mrs French said faintly. Because a mobile library was driving on to the schoolyard. The meanest, baddest, *heavy-metal-est* mobile library anyone's ever seen.

It was the size of a single-decker bus, but its wheels were the sort of massive wheels you'd see on a monster truck, with horned rims that spun backwards like some tuned-up Roman chariot. It was painted a shiny, funeral-hearse black, and a heavy chainmail grille hung from the front, the kinda thing some bloody baron would want on *their* mobile library. Scrawled in red across the side was the word *BOOKS*, looking like the rudest word you can think of, and as this beasting, badass library came to a slow stop right outside the hall, thick clouds of dust kicked up from those gigantic tyres, turning the person who stepped out of its folding library doors into a mysterious, cloud-covered stranger.

A mysterious stranger that walked in the *wrong direction*.

'She's going to the wrong door,' Mrs French muttered, and called out, 'Other door! Use the other door that's the—'

It was too late. As Mrs

French groaned, the figure went straight for the closed-up fire escape we are told to NEVER OPEN because –

WEEEEEOOOOOOOOEEEEEEEEEE!

'Fire!' Mr Wimpole shouted. The alarm blared, and chaos reigned. Kids leaped to their feet and ran around, while Mr Wimpole rushed straight for the exit. Mrs French and the other teachers tried and failed to stop either Mr Wimpole or the kids. Our year laughed their heads off.

And through it all, me, Stefania, Luke and Dimi sat with our mouths wide open, staring at our new librarian. Because in her torn jeans, with her bright pink hair and the piercings in her nose, ears and eyebrows, it had to be one of two people. My dad's punk cousin, Mould, or the person we'd been looking for all summer.

''Ey up, everyone!' she shouted over the blaring alarm she'd just set off. 'I'm Edie Scrap! Noisy here, in't it! Not like this all the time I hope?'

'Come on, come on!' I yelled back down the busy school corridor to Stef and Luke. 'Quick, before there's a queue!'

Our first morning with Mrs French had been tough. She warned us straight away that 'I am preparing you for secondary school', and by the time the bell sounded for break I was beginning to think she'd gone to secondary school in hell. But it didn't matter, because now we were *finally* going to see Edie Scrap, the cosmic twin of Spider Ace, who had helped us solve the last code given to us by the Infinite Race.

'C'mon, c'mon!' I yelled again. 'Hurry up!'

'I'm trying!' Stef yelled back, swatting Year 3s out of the way. 'It's these kids, they're like flies! Wait, that's your sister!'

'Celestine?' I said, and paused. 'Oi, Tines! You coming to meet Edie Scrap?'

Celestine paused. She was with her friends, and they were all going into the hall, where a sign advertised *AUDITIONS: CHRISTMAS SHOW*.

'Errr . . . *nah*,' Celestine said. 'I'm a bit bored of Infinity Racing. I'm going to be in the show this term instead.'

And just like that, she skipped off.

'Eight-year-olds!' I said in disbelief to Stef.

'They're nihilists,' Stef agreed, and turned back to Luke. 'Luke, hurry! C'mon, before we miss . . .'

'I'm coming,' Luke said, scowling. He sounded miserable, and even as I ran ahead, I knew why.

See, Luke's a proper hard worker, perfect for Mrs French's brutal new regime . . . and completely wrong for Year 6. From the very first question she'd asked, he'd eagerly

stuck his hand up, stretching it up with his other hand –
and Alex Bridges had mimicked him. People had started
to laugh, Luke had got that same baffled look he'd had in
assembly . . . and then he'd stuck his hand up eagerly for
the *next* question, only for *three* more people to do an
impression.

By breaktime Luke had two *well done*s and ten house
points from Mrs French . . . and he looked completely
gutted. The worst thing was, while I did *not* laugh along
with the rest of the class (that's my mate, innit), part of me
really wanted him to chill out a bit, be a bit less eager-
beaver, a bit . . . older. But I had no idea how to say this
without sounding mean.

'Come *on*!' I shouted again, barrelling open the door to
the yard and waving Luke and Stef through it like an army
sergeant. 'Move, move, move!'

'*Oi! Ky!*' a voice called out. I looked back, and stopped.

Walking towards us, Dimi by his side, was Alex Bridges.

'Whassamatter?' Stef said. 'Kyan, come on!'

'What's up, Alex?' I said.

'Safe, bro,' he said with a grin. 'I like your trainers.'

I tried to ignore Stef, who was giving me swear-word
faces and gesturing for me to hurry.

'Er . . . thanks!'

'Come and play football with us, yeah?' Alex demanded.

Now I really *was* speechless. See, Alex Bridges is one of those kids who's just, well . . . *cool*. He's *crazy* good at sports – out of us lot, only Dimi's anywhere near as good as him. His crew – Stef calls them the 'boy band', which just tells you what she thinks of them – are the toughest boys in our year, and they hang on *every* comment he makes. And, from his Mod Seven trainers to his *real* crystal ear stud, Alex doesn't just know about the newest trends, he *invents* them. Hassan Asgar even reckons he invented 'Easy-peasy, lemon-squeezy' back in *nursery*, although that might be a bit much. Either way, when Alex Bridges is harsh on your mate then nice to you, it's not just as simple as telling him to bog off.

'So?' he said again now – looking at me and Dimi, but *not* Stef and *not* Luke. 'You coming? Wembley doubles, me and you, bro!'

'Er . . . maybe later?' I said awkwardly. 'It's just, we know that new mobile librarian, Edie Scrap, and we wanted to say hello.'

Luckily Alex didn't take it badly. He just shrugged, and began to turn away.

'Suit yourself, bro,' he said. 'C'mon, Dimi.'

And just when I thought Dimi would say, 'No thanks, I'm going to see Edie Scrap too,' he waved to *us* and began to walk off!

'See you guys later.'

'. . . Do you think he remembers who Edie Scrap actually is?' I said to Stef with a grin, only to see her glaring at me.

'So you're in a hurry till the boy band comes calling, yeah?' she snapped, then turned and began to jog towards the mobile library.

'Whoa, whoa, whoa!' I protested, as me and Luke struggled to keep up with her. 'Dimi's gone with Alex just now, have a go at him!'

'That dum-dum don't even remember who Edie Scrap is!' Stef scoffed back. She shot a *meaningful* glance back to Luke, who was running to catch up. '*And* Dimi isn't in our class. *He* didn't see what Alex did this morning. *You? You* should've just told him to bog off.'

'It's not as simple as that!' I said . . . but didn't carry on with why Alex Bridges was too cool, too popular to just call out (partly because, I'll be honest, I knew it would sound a bit lame said out loud). Thankfully, Edie's heavy-metal mobile library came into view then, and we all broke out into a full-on sprint . . . only to see some kids there already, trying the folding door handles, only to turn away, disappointed.

'*What?!*' I exclaimed, and sped ahead of my friends. It *couldn't* be closed, not on the first break! There were two fold-out steps up to the door, and as I raced up to them, all the frustrations I had with the Infinite Race, its difficult codes and the mysterious Spider Ace, they all built *up*, and I slammed my hand down on the door handle with anger.

'Racer DNA recognised,' a computer voice said.

'What?!' I said . . . and the door *jerked* open with such force that I fell forwards . . .

. . . into complete and total darkness.

'Oh my days,' Stef breathed, coming to a halt behind me. 'This ain't no library.' I struggled to my feet . . . and nearly fell over again, because she was right.

'Welcome, Infinity Racer Kyan Green,' the computer voice said, 'to the Commodore 65.'

We were standing in an endless black space. And I don't just mean it was dark. Nope, even as the closing door behind us still revealed our noisy, busy schoolyard, everything else around us was *pitch black*, left, right, even up and . . .

'Oh my gosh,' I said, looking down.

A *bubble* was drifting up towards me.

It wasn't a normal bubble either. It seemed to glow from within, and as it floated by me, I saw that it was in the shape of a glittering sword. The skin of this sword was translucent, and I could see moving shapes beneath its shimmering skin.

'There's stuff inside it,' I gasped. '*Loads* of . . . Oh my days, it's a whole world!'

It was like looking into an endless golden snow globe. The glittering sword bubble rotated, and I saw whole cities, miles and miles of bright yellow hills where strange and wonderful creatures rolled like massive tumbleweeds, up into red skies . . .

And out to other planets.

'Not a world,' I corrected myself. 'It's not a world, it's . . . it's a universe. It's a whole universe!'

Suddenly a beam of light fired out from this sword. I ducked back, and saw that the light had blasted *into another bubble*, this one a glowing crown. For a magnificent moment the light connected the two bubbles, giving them both energy, and then, as the energy wisped away into nothing, I saw that there were more bubbles in this endless space; *loads* more. They were all shapes and sizes,

beams of light firing between them and then dissolving into nothing.

'It's the Multiverse,' Luke said quietly. He was gazing around at all the bubbles drifting past us, and I could tell straight away that he understood something deeper about all this than I did. 'It's the *Multiverse*, Kyan. It's everything, and –' he pointed as another beam of energy crackled out between two nearby universes – 'and it's all connected.'

I was about to ask him what he meant, when that computer voice spoke again:

'Racer DNA Recognised.'

The door burst open, and Dimi tumbled in, doing a full roly-poly and leaping back to his feet with his fists up, eyes wide with shock. He saw me first.

'It's Edie Scrap, Ky!' Dimi shouted. 'Edie Scrap, Spider Ace's cosmic twin!'

'Welcome to the party,' Stef said, shaking her head in disbelief. But Dimi looked past her and his eyes pure *goggled*.

'*You're not even Edie Scrap any more!*' he gasped.

'Well, you must be top of the class,' came the hard, sarcastic reply, and we whirled around.

Stood, scowling, between the drifting universes, was the only other Infinity Racer I'd met. Her face was similar

55

to Edie Scrap, which wasn't a surprise – she was the same person, just from another dimension. But still, she looked proper different – from her jet-black quiff to the cold glint in her eyes. If Edie Scrap dressed like my dad's punk cousin Mould, this woman was dressed more like Mould's wife, Smash: all smart and threatening, in a long leather coat and with a face on like she's about to hit somebody who asked for it.

'We meet again,' Spider Ace said. 'Welcome to my most prized computer, the Commodore 65. This is its most prized app: the Map of the Multiverse.'

5
The Map of the Multiverse

We stood in a black, endless space that minutes before had been a mobile library. Glittering, glowing, interesting-shaped bubbles floated all around us, as Spider Ace walked between them, looking grave.

'Just imagine the *quadrillions* of children across the Multiverse,' she said. 'The *quintillions* of children born before you, and the *infinite number* of children who will be born after you. Taken like that, you're like grains of sand in an endless desert, except grains of sand don't whinge, or whine, or expect praise for every little movement they make.'

'I'm so glad I skipped football for this,' Dimi quipped, then shrank back as Spider Ace fixed him with an icy glare.

'What I *mean* to say,' she said sternly, 'is that if you tried to picture the sheer size of this magnificent Multiverse as a whole, your head would go *pop*. That's what the Map of the Multiverse is for. Each one of these bubbles is a universe, and in every one of these universes there exists a Kyan Green, a Dimitar and Stefania Anev, and a Luke Smith.'

'So which one's *our* universe then?' Dimi asked. 'The Crown? The Star? The *Heavy Sniper Rifle?!*' he added hopefully, pointing to a golden, mythic-looking weapon that drifted slowly past in the distance.

'None of them,' Spider Ace replied. 'None of the universes in this Sector is yours. This is merely the middle of the map.' For a strange moment she looked almost sympathetic. Then she called out, 'Commodore 65! Take us to Sector Three please.'

At once the bubbles began to speed up, until they were zipping past us at an alarming rate. We ducked and dodged around them, getting increasingly panicked while Spider Ace stood as still as granite rock, letting the universes flow by her.

'The Multiverse exists across a different plane of reality, beyond even the idea of shapes,' she said. 'But if it *did* have a shape? The Multiverse would be shaped like an egg. We are near the centre of that egg – what we call the Nucleus. The Nucleus is bright, glorious . . . and you don't live there. Your cosmic twins who live here are a bunch of rich nits who wouldn't know a crisis if it kicked them up the bum. They've even built a gate, called the Electron Shell, to protect them from outsiders. Here it is now.'

Blasting towards us was a wavy shell of fizzling energy – what looked like an impregnable force field that we were heading straight for! As Luke glanced nervously at me, I couldn't help but step back, then *flinch*, then DUCK . . . as the Electron Shell passed right through us.

'In reality,' Spider Ace said sternly, 'if you tried to hop to a universe through the Electron Shell, you would be pulverised to a pulp.'

'Ouch,' said Dimi. 'They must really not want us to visit.'

'It's not you they're keeping out,' Spider Ace said ominously, then admitted, 'Well, mostly not you.'

'Dude,' Stef said, wrinkling her nose. 'What's that *smell*?'

It was only faint, but you couldn't un-smell it; an aroma of left-out rubbish, of BO and school toilets. The map slowed down, to reveal universes with way less sparkle than the ones we'd seen before. Whereas the bubbles back inside the Nucleus had glowed with some legendary force, these were dull and lifeless. Where they'd been firing beams of bright energy at each other, these ones didn't connect at all. Oh, and where the previous bubbles had been glamorous crowns, and stars, and deadly rifles, these *really* weren't. A wrench drifted idly past me now, close to a toadstool – not a nice toadstool, to give you friendly words or turbo boosts, but a fungusy, *gross* toadstool, the type you're supposed to wash your hands ten times after touching.

'Yo, our manor is a *dump*,' Dimi said quietly, and every downbeat face agreed with him. The toadstool was followed by a hammer-shaped bubble above us, a *wheelie bin* below us, until at last we came to a stop beside a bubble so strange that I couldn't guess what it was . . . until it rotated to face me.

'It's a beaker,' I said. 'Like a *kids'* beaker.'

'Yes . . .' Spider said, and then awkwardly, 'Welcome to your universe. The, ahhh, Sippy Cup 'Verse.'

'*The Sippy Cup 'Verse*?!' I repeated.

'Are you joking?' Dimi muttered.

'The *Sippy Cup* 'Verse.' I said again. 'The Sippy Cup 'Verse . . .'

And as if our floating beaker couldn't get any more drab, Luke stepped closer to it, his eyes squinting.

'What are those red things on it?'

He was right. Our 'Sippy Cup Universe' looked diseased, wrapped in these thin, red, writhing tendrils, as if the veins on your eyeball suddenly came to life and started to *squeeze*. I took it all in – our diseased bubble, our manky neighbours, the stink of our whole Sector 3 – and I felt the kind of deep disappointment that hurts your chest.

'I mean, if our place is such a hole, then why'd I even get given the racetrack to begin with?' I said.

Spider Ace paused, confused.

'You weren't given the racetrack,' she said. 'At least, not by me. I don't know how you found it in your loft. I'm guessing it was just luck.'

'Luck,' I repeated, and let out a laugh that wasn't funny at all. 'So not only are we whiny grains of sand, we live in the dirtiest, stinkiest, *least* important part of the Multiverse – I mean *that* universe is *literally trash!* – and nothing we do will ever matter, and you think this is *luck . . .*'

'*No!*' Spider Ace said, in a way that made me look up. Furious, she marched towards me, between the toadstool bubble and a bubble that looked – honestly – like a pair of underpants.

'Now, this is important, Kyan, so use your ears,' Spider

Ace said. '*What* you are? That means nothing. You, me, everybody, we are all grains of sand. But what you *do*? The actions you take, the battles you fight? That can make a bigger difference than you could ever possibly imagine.'

'Oh yeah,' I scoffed, and waved around at our grotty Sector 3. 'It looks like we're doing great.'

'This map is *out of date by a month*.'

I looked up at her.

'Out of date?'

'I haven't updated the Commodore 65 since *the day before you discovered the Infinite Racetrack*, Kyan Green. So if you listen, and don't have any more mardies, you can see just what five punk kids like yourselves can do.'

'. . . All right.'

'*Commodore 65!*' she shouted. '*Update the map!*'

'Map of the Multiverse: Update Beginning.'

For a moment nothing seemed different. Then I realised that the bubbles were moving in quick, sharp jerks, like TIME LAPSE mode on my phone camera. I opened my mouth to ask a question, then a blast of bright blue energy BURST out from our Sippy Cup Universe.

Instantly Spider held up one hand, and the time lapse paused, leaving the energy beam sticking out like a shard of brilliant crystal. There had been loads of these

62

blue-white energy bursts back in the shiny Nucleus, I realised. But here, in Sector 3, this dark, dingy part of the Multiverse, I hadn't seen one until now.

'This is what happened the first time you activated the Infinite Race,' Spider said. 'You created a Cosmic Connection with another universe.'

'What's a Cosmic Connection?' asked Stef.

Spider turned to face us. Her eyes sparkled in the frozen blast of energy from our Sippy Cup 'Verse, and suddenly she looked more excited than I'd seen her before; almost like a kid.

'Have any of you ever done anything so brilliant that you couldn't explain?' she asked. 'Something that you would never have thought possible before you pulled it off?'

We all paused, thinking. Then Dimi put up his hand.

'At Football Factory,' he said eagerly, 'we were one–nil down, right . . .'

'I knew he was going to say this one,' me and Stef both said, grinning, but Spider Ace held up a finger for us to be silent. Encouraged, Dimi continued.

'Well, I cannot do overhead kicks. Honestly, never. But this cross came in too high and curling out . . . and right then I went for it. I twisted round, jumped higher than I've ever jumped, my feet bicycled up and over my head, and . . .'

He paused, and swallowed. When he spoke again, his voice was a whisper.

'It was the best shot I've ever done. Top bins. And I've never done it since.'

'That,' Spider said, 'sounds like the perfect example of a Cosmic Connection.'

'Really?' Dimi said, brightening.

'It sounds like,' Spider Ace continued, 'in that moment, another Dimitar in another universe was also trying to achieve something they have never done before. In that moment, you and your cosmic twin joined forces. You experienced a Cosmic Connection, where you pulled off an incredible overhead kick . . . and in another universe, another Dimitar pulled off something equally unlikely.'

'He had a wash,' Stef wisecracked. But Spider turned glittering eyes on her, and she fell quiet.

'Used correctly,' she continued quietly, 'this is what the Infinite Race does. It forces a Cosmic Connection, builds a bridge between worlds that have become disconnected. More importantly, given to the right people, it enables you to help your cosmic twins reach heights they despair of ever reaching. Once there were many teams of Infinity

Racers, directed by a trusted Navigator to the universes who needed them the most. Now . . .'

Breaking off, like she'd caught herself saying too much, she turned back around to the Sippy Cup 'Verse. She held out her hand again, and said: 'Commodore 65, CONTINUE UPDATE.'

The Multiverse Map began to move forwards again, the pulsar of energy bursting from our Sippy Cup 'Verse, before it smashed into the Wrench.

'So . . . that was my first race?' I asked. 'I was in the Wrench Universe?'

Spider Ace nodded. 'It was the first time in a long, *long* time that Kyan Green had come up against Kenneth Stringer and won.'

'But I was cheated in that race!' I exclaimed. 'Kenneth Tha Goat claimed to win, and when everybody booed he made a dash for the prize money.'

'Oh, definitely,' Spider said with a grim smile. 'KTG *tried* to cheat. But your final act in the Wrench 'Verse was to shout at him and leap from your car. After you left, your cosmic twin – *and* the entire crowd – chased him for the prize winnings he stole. The first time anyone had *ever* stopped Kenneth Tha Goat from cheating before.'

Another blast of energy burst out then, both from the

Wrench and the Sippy Cup universes, and fired into another *three* universe bubbles nearby.

'These complaints grew,' Spider Ace continued, 'and not just in the Wrench Dimension either. You see, every action you take is felt everywhere else. Your Cosmic Connection caused *more* Cosmic Connections, like a *movement* of people making a stand against Mr Stringer across the Multiverse, fighting a man who had pushed them down in so many ways. And then, because the odds were stacked against you . . . the movement began to falter.'

After the initial burst of Cosmic Connections, the energy blasts began to fade away. Our Sector began to darken again, the red tendrils shuffling closer with a stomach-turning quiet. Even though this had already happened, anxiety rose through me. My eye caught something in the far, dark distance, beyond the floating bubbles of our sector. These huge, squat, red shapes were sat barely visible, in the far depths of the Multiverse around us. They were huddled together, these shapes, as though they'd gathered around to watch us fail. For a nanosecond I had an uneasy feeling, like being watched by a pack of wolves. Above them all, also barely visible, were three words, like a map label almost too far away to bother reading:

THE PURE STATE

'And then,' Spider said, 'You hopped again – this time to the Underverse.'

The moment she said it, another *blast* of energy burst out of our Sippy Cup 'Verse, this time into the boxer shorts-looking bubble. The map was lit up even more brightly than before, and both the red shapes and the label vanished like flecks of dust under full sunlight.

'There you battled with the corrupt Police Officer Stringer. You and your friends *kept* on battling, in fact. You hopped from universe to universe, visiting underground oceans and a village in the eye of a storm. You stood up against Stringer and his wrongdoing.'

'We didn't "visit" that ocean,' Luke pointed out sharply. 'You *chucked* me into it!'

'Yeah, that . . .' Spider replied, and at least looked a *bit* embarrassed. 'I thought you needed a nudge. Besides, I wouldn't have let Chief Stringer take any *vital* organs.'

As Spider blustered, I stepped forward to take in the results of our dimension-hopping. Our Sector was almost completely joined together, straight lines of Cosmic Connections linking every universe to every *other* universe like a neon-bright train map. The stench had gone, replaced by a fresh smell, like the air after a thunderstorm. And those red tendrils, the thin wriggly cords that had been squeezing at our universe? They were melting away, until there were barely any left.

'Update Complete,' the Commodore 65 said. At last, the Cosmic Connections ended, the energy wisped away into nothing, and the time-lapse look of the map returned to normal. Right at the end, with the last beam that fired into the Wheelie Bin 'Verse – where we'd caused mayhem across the Giant Grinster's kitchen table – I could have sworn I heard another noise, like that brief FAIL *beep* you get when selecting the wrong option in an app . . . but I barely noticed. With those thin red tendrils almost eliminated, our Sector 3 looked better than ever. Not perfect, certainly not glowing like the Nucleus, but better.

'So . . . no,' Spider said. 'I didn't give you the Infinite Racetrack. No, you are not royalty, you are not magic, you are not a superhero. You are not default special at all. You are a kid who found a racetrack in their loft, and with his friends, used it to save not one universe, but *many*. Which is infinitely preferable, if you ask me.'

I looked up to see Spider staring at us all intently, a slight smile on her face. Suddenly I felt proud, properly proud.

'Commodore 65!' Spider called. 'Set up Infinity Racer Kyan Green's track!'

'Oh, my track's at home,' I began. Then, with a clatter, a shelf slid out from some unseen wall, and *kept* sliding, stretching far out between us. On the table was the Infinite Race. As in, *my* Infinite Race.

'My racetrack!' I gasped.

'Your next mission,' Spider said, 'will, like all the best missions, also be a *lesson*, a vital way for you to understand the true importance of these Cosmic Connections. There are two worlds you can visit for this lesson. In one universe are beauty and light. The other one . . . involves a lot of dirt.'

'I think we'll go for the first one, please,' I said, and Spider Ace nodded.

'Fair enough. You'll just need to follow the instructions in your latest Level Four code.'

There was a pause.

'Er . . .' said Stef.

'You *have* solved it, haven't you?' Spider smiled, but her eyes were suddenly sharp. 'It's the easiest one you've had yet.'

Nobody spoke: that awkward silence in class when *nobody's* done the work and *everybody's* about to get told off. Spider Ace waved her hand, and the map scrolled around us, so suddenly that I fell over. When I got back to my feet, the others were all staring up behind me, looks of horror on their faces. I turned ... and stepped back. Floating over us, bigger than ever, was the big, ugly toadstool. Close up, its hooded cap looked swollen and pulsating, its green-and-white polka-dot skin muddy and, well, *fungusy*.

'I don't wanna go there!' I exclaimed.

'Of course you don't,' Spider Ace said. 'The Fungiverse is a perfect lesson for Racers Who Don't Do Their Homework. You say that this racetrack is "your" racetrack, Kyan Green, but I say that you are still earning it. You've done well so far, but the work you have to do is too important for you to ignore important codes, understand?'

I stared at the Fungiverse toadstool, and gulped. The idea that I could lose the Infinite Racetrack was something I couldn't bear. But just as I was about to nod, Luke spoke up.

'We only found the code yesterday,' he pointed out, 'and we're only kids. If it's that serious, shouldn't someone else be—'

'We can do it,' I said sharply. What was Luke playing at? Did he *want* to lose me the racetrack?! 'The Fungiverse. Send us there.'

Spider Ace looked from me to Luke, and back again. When she spoke her voice was softer.

'Good,' she said at last. 'Now, the Fungiverse is a strange place, in that the entire universe is connected by one ecosystem. At the moment, that universe's version of Stringer is upsetting the balance in this ecosystem. Your mission is to investigate what he is doing, and stop it. Remember, Kyan in this universe is *also* threatened with losing his home. His situation is every bit as serious as yours was, in their city of Leaferpool.'

'Leaferpool?!' said Dimi.

'Yes,' Spider repeated. 'Leaferpool. What's so funny about Leaferpool?'

Now we were all smiling.

'It just, you know, sounds like a tree pun for Liverpool,' I said, chuckling.

Spider Ace clearly didn't see the funny side.

'You will be riding hexapods called Springfeet,' she continued. 'I'll admit, it was difficult to find a toy hexapod, but I have programmed the Commodore 65 to guide you, and so *these* should work fine instead.'

She reached into her pocket, and deposited four tiny things on to the track. Frowning, I stepped closer to see what they were. Then the four things *scurried*, all in separate directions. With *enormous* dismay, I realised that Spider had placed four little bugs on to the Infinite Racetrack.

'Wait a minute . . .' I began. But the track began to tremble. The smooth, shiny surface began to *bubble* and warp, like something was cooking beneath it. The deep stink of compost hit my nose, and just as I turned to ask what was happening, a torrent of mud *spewed* out of the track like a fountain all over us!

'Euwww!' we shouted. I stepped back, trying frantically to wipe my face . . . but this mud was gripping me, pulling me towards the track. I struggled, but the track grew bigger and bigger, more streams of dirt and mud bursting out to cover us.

'Now,' Spider Ace shouted over the roar, 'you should hopefully not encounter any almost-family or almost-friends in the Fungiverse, but remember – until you progress to Level Five, seeing *anybody* is dangerous.'

'Wait!' I shouted. 'What do we do when we—'

But it was too late.

There was a sucking sound.

There was a tornado of wind and dirt around my ears.

And I plunged, face-first, into the mud and slime of the Fungiverse.

6
The Fungiverse, Where Kyan Meets Another Racer

'Ohhhh,' I moaned. 'Oh, this is disgusting.'

Don't get it twisted, I don't mind nature. I'll pat a dog, when it's clear that the nutty owner ain't gonna stop barking 'SHE'S EVER SO FRIENDLY!' until I do. I can live with cats, even if they care about *naff all* but themselves. I even rode a horse once, although me and that horse will *never* be swapping Christmas cards. But nature in general, outdoorsy nature? I like it a *lot* more when I'm looking at it through a screen. And with bugs *I draw the line.*

And right then, I was sitting on the hard, bristly back of

a bug that looked like an unholy cross between a cockroach, an ant and a hippo.

There was no saddle. No reins either – the only handholds were these two horrible stalk-like antennae that stuck out the top of this bug. At first I thought my feet were resting on a big safety bar – until I shifted and the bar *moved*. Panicking, I floundered about more, and only regained my balance as Dimi's bug-horse ambled past. The safety bar, I saw, was actually a muscly extra leg, looped around the Springfoot in a way that was – yup – also gross.

'They're mental, innit!' Dimi yelled joyfully. 'I've called mine Gary.' And right then, 'Gary' leaned over and *vomited on the ground.*

'Did nobody else see that?' I said faintly. 'That thing just chucked up!'

'I'm going with what Spider Ace called them,' Stef said, ignoring me. 'She called them Springfeet, didn't she? So meet Springer.'

'Mine's called Thumper,' Luke said cheerfully. 'What's yours called, Ky?' And – yep – Thumper went and vomited right then as well.

'There's something wrong with all of you,' I said.

'Funny name,' Luke said, grinning. 'You should call it "Something Wrong" for short.' It was good to see him smiling again at least, I thought . . . before I looked around, and found a whole new list of things to be disgusted about.

We were in a whole herd of Springfeet, moving along a tight tunnel. The walls and ceiling were close enough to touch . . . except they were grotty, and blistered with black-and-white mould like rotten fruit. Thin white tubes travelled along the ceiling, swelling and contracting like they were alive, beads of this rank green liquid forming on them. One caught me – *plink!* – on the forehead. I groaned aloud, and ducked my head downwards . . . only to see that the ground was almost *completely* formed of Springfoot vomit. As Stef pulled up alongside me, *bursting* to share some information about this despicable place, it was *tough* not to swear.

'Don't you talk about wonderful nature or something,' I warned her. 'After this I wanna bath for a week.'

'Buck up,' she said, laughing. 'This is all amazing if you think about it. You know what we're in?! This is a *Mycelial Network*, a massive network of fungus tunnels that carry food and even *information* beneath forest floors. Scientists found that if a bear caught a salmon and left it in one part of the forest, it would rot down into the ground, work its way into the Mycelial Network somehow, and its DNA wound up in the *trees*! Thanks to these fungus pathways, *the trees ate the salmon!*'

I stared back at her, more appalled than ever.

'How is that good *with us in here*?!' I said. 'And how does that explain these . . . sick insects?'

'Well, *firstly*, they're not insects, so that's just lame,' Stef said. 'And *secondly*, that sick is what's *building the entire tunnel*! In this universe, the Springfeet must help *create* the Mycelial Network!'

I looked down again at the vomit floor. Stef was right: it was slowly decomposing as it rose up along the walls, turning into those white thin tunnels by the time it reached the ceiling.

'The worst place we will *ever* visit,' I declared. And as if things weren't awful enough, a SCREAM travelled along the fungus ceiling towards us.

Yeah, that sounds *nuts*, so I'll say it again: A SHOUT started off far away, and raced along those little white tubes above us until it was a SCREAM.

'STRING RIPPERRRRRRRRRRRRR!!!'

'Oh my days, what the *hell* was that?!' I squeaked, as the bellow faded into the distance, 'Was that my grandma's voice?! What's a String Ripper?'

That's when the tunnel behind us began to *rumble* . . .

'Oh no,' I moaned. 'What's that now?!'

The rumbling grew louder, and now even Stef was frowning.

'It's getting closer,' I said, my voice high with terror. 'How do these things go faster? RUN, BUG! CREEP! CRAWL! BUZZ!' It was no good. Something Wrong kept ambling forwards with me on its back, even as the rumbling became deafening until . . .

With a CRASH, the tunnel wall beside me collapsed into clouds of dirt and dust, and the bulging luminous flesh of the biggest, ugliest, *squirmiest* maggot writhed towards us.

Well I have *never* screamed like that in my entire *life*.

'*RUN!*' I shrieked. 'RUNRUNRUNRUNRUN!' *Finally* that hopeless Springfoot sped up, its legs tottering forwards like a toddler drunk on Blue Raspberry Prime, but it wasn't fast enough. Daring to glance back, I saw the squirming maggot smashing its way ever closer through the collapsing tunnel, its pearly white front-mouth folding back into a mushy toothless gob that hoovered up the Springfeet behind me, swallowing them whole.

'RUN!' I screeched, and somehow my voice was even higher than before. RUNRUNRUNRUN—'

That's when my feet caught Something Wrong's safety-bar leg.

It was like a catapult. Instantly the Springfoot's leg snapped open and we shot up through the tunnel ceiling, so fast that I was pinned face down into Something Wrong's bristly back. We ripped through layer after thin layer of mould and mush, through tunnel after tunnel, until I burst out into the open air, soared for a second . . . and slammed back down on to Something Wrong's hard back.

'WHOA!' said a voice nearby. 'NICE SPRING!'

Bleary-eyed and still groggy, I hefted myself back up to sitting, and felt warmth on my face.

I was at the bottom of a huge, rocky chasm. Sunlight filtered hazily down the brown and black cliffs. Tunnels had been dug through the walls on every side, while humongous tree roots, gigantic leaves and quivering toad-stools jutted out to create broken, uneven paths and bridges that climbed all the way up to the ground far above. Everywhere I looked there were glistening, *stinky* pools of fluid and – you've guessed it – mould.

'Urgh,' I groaned aloud. 'It's like Go Ape had a disease.'

'Ha!' the voice laughed. 'That's *exactly* what it's like! I'm guessing Spider Ace just threw you into the new 'verse without any warning, eh?'

So I hadn't imagined it. Dazed, I looked around to see a blond boy sat on another Springfoot with a grin on his face.

'You . . .' I said, stunned. 'You know Spider Ace? And *'verse* . . . You mean *universe*? You know about hopping?!'

The boy's smile widened, and he gave me a cheeky salute.

'Safe safe, Kyan,' he said. 'I'm Edwin. I'm another Infinity Racer. And together we can kick your Cosmic Nemesis Mr Stringer's *butt*.'

I stared at this older boy, still in shock. He grinned right back.

'The others!' I said suddenly. 'I've gotta help them, I—'

'Your friends are fine,' the boy said easily. 'They bounced further along the tunnel, that's all. You did a good job escaping without any warning from *Coach*.'

There was something bitter in the way he said *Coach*, which I guessed meant Spider. But he kept smiling, and I was so shocked to see him that I didn't really notice it.

'You're an Infinity Racer!' I exclaimed. 'You . . . What are you . . . how did you . . . where are you from, Edwin?!'

'One question at a time, cool mint!' Edwin said with a laugh. 'It's mad, I know. Spider Ace is great at the hurling-you-into-danger bit, but not so hot on the teaching. I'm originally from the Hatchet 'Verse, but nowadays the whole Multiverse is my home, bro!'

'And . . . and what are you doing here?'

'Like I said, Chief . . .' Edwin chuckled. 'I'm here to help you with your Cosmic Nemesis, Stringer!'

'What do you mean, Cosmic Nemesis?' I asked.

'She hasn't even told you about that?!' Edwin said with a laugh. 'Wait – I bet she went with the whole "*You're no superhero, you're a whining grain of sand*" bit.'

I nodded slowly. Spider Ace had put it differently somehow, but . . . that was what she'd said.

'She also told us about Cosmic Connections,' I began.

'Bro, your Cosmic Connections are why you are so

important!' Edwin exclaimed. 'You and Mr Stringer – I'm guessing you *keep* finding yourself against him, am I right?'

'Yeah,' I said bitterly. 'Every universe I visit, *he's* trying to squash me, or shoot me, or make my family homeless. No matter who else is there, *he* is.'

'You see, that is *not* usual,' Edwin said. 'There are *thousands* of worlds out there where your teachers are different, your neighbours …. everyone outside your family. There are worlds where you've never met your best friends. So this connection that you and Stringer have . . . it's special.'

'How?' I asked. 'What does the fact he always has it in for my family have to do with *anything*?'

'Think about it. The way Cosmic Connections work, if you win in one universe, then *next* Kyan is more likely to win in the *next* universe, and so on.'

'I get that,' I said, 'but how's that different to anybody else?'

'Because if *you* win, Mr Stringer *loses* . . . and the Mr Stringer in the *next* universe is more likely to lose as well. And who is *next* Mr Stringer fighting?'

Suddenly it dawned on me.

'*Next* Kyan Green.'

'Next *Kyan Green*. It's a *double win*! And if *more* Kyans win? It's winning *squared*, or *cubed*, or whatever the biggest number is you can think of.'

'A *googleplex* win,' I said, chucking the word in, all casual.

'*Exactly*. So don't let me hear you're not special, Kyan Green. You're more special than *anyone* in your universe. And you need to beat Stringer, and keep beating him.'

I grinned back. This Edwin seemed cool. He was older, like fourteen or fifteen, and even watching him control his Springfoot was a lesson. He caught me watching and chuckled.

'What level Racer are you?'

'Oh . . .' I said, a bit awkwardly. 'Probably about . . . I'm Level Four.'

'*Four?!*' he said with a grin. 'No way. I've seen you operate, you're easily Level Five!'

I grinned, feeling delighted.

'What level are you?!' I asked.

'Level Ten,' Edwin said airily.

'*Ten?!*' But already he was leaning in, still smiling, but serious.

'But please listen to my advice now, bro. In this universe, Stringer – the String Ripper, he's called – is psycho. He has a whole army of *beasts* who've been wiping out all the Springfeet that run the Mycelial Network. They're basically stopping food and water getting across the forest! Lucky for you, I'm gonna teach you how to ride.'

It wasn't so difficult, once Edwin showed me. First up, there wasn't any top speed – Something Wrong was gonna bimble about at the speed it wanted to, and that was that. To turn it right I rested my hand on the left side of its head, and to turn left I did the opposite. Once I'd mastered that, the only thing to learn was Something Wrong's terrifying *spring*.

'Two things to remember,' Edwin said. 'First: the harder the surface you're springing off, the further you'll go. Spring off this rock, you'll go flying. Move to this pool of water, though . . .'

He trotted across a huge puddle. His Springfoot's feet didn't dip *in* the water, I noticed with amazement. Instead they pattered along the water's skin.

'Spring off water, and you'll pull off a smaller jump, more controlled.' Edwin pushed down on that strange safety bar, and at once its sprung legs fired down, sending them both somersaulting *backwards* up to a bridge nearby.

A somersault? As Edwin turned back, smiling down at me, I gingerly guided Something Wrong on to the water.

Taking a nervous breath, I pressed the safety bar down – and Something Wrong fired up and *over through the air*, leaving me clutching desperately to its bristly back before I landed next to Edwin with a *Yes!* . . . only to find that he'd already sprung.

'OK,' I breathed, elated. 'Let's do this.'

And I did. I followed Edwin in and out of tunnels, over bridges, and up and down the ravine. We sprang off everything: water, wood, rock, leaves and even a toadstool (which *fired* me, yelping with fear, all the way to the other side).

By the time we returned to the bottom of the chasm, I felt more confident riding Something Wrong than I ever imagined I would feel riding a bug. Following Edwin to a dirt wall, I kinda hoped for a well done . . . but then I noticed something strange about the wall. It looked . . . odd, like it was cut-and-pasted in, with a root sticking out of it, unnaturally straight. Edwin pushed down on the root, and with a groaning metal sound, the wall swung open to reveal an *enormous* cave.

'Oh my gosh,' I said, looking further in. The sound of quiet wrapped my ears in wool, and the floor dropped down *deep*, towering stalagmites climbing up from it like spires.

'Welcome,' Edwin said, 'to the Bug Jar.'

'Did you dig all this?!' I asked in disbelief. Edwin laughed.

'Bless,' he said. 'Nah, I didn't have to. Millions of years ago, there would've been a softer rock here, stuck between loads of harder rock. You've figured out there's trees above us all, yeah? Yeah, well, as the tree's roots burst down into it, so did the rain. After *millions* of years, this whole chunk of soft rock would've dissolved and fed the tree, until all that was left was this cave. You can even still see the roots, look! All I did was give this cave a door. And *this* door has the best doorbell you ever heard.'

Edwin shoved another root lever down, and a strange, chirping noise echoed out of the cave. I was about to ask what it was supposed to do, when Something Wrong darted forwards like somebody had yanked a lead.

'Whoa!' I yelled. 'Oi, bug, *stop*!' But it was no good – no matter how much I turned Something Wrong, it would turn back towards the cave. Finally, with a laugh, Edwin lifted both levers. The door shut, the noise stopped and, at last, so did my Springfoot.

'It's called a Bugnotiser,' he said with a grin. 'Cheesy name, but those bugs can't resist the sound! I found it way away, in the Broomiverse, but I never had a use for it till now.'

'Can we ... do that?' I said slowly. 'Using technology from other universes, that's OK, is it?'

'Bro, have you met the String Ripper's Beast Army yet?!' I shook my head, and Edwin chuckled. 'Those bugs are monsters. But if you can get them near to this door and switch on the Bugnotiser, they'll flood inside. Shut the door, bish-bosh, no more army to worry about.'

'That does sound good,' I admitted.

'Sure does!' Edwin replied, laughing. 'Good luck, Kyan.'

'Ky?' Luke's voice called out nearby. 'KYAN?!'

'Oops, somebody's a keen Jean!' Edwin said with a grin. I grinned back, but then he added something strange. 'You two are *friends* in this universe, then?'

'Yeah,' I said, 'Er ... wait, how come? Are we not—'

But Edwin was already steering his Springfoot away.

'I have to go myself now, bro. Remember – *don't let Stringer win*. Oh ... and maybe don't tell Spider I helped you, yeah? She might actually give a Racer some credit for once.'

'Wait,' I said, a million questions suddenly occurring to me. 'What about you? What's your mission? Where's the other Edwin in my universe – I mean 'verse?'

'Ha, you've got to work on that one-question thing,'

Edwin said with a grin. 'Remember – this is between you and me, bro, yeah?'

And with a flick of his feet, Edwin was soaring up, bouncing from every platform above me, until his Springfoot disappeared over the top of the rocks, and was gone.

'Kyan!' Luke said in the entryway, before turning back. 'He's here! Kyan's here! PHEW, I was worried where you'd gone!'

'Chill out, keen Jean!' I laughed, using Edwin's phrase. Luke's smile faltered a bit, but I barely noticed.

'Where've you been?!' Dimi said, entering the hallway with Stef before looking around. 'Whoa. What is this place?'

'It's a training hall,' I said confidently. 'And before long it's going to be a battleground. I've just met a *Level Ten Infinity Racer*.'

7
The String Ripper

'So the whole Multiverse hangs on you versus Stringer!' Dimi said, impressed.

'Well, that's how he made it sound,' I said back, glancing nervously at Stef, expecting a cutting reply. But she was nodding.

'That makes sense,' she said. 'He *has* been the bad guy in *every* universe.'

Luke, however, looked doubtful.

'So you've got to ... what?' he asked. 'Destroy every Mr Stringer? I thought Spider Ace said we had to find the balance in the ecosystem or something?'

'Yeah, and *that's* how we'll find the balance,' I said, feeling a pang of annoyance. 'His beasts are eating too many of our Springfeet, and we're going to trap them all. It's not like Edwin wants me to *kill* Stringer or anything!'

I showed my friends the Bugnotiser, which almost dragged *all* of our Springfeet into the tree-root cave. We had a laugh trying to switch it off, but again, when Luke saw the futuristic mechanics behind the hidden door, he frowned.

'And this was always just *there*?' he said doubtfully. He was being so *negative*, it was doing my head in. That's why I didn't tell the *whole* truth, about how Edwin had put it in from another universe.

'I s'pose so,' I said quickly. 'And hey, you should see the moves Edwin showed me! If you bounce off water you—'

'Bounce lower and do a somersault. Yeah, we know,' said Stef. 'We've been riding these bugs around looking for you, remember?'

Expertly she guided her Springfoot to the toadstool . . . and they *bounced*, pirouetting across the chasm. The others all began to spring from different surfaces towards her, and as I joined them, I realised with annoyance that my gang were a *lot* better on Springfeet than I was.

Still, with each jump, I grew more and more confident. Dimitar – easily the best on his Springfoot, Gary – led us all to the top of the chasm until the platforms became smaller and the ground seemed *terrifyingly* far below. By the time I managed to bounce up to the very top, standing over the waterfall, I didn't care that my friends had reached it ages ago; I felt ready.

And then I looked around.

'Oh. My. Gosh,' I said. 'Er – why does Fungiverse Kyan spend so much time down there when up *here*'s like this?!'

It was a prehistoric paradise. A *gigantic* flower hung over us, surrounded by blades of grass the size of trees. Above us stood a tree trunk wider than our school building, climbing so tall that I couldn't see where it ended. Bugs the size of birds soared above us; and swooping down on *them* were birds the size of dragons. Everywhere there was chattering and noise, like our street on a sunny Sunday. Even the tree was – and all right, I'm sounding *proper* drippy now – even the tree was *speaking*, this deep warbling voice that made the ultimate background noise, like Mr Wimpole in Singing Assembly. *All right, Nature, you're not* all *bad*, I thought, then leaned forwards and stroked Something Wrong's scabby head.

'You're a good bug, aren'cha?' I said gruffly. Something Wrong turned, and snuffled my face with its mouth. 'Gerroff, you!' I laughed, pushing it back gently.

'You *do* know that mouth has been vomiting up mould this whole time,' Stef reminded me, and I flinched.

'Seriously, geddoff, bro that's disgusting,' I said sternly to Something Wrong. 'You should be ashamed of yourself.'

'Hold up,' Dimi shushed. 'You hear that?'

We stopped and listened. Dimi's hearing is *crazy* sharp, and for a long while it seemed like there was nothing. Then, very faintly, a rumble began to build, faint and deep, coming from the rocks far below.

'Down there,' Dimi murmured. The others leaped swiftly down the rocks into the chasm and I followed, hoping nobody would turn to see my bouncing butt and my panicked lurch-face with every jolt. By the time I'd caught up, Dimi had stopped halfway along a rocky bridge, listening hard.

'Over there,' he murmured, and pointed to the tunnel above us. Then he turned, pointing down to the soft ground at the bottom of the chasm. The rumble grew louder, and soon he was pointing left and right, up and down.

'It's coming from *everywhere*!' he muttered.

'It sounds like . . .' Luke said nervously. 'It sounds like a stampede!'

Because it was.

With a sudden burst of noise, *hundreds* of Springfeet exploded out on every side.

'Kyan, look out!' Luke yelled, as the trundling hippo-cockroa-bugs rampaged across the bridge towards me, and just in time we dropped down to a small platform below.

'Phew!' I said. 'That was close, thank you, Lu—'

But Luke's face was frozen in sheer terror. He lifted one trembling hand, pointing to the bridge below us.

'Is that the String Ripper?!' he gasped.

He was Mr Stringer's cosmic twin, that was for sure. But where Mr Stringer was scary in an officey, teachery sort of way, the String Ripper was just flat *heinous*. He was riding a scorpion, for one thing; a *scorpion*. He was flipping *hench*, like the old action-movie stars Mum and Dad like, and his arms, chest and face were greased in this greeny-brown stuff I *prayed* wasn't poo. He lifted what looked like a carved-out beetle-shell to his lips and blew it.

With the chasm-shaking sound of this horn, his army appeared.

First, the giant maggot that had

nearly eaten us down in the fungus tunnels burst on to the bridge above, more bloated and slimy than ever. A pack of huge spiders scuttled out across the ground below, ripping through panicked Springfeet with legs like spindled blades. Oh, and just in case we felt too safe, there was a *swooping* sound above … and a swarm of giant mosquitoes flew down, plucking the Springfeet off their platforms.

'Take the Springfeet!' the String Ripper roared, beating his chest. 'Take them and eat them *allllll!*'

'NO!'

For a moment I wondered which *idiot* had shouted that. Then I realised it was me. The cavern fell into silence. The Stringer Ripper stepped forwards, looking up at me, and it took everything not to run away.

'Well, well, well,' he snarled, and let out a laugh like a hyena. 'Some sprats from the DUNG patrol. What are you doing here? Don't you know who I am?'

Word of advice? Never ask someone with smarts that question.

'Er, *no*,' I said. 'Who are ya?'

'I – I'm …' the String Ripper said, suddenly flustered. 'The String Ripper doesn't need to explain himself to a little sprat like you!'

'Good for the String Ripper,' I said. 'Who are you though?'

'I'M the String Ripper!'

'The *Sling Dipper*?' (I mean, this is all like basic level wind-up, innit.)

'STRING RIPPER!'

'The Strong Rapper?!'

'THE—'

'You're upsetting the balance of the ecosystem!' Luke shouted at him, and I cringed a bit. 'You're not supposed to be here.'

That was a setback.

'Not supposed . . . not *supposed* to be here?!' The String Ripper let out a bark of wolfish laughter, and a horrible sawing sound echoed across the ravine. His grim army was laughing along with him.

'There is *nowhere* I'm not supposed to be,' he snarled with a sudden manic rage, and the laughter stopped dead. 'I *strongly* suggest you leave, little sprats.'

I stepped forwards, anger at this bully warming my veins. *Cosmic Nemesis*, I thought, and the fury felt good. *You're my Cosmic Nemesis.*

'You haven't been told yet, have you?' I shouted. 'Things. Are. Changing.'

95

The String Ripper stared up at me, and I stared down at him. A thunderous sound built around us, his 'beasties' hammering a beat of war on the rocks.

'Have at it then!' he frothed. 'Have at it!'

'Ky?' Dimi hissed, as he and Stef dropped down to us. 'Er . . . what was the plan again?'

'We've got to get the String Ripper's army chasing us, and get them all down there,' I said, nodding to Edwin's hidden door in the earth far below. I'll admit that, right then, that plan seemed a lot less straightforward. Fortunately, Stef was locking *straight* into full strategy mode.

'Right,' she whispered. 'So, we need them *behind* us, yeah? So we should climb up, all the way to the top. *Then*, when they form this stream chasing us, we turn back round past them, one of us races ahead and switches on the Bugnotiser. Yeah?'

'Yeah,' I said, grateful for the plan.

'Unfortunately,' she went on, 'because he knows how the door works best, it'll have to be Kyan in front so we'll have to slow down to allow for his riding, yeah?' (I *tried* to not get offended as Dimi and Luke both grumbled.) 'Then we bounce outta the way *just* before we reach the door. The beasties flood in past us, Kyan shuts the door, *bam*, we've saved the universe. Safe?'

'Safe,' I agreed. But Luke *still* didn't look happy.

'This doesn't sound like balance . . .' he began, but before I could point out that we didn't have time for debates, we *really* didn't have time for debates.

'ATTACK!' the String Ripper roared. All at once the swarm went for us, spiders scurrying up, mosquitoes swooping down, and the Multiverse's most overfed maggot rolling towards us.

'UP!' I shouted. And we leapt up away from those snapping jaws. The next platform up was a winding path that ran along the cliff. We ambled up it *frighteningly* slowly, as the monsters followed *right* behind us and – SNAP! – I leaped to safety just in time. The platforms got shorter as we climbed, the jumps faster, as we fled the buzzing, scuttling and slicing stream of death *right* at our heels. One spider with extra-long front legs and seven gouged-out eyes seemed to go for me in particular, springing ahead of my friends and slashing at me with those venomous fangs before I sprang out of its reach, up to the top of the chasm and –

'BACKDOWNBACKDOWNBACKDOWN!' Dimi roared, as a swarm of spiders, mozzies and tumbling maggots buzzed up towards us. Something Wrong finally acted on its own, tottering cheerfully around and off the edge to –

'NonoNO!' I yelled, and we dropped like a stone, plunging from rock to leaf to toadstool, faster and faster, past the roaring beasties. It was all I could do to cling on to Something Wrong's antennae, but it was *amazingly* nimble, dropping down almost as soon as it reached each platform and barely jostling me . . . until we dropped down to a huge fern leaf, and another creature landed on it just before we did.

It was disastrous for Something Wrong's landing. The platform wobbled as it landed, and those tottering legs buckled, flattening me painfully into its hard back. There was no time to recover either: our attacker was the one-eyed spider, and as it hissed and spat, Something Wrong backed away, and the entire leaf began to droop beneath our weight.

'Mmmm, *nope*,' I said, and kicked the safety bar out. And the timing was *seriously* lucky. Thanks to the leaf, we sprang horizontally across the chasm to safety, bouncing the spider off the leaf entirely. It wasn't the only beastie to fall either. As we kept dropping down, I had a chance to look up and see the others just behind . . . along with a gruesome rain of beastie after beastie missing their landing and tumbling past to splatter on the ground below.

'No!' The String Ripper's scream echoed around the chasm. 'Careful, my precious buggy-wugs, CAREFUL!!'

We dropped down the final three platforms, and at last reached the bug-spattered ground, about five metres to the hidden door. I pointed Something Wrong at it, yelled for the Springfoot to '*Go, Something Wrong, GO!*' . . . and the bug took forever. Seriously, considering the *petrifying* chase we'd endured just to get here, it was the laziest, most ambling-est stroll yet. Through some evil miracle, that one-eyed spider staggered to its spindly feet, and even before I could shriek '*You're still alive, how are you still alive!*' began to scurry towards us with a bloodthirsty leer.

'You're trapped now, little sprat!' the String Ripper cackled. 'Time to be mincemeat for spider supper!'

'Please, Something Wrong!' I sobbed. 'Please go faster!' And would you believe it, that stinky, sicky creature finally listened. Those brilliant little legs whirled back and forth, boosting us a *tiny* amount, just as the vicious spider scrabbled towards me, just as my friends screamed at the ravenous horde of nightmares slobbering and snarling just behind them, and . . .

. . . just as I reached the root levers and SLAMMED them both up as hard as I could before *pushing* Something Wrong's wonderful spring down with both feet.

'Eh?' was all I heard the String Ripper say as I bounced up to the safety of a platform. And it all seemed to happen at once.

The hidden door creaked open. That strange chirruping sound blared into the cave. And the others reached the doors before *SNAPping* upwards to safety from . . .

'Yes!'

Because the String Ripper's army of monsters *poured* into the cave. The String Ripper let out a howl of fury, and blew on his weird leaf horn, but it was no good – Edwin's Bugnotiser won. The String Ripper roared, and I was about to gloat at him, when –

'LUKE!' Dimi called out. I looked down . . . and felt a deep terror.

Luke's Springfoot had fallen under the Bugnotiser's spell, and was caught up in the final tumult of frenetic bugs. No matter how hard he struggled, he was being dragged inside, and there was only one thing he could do.

'JUMP!' I shouted. 'YOU'VE GOT TO JUMP, LUKE!'

'NO!' he shouted back. 'THUMPER'S CAUGHT!'

'JUMP!'

Finally Luke flung himself clear of the bug. Thumper and the last of the String Ripper's Beast Army streamed into the gigantic cave. Dropping down from the platform, I slammed both levers down. There was that metal creak, the doors closed . . . and the String Ripper let out another howl.

'NOOOOOOO!'

He leaped down, banging his fists against the wall, yelling and gnashing his teeth.

'What did you do with my beasties!' he gibbered. 'Where are they?!'

We all stared at him. I mean, it seemed obvious where they'd all gone. With a final, wailing scream, the String Ripper leaped back on to his scorpion. Weeping, he bounded away, down the tunnel and out of sight.

'YAAY!' we shouted, but even right then, I caught Stef's eye and I *knew* we were both thinking, *This doesn't feel right*. And then I noticed Luke, facing away from us, standing close to the hidden door.

Luke didn't turn around.

'This wasn't a good idea,' he said quietly. 'I told you that.'

'But, Luke,' I protested. 'We took him down! Another victory, it—'

'I lost ThumpThump,' he said louder, and the quiet anger in his voice suddenly made me worry.

'ThumpThump?' I asked, for a second unsure who he meant.

'Where did he go?' Luke said. 'Where did he go, thanks to *your* plan?'

'I . . .'

'I told you,' he said. 'I told you we should listen to your GranGran. Now . . .'

'GranGran? Luke, what's—'

'Ky,' Stef whispered. I looked up, and her face was urgent. 'Ky, we need to go.'

And a load of things occurred to me at once.

Luke called his Springfoot ThumpThump instead of Thumper.

Luke came off his vehicle.

So Luke isn't our Luke any more . . .

Almost-Luke turned, and it was all I could do not to gasp.

It definitely wasn't him, it definitely wasn't our Luke. This Luke was slightly taller, his face slightly thinner, tougher, his cheeks more hollow.

And then he said something that completely stunned me.

'Thumper. The String Ripper's beasties. Where did it all go?'

I looked to Stef and Dimi. They both looked concerned.

'What?' I said.

'They were here,' Almost-Luke said, puzzled. 'Then they went . . . missing. Why did they go missing?'

That's when he turned to face me . . . and froze, his tough face so shocked that he almost looked like our Luke again. For a moment we all stood there, too stunned to speak.

Then he turned and sprinted away.

'Luke, wait!' both me and Stef called at once. 'LUKE!'

But he was gone.

'Luke-Luke!' Dimi shouted. But whatever his name was, it was too late. Almost-Luke had already disappeared down the tunnels, and I felt a horrible guilt. How had this mission gone so wrong?

'If winning helps our cosmic twins win,' I said, 'then what did we just do? Is Luke going to stop trusting us or something?'

'I don't think it's good,' Stef admitted. 'And why couldn't Almost-Luke even remember the String Ripper's beasties going in through that door? It was like he couldn't even see it.'

Before any of us could answer, there came a whoop from the top of the ravine. There, somehow managing to make his Springfoot *rear up on its hind legs*, was Edwin, Level 10 Infinity Racer.

'Whoa,' Dimi said, impressed.

'You did it!' Edwin yelled again, laughing. 'I knew you could! The Mighty Trio! Well done! Now keep up the good fight against the Stringer in *every* 'verse, bro!'

And with a spring and another *whoop!* Edwin and his Springfoot were gone.

'Cool,' Dimi said eventually. 'I guess we completed the mission.'

'Yeah!' I said, trying to sound enthusiastic after all the effort we'd put in. But as I gratefully patted Something Wrong goodbye (and even *more* gratefully leaped off it), letting the world dissolve into strings around me, my doubts stayed put. Spider Ace had said this mission was about 'restoring balance'. Had we really done that, using technology from another universe to lock our enemies away? If so, then why did Almost-Luke think we'd done something wrong – and why did he not seem to remember how we'd done it, with the cave, with the Bugnotiser? And what about that thing Edwin had called us, 'The Mighty Trio'? There were *supposed* to be four of us. Was Luke . . . leaving our team somehow?

The strings clumped back together again, forming old carpet, shelves, *stacks* of books . . . and an uncomfortable-looking box that I landed on, bum-first. I looked around, taking in Edie Scrap's mobile library. *Stacks* of books and random mechanic's tools stood in every free space. The Map of the Multiverse was gone. There was no sign of Edie, or her cosmic twin, Spider Ace. And, as Stef and Dimi both struggled to their feet, and I heard the end of break bell, I looked through the open library door and saw that somebody else was missing.

Running across the playground, hurrying away from us as fast as he could, was Luke.

8
The Shoplifter

That afternoon was *tough*. I was exhausted from our adventure. We were so muddy that Mrs French shouted at us to go back to the bathroom and wash, but still I *reeked*, so bad that Emma Gray's nostrils started twitching like a rabbit's when I sat down next to her. Oh, and Luke sat at the *other* end of the classroom to me, looking *seriously* downbeat, not even putting his hand up for questions *at all*. When at last the final bell rang I hurried out of the classroom ahead of Luke, determined to stop him at the school gates and make him listen. But before I could find him a voice yelled at me from the football goals.

'Ky! Yo, Ky, come and join our game, bro! Quick, before Wimpole kicks us out!'

It was Alex Bridges, playing football with a few of his hangers-on. Looking desperately around for Luke one more time, I joined in . . . and it was worth it. Alex was *amazing* to play with – sometimes it felt like playing with an older kid, the way he could position himself and properly link up. I had a great game myself, scoring the first goal and setting up the second, and we only needed one more goal to win . . . when I saw Luke walking out through the gates.

'Luke!' I shouted. 'Hey, Luke! Come join our . . .'

'Not him, not him,' Alex muttered.

'. . . game!' I finished, and glared at Alex. Hey, Luke's my mate, and I wasn't about to ignore him just because the cool kid says otherwise. But as though he didn't hear me, Luke kept walking.

'Ah . . .' I swore, annoyed, but didn't even think twice. 'Alex, I've got to go, mate – carry this on tomorrow, yeah?'

'What?!' Alex said, 'But it's next goal wins!' Luckily, Mr Wimpole came out to do his comedy *Leave or I'll call the police!* bit, and so without the need to argue, I ran out through the school gates, and caught up with Luke at the traffic lights.

'Eesh, that afternoon was *rough*,' I said lightly as we crossed the road.

Luke grunted, saying nothing, and again I felt a twist of anxiety about what had happened in the Fungiverse. As we walked down the road, ahead of a group of secondary school girls, an awkward silence fell down over us, and that throwaway comment Edwin had made went through my mind. *You two are* friends *in this universe, then.* How many universes had he been to where Almost-Ky and Almost-Luke *weren't* friends?

'It's your grandma – look, Ky!' he said suddenly, and pointed ahead. 'Ky! I said it's your grandma!'

He wasn't wrong. My grandma had picked up Celestine from school, and they were walking down the alleyway ahead of us. But with those secondary school girls behind us, it was so loud. One of the girls said something to her mate and her mate laughed.

'Yeah, bro, I get it, it's my grandma,' I muttered. 'Chill!'

'Don't you wanna catch her up? We could go into the Community Gardens – remember that massive tree we always used to climb? Maybe she'll get us a Freezie Pop, man I'm *plare* peckish!'

'*Plare?!*' I muttered. 'Luke, what does that even mean?!' I suddenly felt caught between wanting to hurry on away from the sniggering Year 7 girls, and wanting to let my grandma and Celestine get *far* away ahead. I went with the second option and slowed down as we crossed the road to the alleyway, letting even the giggling older girls overtake us, and relaxing as Grandma and Celestine disappeared round the corner.

'So . . . how come you're walking this way again?' I said finally. 'Your house is the other way!'

Now it was Luke's turn to look a bit bashful.

'I'm, uh . . . My dad's picking me up from the end of the road. He's got a meeting on with his work so I'll have to wait in his office.'

'Wait, so you don't just get to go straight home? That's torture! That's like home-made detention!'

'It's not so bad,' Luke said quickly. 'I've got the Proton Wars manual in my bag, so I just read that.'

'Ohhh, bro,' I sympathised. 'What did you do wrong? Why won't he let you just walk home?'

'He does. He's fine with it. He wants me to – I just . . .'

Luke trailed off into another awkward silence. I was *really* worried now. This was Luke, my bestie. Why couldn't I talk to him? Then, as if things couldn't get any worse, Alex Bridges came cycling past in his yellow jacket, and clapped me on the shoulder as he did.

'Match again tomorrow, bro!' he shouted, waving back.

'Yes, bro!' I yelled back with a grin, before realising that he hadn't even looked at Luke. *I'll sort it out*, I decided as we walked over the railway bridge. Suddenly, with an older kid like Edwin giving me props as an Infinity Racer, with popular kids like Alex inviting me to their football matches, I felt like a boss. *I'll sort it out*, I thought again. *Tomorrow, I'll get Luke involved in the football match.* We reached George's Shop on the corner, and I nudged Luke, hoping to cheer him up.

'Oi, Luke,' I said with a grin. 'You know George, in the shop? Yeah? My mum reckons that he fancies my grandma, but she's always rude to him—'

But before I could finish, somebody *burst* out of George's Shop in a bright yellow windbreaker, hood up.

'Isn't that . . .' I began, and was about to say '*Alex*', when George ran out after him.

'Get back here, thief!' he shouted. 'Get back, THIEF!'

'*What?!*' I exclaimed. Alex? *Shoplifting?* Whoever it was, George was *fuming* at them. He sprinted out to the zebra crossing, made a swipe for the yellow windbreaker . . . and tumbled to the ground.

'George!' I shouted out, and ran towards him, as Alex ran off down the street. George seemed OK, struggling to his feet by the time I reached him, but he was wheezing heavily. He let out a big sigh, turned . . . and saw us.

'Kyan!' he exclaimed. 'Did you see who it was? Did you see? I'm positive he's been nicking stuff out my shop all week – did you see who he was?'

This was it. I *did* know. But did I want to tell on Alex Bridges just as we were becoming friends? George stared at me, and just as Luke opened his mouth to speak, I cut in quickly.

'We didn't see,' I said. 'They ran the other way, I couldn't make 'em out. They looked older though.'

Luke stopped abruptly, his face falling into confusion.

For a long moment, George looked at me, and I felt heat rise up to my face.

'You couldn't make them out,' he repeated. *He doesn't believe you. He's going to get the police involved, get you in trouble . . .*

But then the shop door opened. Celestine was holding it, a bundle of Freezie Pops in her arms. Behind her, my grandma pointed at her shopping on the till.

'Can we pay then, George?' she said in that strange, strict voice she always has for him. 'I went to the back room to get a mophead, and when we got back to the till you were gone!'

'That stinking thief's pinched three packets of crisps!' George said, his voice high with frustration.

'Again?' my grandma said, and her voice softened slightly. 'Oh, I'm . . . I didn't hear a thing! What's the world coming to?! Did you see anything, Kyan?'

'They ran the other way,' I said. Now both George and my grandma looked unconvinced. But George was also glancing at my grandma, as if looking to her for advice. When she didn't say anything else, he sighed, and clasped one hand to my shoulder.

'You know, I'm glad I'm getting that helper, Kyan,' he admitted finally. 'I'm too old for this running about.'

'Who's helping you?' I said. 'Can I work Saturdays?'

George laughed. 'All right, old timer, we're not allowed to have kids working for us any more! No, he's just started this week, *not that he's much help, out on his CRIPPIN' phone all the time!*' He said this into the shop, loudly, and my grandma – who's *proud* to be a nosey parker – craned in to look.

When she turned back though, her face was stunned. She shot me a look – a concerned look, which made no sense until she stepped back and George's new assistant hurried to the doorway.

'Sorry, George,' he said. 'I had to take that call, it was my solicitor . . .'

And George's new assistant saw me, saw Grandma, saw Celestine . . . and stopped, his mouth dropping open.

Because George's new assistant was my Cosmic Nemesis.

George's new assistant was Mr Stringer.

'You took your sweet time,' George snapped. 'You know I've got bad lungs? You know we just got *robbed*?'

But Mr Stringer, aka the String Ripper, aka the Giant Grinster, Officer Stringer, Kenneth tha Goat and more . . . he hadn't moved a muscle. My enemy from countless universes was working in George's Shop, and if I was completely speechless at seeing him there, it was nothing compared to the horror, the absolute horror that now froze his face.

'I . . .' he began, then stopped. 'Sorry, boss. I really had to take that call.'

'And while you deal with all your cases, my shop gets looted to *crippin'* death!' George snapped. His voice was harsh, harsher than I'd heard it before, and he seemed to realise it, glancing hurriedly at my grandma before calming down.

The look of dismay was pulling Mr Stringer's face further downwards. His hair was drooping with it, and his suit had been replaced by too-blue jeans and a green polo-neck workshirt, like he'd tried to dress as my dad for work and got it wrong. For one foolish second I *almost* felt sorry for him. Then I remembered the unhappy faces my mum and dad used to have when he was bothering them about our flat, the terror he'd given us about losing our home, and my anger returned stronger than ever before.

Course, George had finally noticed the awkward silence between us all. He looked from me to Mr Stringer, his beefy tattooed arms crossing in suspicion.

'Hang about,' he said, looking from me to Mr Stringer. 'What am I missing?'

This was it. I've been getting sweets and lollies at George's Shop forever. All I had to do was tell him what kind of bully he'd hired, and Mr Stringer would be gone before you could say *revenge*.

'He . . .' I began, but then my grandma – my *own* grandma! – cut in.

'You're missing nothing, George,' she said crisply. 'It's just strange to see somebody new at the shop.'

George stared for a moment. I wanted to say something more, but Grandma fixed me with a look at Gale Force 6, the kind you don't ignore, and bitterly I shut my mouth.

'Hmm,' George said. 'Are you sure?' He said it in a concerned way, but my grandma – *my own grandma!* – nodded curtly, with that flat look that says *We're finished talking about this.*

And George wasn't going to argue, not with my grandma anyway. He gave me one last curious look, then shrugged.

'Well, you'd better go and tidy the shop then, Kenneth.'

'OK, George,' Mr Stringer said, his eyes lowering and his mouth set. He disappeared back inside, and my grandma turned to me.

'Let's go to the Community Gardens and enjoy these Freezie Pops,' she said. 'I bought you bubblegum flavour, Kyan. Did you want one too, Luke?'

Luke, who'd been staring speechless at Mr Stringer, was roused out of his stupor.

'Oh yeah!' he exclaimed. 'I love bubblegum flavour.'

'Tch,' I said dismissively, still furious with Grandma for not getting Mr Stringer fired. 'Bubblegum's for babies. It doesn't even taste like bubblegum.'

'Fine then,' Grandma said wickedly. 'Don't want the Freezie Pop? You can swap with my Milk Lolly instead. Goodbye, George.'

And to my amazement and absolute fury, Grandma handed me the ultimate toddler treat, a milk-flavoured lollipop, and walked on with Celestine grinning by her side. I watched them leave, outraged.

'I wouldn't even put it past her to have bought that just in case I moaned,' I said to Luke.

And then I caught the hurt look on his face.

'I don't see what's so wrong with bubblegum flavour,' he said.

No! I thought. I hadn't meant to hurt his feelings again. It was like we suddenly didn't get each other at all. With my spirits well and truly lowered, I traipsed off to the Community Gardens alongside Luke, the silence longer and more awkward than ever.

9
The Code Is Solved
(Almost)

The next few days shot by. I couldn't think of a way to ask Alex about George's Shop, so instead we played football. A lot of football. See, Alex and his mates didn't really talk much about ... anything, really. Most of the time he would brag about all the great goals he'd scored – 'Bro, I curled the shot, from outside the box, bro, and it went BOOOOOSH, bro, top bins!' Then we'd all call out, like 'Sick!' and 'Nah!', and one of his mates would repeat him, like an echo: 'Top bins, cuz. Squad goals.'

Still, he really was good at football. I tried to get Luke involved, but he didn't want to know. Alex blatantly didn't want Luke to join either, but he did stop making fun of him in class after I said Luke was all right.

Not that Luke seemed to appreciate it. It was gutting, we were *still* awkward, like we suddenly needed a *reason* to hang out, when we hadn't before. Fortunately we had those reasons: I promised to play his beloved Proton Wars game the next time we were free, and we still had that head-scratching Level 4 Infinite Race code to solve:

DANNY LA RUE (CLUE):

1. WITHOUT ANT AND DECS, LEVEL 4 WILL CAUSE YOU BUNNY EARS SOON AS ANY ALMOST FRIENDS BUTCHER'S HOOK AT YOU.
2. WITH BINS ON? HAVE A BUBBLE BATH EVERYWHERE AND YOUR GARDEN GATES WILL ADAM AND EVE IT'S YOU.

Except we weren't getting anywhere solving it. The only person we could think of to help us was Edie Scrap, our new mobile librarian and Spider Ace's friendlier cosmic twin. Edie had helped us solve a tricky code for the Infinite Race before, just that summer. The only trouble now was getting to see her. Since opening on the second day of school, her headbanging library had been open all week, and it was *insanely* popular.

'What's *wrong* with the kids in this school?' Dimi groaned, after we'd raced out of class, only to find a queue already snaking across the yard again. 'Don't they have a screen to watch?!'

'I think it's because of Edie,' Luke said. 'I saw her yesterday, and she was actually *choosing* the books for people.'

'*Choosing* the books?!' Stef scoffed. 'What kind of library doesn't even let you pick your own . . .'

But she trailed off then, because the long queue turned a corner and we saw Edie, standing *outside* her library, chucking books like confetti.

'Name and interest, duck?' she hollered to Ronnie Jones. 'C'mon, time's wasting, 'ey up, Ronnie, what's your interests? Conspiracy theories? You'll want *The Demon Headmaster* then, it's a bit eighties but the plot's mint!'

As Ronnie caught a crinkly old paperback book and hurried away, our new librarian moved on to the next kid.

'Name and interests, duck?
Cara Grace and magic?
Read *Harry Potter* already?
Narnia too? *Skandar*?
Fablehouse? Flippin'

heck, Ems, check *Amari* out then, marra, you'll be on the sequel soon enough.'

'This is *nuts*!' I breathed, as Cara hurried away, looking delighted. 'Mason's queueing for a book, and he moaned when I switched on captions on YouTube!'

Still Edie kept going, getting faster and faster, until she started to sound like the call and response they do at Grandma's church.

'Name and want?'

'Tyler, and something easy that rhymes!'

'*Oi Frog!* for you! Name and want?'

'Mahalia, and I don't know!'

'*The Phantom Tollbooth* for you!'

Soon the queue was moving rapidly – but so was our dinner hour. Finally, just as we got close to the front, Edie called out.

'Sorry you lot, that's it for today. Maybe come by tomorrow, eh?'

There was a groan as the other students walked away.

'Mmmm, *nope*,' I said, and I raced on to the library, leaping up the steps just as she was shutting the door.

'Edie!' I shouted. She looked up . . . and her face broke out into a smile.

''Ey up!' she said. 'I remember you – Crayon Green, in't it?'

'Er . . . close enough!' I said. 'Edie, we've got a code to break and we need your help!'

Edie stared at me for a moment, then sighed.

'I've got a corned beef and brown sauce sandwich in the staffroom, and your Mr Wimpole looks like a fridge raider so we'll have to be quick. Come in.'

'Great!' I cheered. I grabbed the door handle . . . and paused, bracing myself for a computer voice to greet me, and the library inside to transform into a Multiverse Map like before.

Nothing happened. That's when I caught Edie watching me curiously.

'I get nervous about doors sometimes,' I lied, and went in.

Edie's 'library' felt less like a library and more like an old-school caravan being used as a skip. It was *chaos*; towering stacks of books were piled everywhere I looked, each one wobbling dangerously every time somebody moved and rocked the van. A whiteboard had been jammed between two stacks towards the front, and as Edie scribbled the code I'd given her across it, I sat my bum on a painful hardback with *Bartimaeus* written on the cover, and wondered how this dusty old van ever contained a map of the entire Multiverse.

DANNY LA RUE (CLUE):

1. WITHOUT ANT AND DECS, LEVEL 4 WILL CAUSE YOU BUNNY EARS SOON AS ANY ALMOST FRIENDS BUTCHER'S HOOK AT YOU.
2. WITH BINS ON? HAVE A BUBBLE BATH EVERYWHERE AND YOUR GARDEN GATES WILL ADAM AND EVE IT'S YOU.

'Any ideas?' Edie asked when she was done.

'I already said,' I replied. 'We're stuck.'

'I know, duckie,' Edie said cheerily. 'But if empty pipes make the most noise, maybe sometimes just act full and hope for water?'

While I tried to work out if that was a diss, she circled two parts of the code.

'"Ant and Decs",' she said, 'and "Bunny Ears". Do these look similar in any way?'

Nobody spoke, because they didn't look similar at all.

'Maybe take a look at it differently,' Edie offered. 'You'll remember from the summer club, solving a code isn't purely a maths problem. Now, don't worry that you don't know what these things *mean*, what exactly do you think they are in this sentence?'

Still nobody answered for a long moment. The silence was thick with confusion. Finally, Dimi raised one hand shakily.

'Er . . .' he said. 'They both *sort* of look like . . . *things*.'

He glared at us, daring us to make fun. But Edie made an impressed noise.

'That sounds interesting,' she said. 'What do you mean by *things* then, Dimi?'

'Well . . . with those words,' Dimi said, 'the sentence leads up to them. So it says "*Without* Ant and Decs" and "*Cause you* Bunny Ears". Like those are things you need or things you'll get.'

'*Nouns!*' Stef said, her eyes lighting up, genuinely impressed. 'He means they're both *nouns*!'

'Exactamundo!' Edie said, and gave Dimi a salute. 'Nice work, Mr Anev!' And as Dimi looked pleased with himself, she drew an arrow pointing to the circle around 'Ant and Decs' and 'Bunny Ears' and wrote 'NOUN' next to it.

'Now,' Edie said. 'What about 'Butcher's Hook' and 'Adam and Eve'? If we take that whole phrase, and think of where it is in the sentence, what do we think it is. A noun?'

'Nah,' Dimi said. 'It's in the middle. It's more like a . . . like a . . .'

As Dimi trailed off into thought, Luke gave a sudden start.

'They're *doing*-words, er – *verbs*! Somebody *will* "Adam and Eve" you, and Almost Friends "Butcher's Hook" *at* you.'

'Top mega!' Edie said, and as Luke grinned, she went through the whole code, sorting out each type of word, until the whole thing looked like this:

DANNY LA RUE (CLUE):

1. WITHOUT NOUN 1, LEVEL 4 WILL CAUSE YOU NOUN 2 AS SOON AS ANY ALMOST FRIENDS (NOUN 3) VERB AT YOU.
2. WITH NOUN 1 ON? HAVE A NOUN 2 EVERYWHERE AND YOUR NOUN 3 WILL VERB IT'S YOU.

'Hold up,' I objected. 'You've marked "Friends" as "Noun Three", but it's not in code.'

'It's still a noun though,' Edie said. 'It's still a *thing*. And marking them as *things* shows something quite similar about both Sentences One and Two. What do you think that is?'

I stared at it, my eye drawn to the nouns Edie had highlighted.

'Noun, noun, *friends*, verb . . .' I murmured, then read Sentence Two. 'Noun, noun, *noun*, verb—'

'I've got it!' Stef exclaimed. 'The nouns mean the same! Noun Three must be "Friends"!'

'Bang on!' Edie exclaimed. 'And . . . that's about it for deciphering.'

'*What?*' I said, my hopes dropping fast. But Edie smiled.

'Don't despair. This is a type of code called Cockney Rhyming Slang. It's an old code – at least two hundred years old – and it's been changing ever since it started.'

'My dad's always on about Rhyming Slang!' I exclaimed. 'His mates at work use it! The words are swapped with other words that rhyme, so . . . "Garden Gates" . . . friends . . . *mates*! "Garden Gates" is *mates*!'

'Exactly,' said Edie. 'And there's a big clue about this at the beginning. "Danny La Rue" was a famous performer in olden times, so famous that Cockneys used him as rhyming slang for "clue" – which is right next to it.'

'But how do we solve it,' Dimi moaned, 'if we don't know what this stupid code is?'

'Don't get lemon,' Edie warned sharply (though none of us knew what 'lemon' meant). 'The clue's in the rhyming. Each of you, take a word, and rhyme it with every word you can. Just remember – *look at the whole sentence* to see if it fits.'

Soon we'd all picked a word. I had 'Butcher's Hook', and tried desperately to rhyme it: *butcher's HOOK, COOK, SHOOK* . . . Then I stopped to think.

Look at the whole sentence, Edie had said.

Take a Butcher's Hook at you would be the same as . . .

Take a —— at you . . . which would be . . .

'GOT IT!' I shouted, first out of everyone, to my happy surprise. 'Take a LOOK! That fits the sentence best . . . doesn't it?'

'I think you're right there!' Edie said. She was looking at her own rhyming code – a bit puzzled, I thought – but she gave me a thumbs up. I was going to ask if I could help, when Stef jumped up.

'BELIEVE!' she exclaimed. 'Adam and Eve rhymes with "believe". Have a Bubble Bath everywhere, and the *mates* will BELIEVE it's you.'

'Brilliant!' Edie said, but she was still frowning down at her code. 'Does that help you with your clue, Luke?'

'Er . . .' Luke said, concentrating hard on his word. I glanced at it – 'Have a Bubble Bath everywhere' – and wondered . . .

Have a bubble bath . . . Have a -ath . . .

Have a -aff . . .

'Mate,' I muttered to Luke. 'Have you tried . . . ?'

'Don't, I've nearly got it,' he said, screwing up his face, but I couldn't stop myself.

'I really think it's—'

'Don't tell me—'

'Have a Bubble Bath – have a *laugh*—'

'LAUGH!' Luke whirled around furiously. 'I was going to get it, why did you do that?!'

I stared at him, taken aback by his anger. My friends all looked shocked as well.

'Luke,' Stef said bluntly. 'Stop getting annoyed. It's only fun.'

I blinked in surprise. Normally it's *me* Stef's telling to stop getting wound up so much. And Luke, to his credit, did let out a smile.

'You're right,' he said finally, and grinned at me. 'Sorry. Just . . . I *really* wanted to get it.'

'No worries, bro,' I said – but there it was again. Just as I said 'bro', Luke's grin dropped slightly and he turned away to Dimi, who was still struggling.

'Hurry up, Dims,' Stef said brutally.

'Don't get lemon,' he snapped back. 'All yours make sense. But how's mine work?'

We all stared at his part of the code – 'LEVEL 4 WILL CAUSE YOU BUNNY EARS' – and all fell silent, *blatantly* racing to solve it.

Bunny ears . . . funny beers . . . honey gears . . . sunny cheers . . . money fears . . .

'RrrrrrARGGGGH!!' Dimi groaned. 'It makes me wanna cry!'

We all nodded agreement. Then me, Stef and Luke looked at each other.

'You want to cry . . . *tears*?' Stef said.

'Yes, tears,' Dimi snapped. 'Of course tears – what am I gonna cry? Chocolate?'

We stared at him for a *long* second. Suddenly he shouted out.

'TEARS! The answer's TEARS! I've got it!'

'I mean . . .' I began, but Stef shook her head.

'Allow it,' she said with a grin.

So we'd all solved our coded rhyming slang words, and the answer looked like this:

CLUE:

1. WITHOUT ANT AND DECS, LEVEL 4 WILL
   CAUSE YOU TEARS AS SOON AS ANY

ALMOST FRIENDS LOOK AT YOU.
2. WITH BINS ON? HAVE A LAUGH
   EVERYWHERE AND YOUR MATES WILL
   BELIEVE IT'S YOU.

'*Tears as soon as they look at us!*' Stef whispered quietly. 'It's like in the Fungiverse, when Almost-Luke saw us!'

At that memory, Luke grimaced. Again I wondered what *he'd* felt when Almost-Luke looked at the kids he thought were his crew . . . and saw us, a bunch of imposters.

'So what are Bins? I asked. 'What are Ant and Decs? What *is* Noun One?'

'I'm . . . not sure.' Edie groaned. 'Everything about the way the first and second sentences are made up makes me think it's talking about the same thing. This Level Four will cause you problems as soon as your friends on that level see you, *unless* you have "Ant and Decs" or "Bins". I'm sure that "Ant and Decs" and "Bins" are the same thing, but those two things don't rhyme!' Finally, she sighed. 'I'm Hank Marvin, kids: starvin'. I've gorra eat.'

I was *gutted*. The *most* important part of the clue, the thing that we needed to advance to Level 4 Infinity Racers, was just out of reach. But just as the whole visit began to seem like a washout, Luke noticed something in the corner of Edie's van and put up his hand.

'Can I quickly check something on that?' he asked. He pointed at a dusty old computer – I mean like, *really* old; like the keyboard was the size of a desk and the screen looked green.

'That rust-bucket?' Edie chuckled. 'Knock yerself out, I doubt you'll find owt on it though.'

As Edie left, Luke hurried to the old computer, shifting some paperback *Goosebumps* books off it. We gathered around as he pushed the POWER button, and a tinny trumpet blared out.

'What *are* you trying to find on this thing, Luke?' Stef said with a smile.

And as Luke pointed at the *very faded* plastic logo on the computer box, the same word came up onscreen. It was familiar; the same name that Spider Ace had called her computer the last time we were here:

Welcome to the Commodore 65

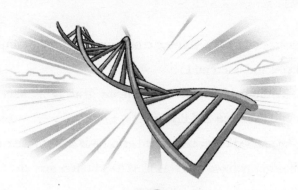

10
The Commodore 65

'**Y**ouuuuuu *GENIUS*, Luke!' I cried.

'It might not be the *actual* Commodore 65 that Spider Ace used,' Luke said, but he looked pleased with himself. As we waited with bated breath around the dusty computer, it hummed, rattled, and actually *clattered* . . . and the hazy, green-tinged screen flickered to show lots of small, pixelly icons.

'Tch, gutted,' said Dimi. 'Looks like just some rubbish old game left on here. Nice idea though . . .'

'Wait a sec,' said Luke. 'I recognise this.'

He pointed at a shimmering ♛ symbol, right at the centre of the screen. The symbol was moving around, very slowly and jerkily . . . In fact *all* of the symbols were moving slowly and jerkily – shining crowns and swords, gleaming rockets and lasers and . . .

'It's the Nucleus!' he said excitedly. 'This is the Map of the Multiverse *in 2D*! BASH!'

As me and Dimi exchanged grins over Luke's made-up slang, Stef pointed at a NAVIGATION button near the top of the screen.

'Can you find our Sector?' she asked. 'Sector Three?'

Luke took the massive mouse, and clicked on the button. At once, a whole list of numbers and charts appeared, all of them written in green old-fashioned computer font. There were different statistics, and *loads* of maths symbols like % and ° – *none* of which made sense to me.

'Huh,' Luke said. 'Where've I seen all of this before?'

We stared at him as he tried to think . . . but, frustrated, he shook his head.

'Luke, my head's hurting,' Dimi groaned. 'Where's Sector Three?'

Rolling his eyes, Luke clicked on a search box at the top of the screen before typing out *SECTOR 3*. Section by section, the screen went to black . . . and another screen slowly loaded in its place.

'Was this really how computers used to be?!' said Dimi

in disbelief. 'How did anyone live? How did they watch YouTube?'

'Hush up,' said Stef. 'That's our universe. The Sippy Cup 'Verse.'

I wasn't *ever* going to get used to that name, but there it was: our manky, baby-beaker-shaped bubble loading up, other universes nearby. Near to it, I saw a 🍄 icon load up.

'The Fungiverse!' I said. 'How do we know if we helped it?'

Suddenly, as if answering me, a thin red line fired jerkily across the screen. It was one of those tendrils I'd seen on the Multiverse Map before, I realised, the ones that had caused our universes so much damage. This one snaked across and collided into the Fungiverse Bubble. The 🍄 shook, and *changed shape*, into a red skull-and-crossbones symbol: ☠.

'Oh, no,' Stef breathed. 'That can't be good.'

'It doesn't make sense,' I said. 'We stopped the String Ripper. We're beating Mr Stringer in *every* universe, just as we did to transform our whole Sector. How come things are suddenly getting worse now?'

'And what even *are* those skull-and-bones?' Luke murmured.

Clicking on the '–' sign, he zoomed out. First we could see our entire manky Sector 3. Then the Electron Shell came into view, protecting the glitzy Nucleus middle, and then . . .

'Ce puii mei?' Dimi murmured, horrified.

Because those red skull-and-bones were *everywhere*, surrounding us like a hand about to squeeze. And I mean *everywhere*: all around the Electron Shell, all across the screen, in fact. Across the middle of this red-coloured area were a set of pixelly capital letters that I had seen once before:

THE PURE STATE

'I know Spider Ace said things were bad,' Stef muttered, 'but this?' Nobody answered. For a stunned moment, there was only the click of Luke's mouse, and the occasional rattle from the Commodore 65. Finally, Luke leaned back, his face pale.

'What even *is* the Pure State?' he said shakily.

'*GOOD QUESTION!*' Spider Ace shouted through the screen, and we all *screamed*.

We screamed for three reasons: (a) after Edie's bouncy pink hair energy, Spider Ace was like a scary undead version of her that we hadn't expected to see; (b) the scratchy Commodore 65 speakers honestly made it sound like she was farting – '*PRRT PRRT-PRRT!*' – in time to her own words. Oh, and (c)? A battered, blocky, pixel version of her face flashed up onscreen with every syllable. It was literally like she'd been squeezed – painfully – into some ancient video game, one blocky eyebrow shoved low, her lips chopped into squares.

'What are you doing, Spider?' Luke said, staring aghast at her butchered cartoon face.

'*WHAT'S THE MATTER?*' Spider fart-said, and her blocky eyebrow waggled. '*AMAZED BY THE COMMODORE 65'S GROUNDBREAKING TECHNOLOGY? IT ALLOWS ME TO SPEAK FACE TO FACE.*'

'So . . . it's FaceTime,' Stef muttered to us with a grin.

'Mangled-FaceTime,' I added.

'Fart-Time,' Luke said, and we all started snickering.

Spider Ace's pixelly face got exclamation marks for eyes, and a load of @£*%£ symbols appeared next to her mouth, like she was swearing. Then the screen went blank.

'D'you think it's crashed?' I began.

'The Commodore 65 does not crash,' Spider's voice said behind me, and I jumped.

She was standing in the room – or at least, her hologram was. It was being beamed out by the Commodore 65 itself.

'Congratulations,' Spider Ace said with a scowl. 'You're the first Racers too immature for Face-Speak. Woe betide you if I'm caught here. Now, you asked me what the Pure State is. And the best way I can describe it is to tell you about a particularly nasty illness called the Zombie Virus.'

'So TikTok was right!' Dimi cried, his face going pale. 'Zombies do exist!'

'I'm not talking about your numbskull numpty news, numbnuts,' Spider snapped. 'This is a true virus, one that latches on to your cells, and feeds on them. But what makes the Zombie Virus special is how it spreads. You see, the Zombie Virus is very subtle, very difficult to spot. Rather than devouring your cells, like other viruses, it makes tiny changes to your organs, your heart, lungs, even your brain. You'll still be alive, but little by little, more of the work your body does will go to helping the virus. Until one day, without ever suspecting you were ill, you are all but a zombie, a creature run by the virus.'

We took this in. It was a horrible idea.

'I'm telling you this,' Spider continued, 'because the Pure State is like a Zombie Virus across the Multiverse. It has spread across thousands of dimensions, and most of the people in those dimensions have no idea that they are being controlled, don't even know that the Multiverse exists. By using Cosmic Connections, the denizens of this Pure State can *change* and *control* society in ways you can't imagine. They don't always have to do big things either. If they had helped Mr Stringer to evict your family, Kyan, it wouldn't have made the news, would it? Who would care?'

'Charming,' I murmured to Dimi, who grinned.

'And yet,' Spider continued, 'because of your connection to Mr Stringer across different universes, the knock-on effect of your family losing their home might help a Stringer in another universe topple an entire civilization. It is unusual, this connection that you have with Stringer in universe after universe. It is what makes your battles with him have such a big effect.'

I thought about this. So Edwin had been telling the truth: my Cosmic Connection with Stringer was important. But just as when she had compared us to grains of sand, the way Spider Ace described it was somehow different, more complicated than Stringer being my Cosmic Nemesis. As soon as she was finished, I decided I would tell her about Edwin, would even 'fess up about using other technology to defeat the String Ripper.

'So . . . if the Pure State is like a Zombie Virus,' Stef said slowly, 'then how does the Commodore 65 work out how infected we are with it?'

'Excellent questions,' Spider Ace said. 'As old and rickety as it looks, the Commodore 65 is an exceptional computer. It takes in enormous amounts of data from each universe it watches, and uses it to measure how much control the Pure State has over a universe, literally like it is measuring the amount a disease has infected a body by using a sample of blood.'

I shuddered again. Now it was clearer what those red, writhing veins were that stretched out from the dark to smother our Sippy Cup 'Verse, it felt even more crucial to eradicate it.

'I don't get it though,' said Dimi. 'We completed our mission in the Fungiverse. The String Ripper was defeated! How is this Pure State still invading it?'

'The short answer? I don't know,' Spider admitted. 'The long answer . . .'

She sighed, and gave us that side-eye adults give when they want to tell you something, but don't know if you're old enough to take it. Finally, she focused on something past us, and tapped her finger.

At once the Map of the Multiverse blinked into view around us . . . only this time the bubbles were ones I hadn't seen before: an axe, a football, a broom and –

And suddenly a red rope *shot* out from the distance to

seize the football. More red ropes shot out – three, four, ten, *twenty*. The Football 'Verse was shaking as though the red tendrils were sucking the life from them, until red points *gushed* out of it, shooting into the nearest universe. The same thing happened, quicker and quicker, until the entire Sector was almost entirely painted red, almost completely lifeless, and the Quantum Space around it was gloomy as death.

'Some time ago,' Spider Ace said, 'I found a daring young rider, a bit like yourself, Kyan, if not as blessed with his friends. The Pure State had stretched its terrible tendrils across every universe of his Sector. The people who lived there didn't realise this, of course. To them, times just seemed unusually hard. But without knowing it, without seeing any signs of the Pure State except for perhaps a few of its more powerful weapons, like, say, the Happy Corporation, they were being silently conquered.'

'Was it Stringer?' I asked, my anger flaring.

'No,' Spider replied. 'But one villain in this story was a *lot* like Stringer. And, like you and Stringer, when this boy found an Infinity Racetrack, he encountered this same villain in many different universes. And, just like you, this Infinity Racer started to *win*.'

Suddenly a blast of cosmic energy burst out from one of the bubbles – the one shaped like an axe – and fired into the Football 'Verse. The two bubbles trembled like they'd had a power-up, and the red tendrils gripping them *burned* away.

'The Racer's fightback worked,' Spider said. 'He won battles and races, and the more he won, the more others in this Sector fought back against the Pure State. Do you remember me saying before that there were once whole teams of Infinity Racers, guided by a Navigator? Well, at last I saw the possibility of that happening again. I could find more riders, I would be their Navigator, and we'd turn the tide against the Pure State.'

As soon as that beam ended, *another* beam burst out of the axe, this time connecting *two* – then *three* – universes nearby, all of them trembling like zapped lines on the bubble-drop games my grandma loves to play on her phone. Red tendrils everywhere flinched back or were burned away. It was bright, it was *amazing*! And then Spider Ace's voice suddenly dropped.

'Then,' she said, 'with no explanation, things began to go wrong.'

Another beam of energy fired out from the Axe, this time into the Broom. Only *this* time there was a FAIL sound, like when you press the wrong button.

'That sound!' I said, shocked. 'I heard that sound

before, when the map was updating last, and our Cosmic Connection fired into the last universe we'd visited.'

Spider Ace nodded sadly. 'Like I told you, your actions can have huge waves of effect. Suddenly our efforts were making things *worse*. We would sabotage one of the villain's plans, and it would turn out to have helped in two other schemes the Pure State had bubbling under their surface. It didn't help that the Pure State will do *anything* for power, that it will use technology from one universe to obliterate another, even though the effects of doing this are terrible for both.

'Terrible?' I asked, thinking of the special door Edwin had given me to trap the String Ripper's beasties in a cave.

'Terrible,' Spider repeated. 'You see, when another technology is suddenly inserted into a world that is not ready for it, the people of that 'verse might not be able to even compute it. If lucky, their minds will just blank it out, although this can leave them with some frightening confusions. If unlucky? Their minds will crack under the pressure.'

I stared at her, my throat going dry. Back in the Fungiverse, Almost-Luke hadn't understood what happened, almost like he hadn't seen it. Was it because he was witnessing, without explanation, some technology that made no sense? Suddenly I had to tell Spider Ace about meeting Edwin, and the terrible mistake I'd made. But she was still talking.

'I tried to reason with the Racer, tried to convince him to pause in his efforts, until we'd figured out what was going wrong, and why, when he was beating his arch-enemy so thoroughly, the Empire was *still* overcoming his Sector. But he was desperate . . .'

Then Spider Ace broke off. She didn't speak, as more bursts of energy fired out from the axe, getting faster, more urgent . . . and none having any effect as those red tendrils *squeezed* ever tighter around every universe in the Sector. One by one the axe's neighbouring bubbles were smothered by the blood-red disease of the Pure State, until there was only the dim glow of the dying axe itself. Then, at last, the axe itself blinked out. We were left standing there, with featureless red orbs tethered silently together by ever-winding red rope. The Sector, the 'verses . . . they were all defeated.

'What happened to the Infinity Racer?' I asked. 'The kid trying to save his universe?'

'I don't know,' Spider Ace said. Suddenly, shockingly, her voice cracked with emotion. 'I went back there trying to find him . . . and I barely escaped alive. The Racer was nowhere to be found. That's when I realised I wasn't cut out to be a Navigator after all.'

I wanted to speak, but I couldn't. Up till now, even when things were at their worst, this had felt like something a kid – at least a kid who could steer – could handle. Now the Infinite Race seemed dangerous and dreadful. A voice in my head urged, *screamed* at me to tell Spider about the Fungiverse, about Edwin. But then she spoke again.

'Have you solved the code yet?' she demanded.

We all sat there, looking awkward.

'Almost,' said Stef. 'We're going to solve it tonight.'

'Yeah,' added Luke. 'While we're playing Proton Wars.'

I glowered at him. After being told about this evil force that was ready to swamp our universe, didn't he think role-playing dice games was a childish thing to worry about?

'I'm not going to make the same mistake again,' Spider Ace said. 'That's why, if I tell you to crack a code, to *earn* your next level, you need to make sure you do that. You don't go to places I tell you not to go, and you tell me about any strange things that happen when you're there. The Pure State is more dangerous than you can imagine, and I hate that things have got so bad that you have to be placed in danger. If I think that the danger is too great, or that you're not following my orders, then that'll be it – I'll take the Infinite Race away and you won't see me again until I think it's—'

BANG!

We all yelled in shock, looking around to see what had made that noise. There was a football-shaped dirt mark on the window of Edie's library.

'Yo, *Ky*!' a voice shouted from outside. 'You playing or what?'

'Somebody's coming...' I began, but Spider had already vanished. We all sat casual in that way that *never* looks casual at all, just as the library door swung open, and Alex poked his head in.

'Come on then!' Alex bellowed. 'Break's nearly over and we're a player down. Dim, you coming an' all?'

And you know what I said about Alex, how he's not the kid you can just tell to bog off? Well, I have *never* been closer to doing that than right then.

11
Now the Code Is Solved
(Er . . . Almost)

'But you're always on about Cockneys,' I moaned to my dad. 'How do you *not* know what Ant and Decs or Bins means?'

'I told you!' my dad said. 'I'm no expert. You'll have to wait for the lads at work to message me back. Enjoy your Hungry Hungry Hippos, and let me go put Robot Pattinson on.'

'Hungry Hungry Hippos?!' I scoffed, but as he left, I turned back . . . and I *wished* that's what we were about to play.

We were all in my room, with the still-unsolved Infinite Race Instruction Manual on my bed . . . and the open box of Proton Wars all across my floor. Stef was sorting through a whole bag of dice, (some of which had *twenty-five* sides), and Luke was happily opening the thick book – yes, *book* – that came with the game, going over character stats, and maps, and *shipping charts*. Me and Dimi, meanwhile, were watching them both, and shooting each other desperate looks that screamed *HOW DO WE GET OUT OF THIS?!* a bit louder each time.

'This game looks, like, really complicated, Luke,' Dimi said unhappily. 'Shouldn't we just concentrate on the code?'

'It's just what we need!' Stef said happily. 'Something light to take our minds off it. That's when we'll get our best ideas!'

That's when Celestine poked her head into the room. She was cleaning her new glasses for the fiftieth time that evening. I think she thinks it makes her look grown up.

'Whatcha playing?' she asked, that *Am-I-bothering-you?* look on her face.

Don't get me wrong: after some *massive* adventures with my sister this summer, I get how lucky I am to have her. Even now, after she'd lost interest in Infinity Racing just like that, she *still* hadn't said a word about it to my mum and dad, which I really appreciated. But also don't get me wrong: she's *still* younger; she *still* has half the cares I do; and she *still* views winding me up as her *job*. However, what Celestine foolishly didn't realise was that, right then, she was distraction *gold*.

'Celestine!' I said. 'You wanna play Proton Wars?!'

'What's that?' she said, wrinkling her nose.

'It's great!' I said feebly. 'It's got all these different worlds to visit, but it's really hard to visit them, and so you have to roll dice, and read charts, and learn different equations, and—'

'Ky!' my dad yelled, just as Celestine's face was scrunching up with disgust at our board game. 'Oi, Nige has got back to me. *Bins* is old-school Cockney, apparently. It might not rhyme though, exactly – he reckons it's either short for *Bin*oculars or "*Bins* and Receptacles" – so, *spectacles*. Either way, *Bins* means *glasses*. He hadn't heard of Ant and Decs, but then he's not heard of much past 1986, so you'll have to wait for Jack or Lee to answer before you—'

Just then my dad's message alert sounded, his beloved old Garage song.

'Huh!' he said. 'That's Jack . . . You'll never guess what *Ant and Decs* means too, Ky. It means *Specs*! It's glasses, just like *Bins*!'

'Thanks, Dad!' I said. Grabbing a pencil, I stared at the code and began to write the possible answers above the original. My excitement grew, the more my dad's solution made sense:

DANNY LA RUE (CLUE):

1. WITHOUT <u>GLASSES</u>, LEVEL 4 WILL CAUSE YOU <u>TEARS</u> AS SOON AS ANY ALMOST FRIENDS <u>LOOK</u> AT YOU.
2. WITH <u>GLASSES</u> ON? HAVE A <u>LAUGH</u> EVERYWHERE AND YOUR <u>MATES</u> WILL <u>BELIEVE</u> IT'S YOU.

'We're supposed to wear glasses!' Stef said, and turned to Celestine. 'Of course! Back on the Grinster's kitchen table you were in the tank with your Almost-Grandma, but she didn't notice any difference in you. Your glasses must've helped change the way you look!'

'We have to test this,' Dimi said. 'Kyan, you got any swimming goggles or anything?'

As he and Stef opened the Infinite Race box and began to assemble the track, I tossed the Instructions to the floor, and rifled through my wardrobe looking for eyewear. I'd soon found sunglasses, swimming goggles, and these plastic comedy glasses with a moustache attached, and like everyone else I was feeling excited about going to other 'verses in disguise . . . Everyone but Luke, that is. He'd quietly picked up the Instructions and was staring at them in a sad way that, I'll admit, made me feel a tiny bit guilty that we were abandoning his beloved cure-for-insomnia Proton Wars so quickly.

'We'll definitely play next time, bro,' I said, and after tossing the swimming goggles to Stef, I handed him the comedy-moustache glasses with an encouraging grin. 'I promise.'

Luke took the comedy glasses and even slid them on . . . but he didn't grin back, and I felt a stab of annoyance. Hadn't he seen what Spider had showed us – universes being swamped by the evil Pure State? Didn't he know how important this breakthrough was?

'OK,' Celestine said, rummaging through our old toy car box. 'I've got . . . this Happy Meal toy or a broken ice-cream van. Where do we wanna go?'

I thought hard. Unlike the Multiverse Map, our Racetrack decides where we travel, based on the vehicle we put down on it and – according to Spider Ace – where the track thinks our help is needed most. But I couldn't think of a vehicle that would send us to a good place for this situation – testing out some face-changing glasses. I was just about to suggest the ice-cream van when Luke said, 'Wait.'

I looked over . . . and saw the Instructions vibrating in his hands like a dodgy controller.

'The words!' I said excitedly. 'Are they changing again?'

Luke nodded, struggling to speak while he clung to the buzzing sheet of paper.

'Y-y-y-y-yep,' he stammered, his voice climbing. 'It's paiiiiiiinful!' But then, finally, the vibrations stopped, and with a deep breath he looked down at the Instructions. As he read, a strange, awkward smile formed behind his comedy moustache.

'We made *Level Four*,' he said, and handed me the piece of untearable paper:

Prepare for the Ride of Your Lives

Congratulations! You are now at Level

4

Level 4 Infinity Racers are given Kinetic*
Face-Morphing Goggles, eliminating the need
for Metamorphic Headphones OR a weapon
to defend against your own grandma when
she doesn't recognise you.**

* Goggles are powered by Kinetic Energy. So stay in the jam jar
and off the scotch pegs if you don't want your charm and
flattery flat.
** Not to be used without a Level 5 Racer present!!

'*Kinetic Face-Morphing Goggles,*' I read, and put on my
shades with a grin. 'Perfect. Now we just need some
"goggles" for Dimitar, and we can roll out. Squad goals,
innit.'

But Luke's smile faltered.

'No, Ky, um . . . Didn't you see the warnings?' he asked.
'The two asterisk bits at the bottom.'

I looked at the sheet again, and this time my heart sank.
At the bottom, where all the bad news is kept, was the
small print:

** Not to be used without a Level 5 Racer present!!

'*Not to be used without a Level Five Racer present*?!' I read. 'What's the point of reaching Level Four then?!'

Luke shook his head.

'I don't think . . . I don't think we can go right now.' But he still had that smile, that tiny relief about the fact, and it proper wound me up.

'Well . . . Edwin said he thinks I'm Level Five,' I said dismissively. 'And he's a Level Ten Racer. So I might just go anyway.'

'What?!' Luke said, his smile slipping finally.

'HA! I knew it,' I shot back. 'You just don't want to go!' But before I could accuse him further, Stef chimed in as well.

'That won't wash, Ky,' she chided me. 'Your friend Edwin doesn't decide what level we are, does he? And besides – look at the first asterisk, that "charm and flattery" bit. Spider Ace just told us today that we have to figure these things out in order before we do anything stupid. We'll have to wait.'

I thought unhappily of the Multiverse Map, of everything around us flickering red, of skull-and-crossbones and red tentacles choking us all, while we sat here playing a stupid board game like Proton Wars. Again. But Celestine was already looking bored. Luke was *still* annoyingly upbeat. Even Dimi, who'd built the Infinite Racetrack and was kneeling by it with a toy car at the ready, didn't look convinced.

'All right,' I said, but couldn't resist one final shot at Luke. 'But you blatantly didn't want to go anyway.'

Luke opened his mouth to retort, but before he could speak, a noise came trundling up the hallway towards us. It sounded like a jet engine with a chest infection, and sadly, I knew exactly what it was.

'What's that?' Stef asked. 'It's so loud!'

'Huh,' I grunted moodily. 'It's Robot Pattinson – er, it's my dad's robot vacuum cleaner. It doesn't work properly. It'll try to get in my room and get stuck – look.'

We all watched, amused, as Robot Pattinson turned to go through my bedroom door . . . and got caught on the gappy floorboards. It began to swivel about in that mad way it does, backwards, left, forwards, right . . .

'C'mon, Ky,' Dimi said. 'I'm starting to feel sorry for him.'

'I'll get it out,' I said with a grin, and walked to the door. That's when everything went wrong.

Just as I was reaching him, the hopeless robot vacuum swivelled one way, then another . . . and made it into my bedroom! Without turning, it drove straight for my trainers, making me yell out and skip out of the way, leaving it with a clear path to –

'Robbie, no!' I shouted. It was too late. The vacuum cleaner trundled all the way along the Infinite Racetrack, one wheel keeping in contact all the way along to the end. Then, the moment it touched the chequerboard finish line, that crazy cleaner spun slowly around 180 degrees, turned back and began to drive the other way!

'RED ALERT!' shouted a voice from somewhere, and again, louder, 'RED ALERT!'

'Whoops!' said Dimi, and reached out to yoink the robot off the track . . .

'Dimi, NO!' *we* all shouted, and leaped across the room to snatch Dimi off the robot . . .

'RED ALERT!' the voice shouted again, and all of us – me, Luke, Stef and Celestine – seemed to connect with Dimi at the same time. An electric wind blew through the room, and as the world around me grew *enormous*, I felt my sunglasses grow, around my head and then my entire body, until it felt like I was encased in an invisible bag. Then, as if I were trying to fill this bag, my entire being began to expand, from my head to my feet, from my skin to my stomach.

'What the—?' Dimi gasped in horror, and he was looking at *me*.

'What's happening?!' I cried – and gripped my throat, because my voice burbled from high to *deep*. Still the world kept growing, Robot Pattinson looming *gigantic* above me, *still* shaped like an enormous hockey puck, only now the wheels were gone and the white heat of a futuristic engine *blasted* out of the bottom where the sucky hoover bit had been.

I whirled through the air, cartwheeling around what was transforming into a spacecraft, past window after small window dotted along the side. *Frantically* searching for my friends, who'd blown away somewhere else, I reached the front of the ship, where the biggest, widest windscreen stretched all around to show *people* inside, an actual *crew* of people standing and walking and talking . . . *and I tumbled towards it.*

'NO!' I shouted, and *again* flinched at my warbling high-low voice. I was going to smash through that widescreen windscreen, I was *sure* of it . . . only now the ship, the world, *everything* was dissolving into strings.

Those strings look like hammers, I realised. Did that mean this was the Hammer Verse? I landed with a *whoomph* into a chair, the *comfiest* chair my butt had ever visited. I felt a crushy carpet beneath my feet, and just as I was getting cosier than I had in *any* universe I'd visited so far, that urgent voice ripped through the air again, louder than ever.

'RED ALERT! RED ALERT! THERE'S A CATASTROPHE!'

12
The Good Ship *Vengeance*

'Red Alert, we're under attack! Orders, sir?'

My butt hadn't been lying. I was sitting in a comfortable bucket-shaped swivel chair, on the bridge of a starship that was *miles* nicer than any vehicle I'd landed in so far. The last time I'd visited outer space, our craft – called the *Europa Quest* – had been small, rusty and uncomfortable . . . and turned out to be a submarine. This place was *completely* different. Holographic screens showing star maps and engine controls dotted the spacious room, each with a quiet, serious-looking adult tapping seriously away at it, dressed in those pyjama-looking uniforms they always wear in films. A ma-*hoo*-sive viewscreen at the front showed distant stars whipping past us at high speed, the image sharper than Grandma's new telly. And, unlike every other vehicle, I couldn't feel our speed at all, any more than you can feel the earth spinning. I rose to my feet . . .

. . . and *very* quickly sat back down.

I was higher up than normal. Like, *way* higher up. I looked down at my hands, which didn't look like my hands at all. They were grown-up hands, rough with scars up them. My whole body felt different, heavier, because . . . well, it was. The goggles had worked! I had transformed into the Kyan Green of this universe . . . and he was a full-on grown-up adult!

'Sir? The Viper drones are right ahead. What are your orders, sir?'

I looked up to see a woman smiling nervously at me. She was wearing a red pyjama uniform, and stood more upright than a Reception kid trying to get picked for Lunch Monitor. Could she be . . . ?

'Stef?' I said, extra quietly.

'What was that, Captain?' she asked. 'I'm Officer Mirks, sir, your First Officer, sir?'

I stared at her for a moment as something she said sunk in.

'Did you just call me "Captain"?!' I said, but flipping

heck my voice was so deep! Without thinking, I lifted my hand to my throat and tested it out again.

'I'm the Captain. That's *me*. Hey. Hey.'

'. . . Sir?' Officer Mirks's smile was strained now, but before she could say any more a woman in a blue uniform yelled from the controls at the front of the bridge.

'Captain!' she shouted. 'Captain, we're being targeted!'

'Targeted?!' I exclaimed. 'Who's targeting us?!'

'Who'd'you think?!' the woman in blue snapped back, and pointed at the viewscreen. '*They* are!'

Two small but deadly-looking ships were ahead of us. They were shaped like a letter 'M' – if the 'M' had been slashed by a *really* angry person with daggers for hands who was going to follow the 'M' up with 'urder'. At the point of each wing were vicious-looking blasters, and as I watched, a steady stream of red energy fired out into our shields.

'Oh my days,' I said, as the entire ship shook around me. I got to my feet, and I *winced* as aches and pains twinged my back. 'Ow! Why's it hurt to get up?!'

'Captain,' the woman in blue said impatiently, but I was gripping my side.

'I mean, *seriously*! Was I in an accident? My back hurts just moving around, and my legs feel so *heavy*! Is it – is this what all adults feel . . . ?'

'OI!' the woman in blue shouted, and everybody gasped.

At last I looked properly at her . . . and felt a sudden sense of relief. Her hair was cropped shorter, and a single, thin scar lined down across the side of her face, but it was her.

'Stef!' I said, just as another red blast fired into us from the drones.

'Those drones are wiping the floor with us, Captain,' Stef replied pointedly. 'So do you want to give us an order or what?'

'Er, I *don't* think that's how we speak to our commanding officers, is it, Navigator Anev?' said Officer Mirks, her smile getting sad for a moment. Then, after a pause, she gave a nervous little cough-giggle.

'*Did* you have orders though, sir? We need one of those brilliant Cap-KG plans that are so famous across the galaxy!'

'Famous?!' I said, impressed with my other self.

'*Very* famous, sir,' Officer Mirks added with a proud smile.

This was different to my previous missions. I wasn't just racing, or flying, I was playing a part. I would have to *be* the daring Captain. So, slowly, I began to pace my little area of the bridge, rested one finger on my chin like I was thinking deep thoughts, and put the most faraway, most *staraway* look in my eyes you could possibly imagine.

'Give me strength,' Navigator Stef muttered.

'What...errr...what...would...*you*...do...Officer Mirks?' I said at last.

'Thank you for the opportunity, sir,' Mirks replied eagerly, 'I would blast the Vipers out of the sky before they could get any closer. Make it clear to Stringer that Captain Green and the good ship *Vengeance* is coming for him no matter what drones he throws at us.'

'That sounds *good*,' I said, impressed. 'Nice plan! I knew you could do it! And – wait, there's nobody on them, is there?'

'. . . Sir?'

'No people. I'm not going to go back and find I wiped out Mrs French or something.'

At this, Officer Mirks blinked, her smile a bit doubtful. Phew, this whole *being here* thing had started with a lot more attention on me than I'd expected!

'The, ah, the Viper drones are unmanned craft, sir,' Officer Mirks said.

'Hence *drones*,' Navigator Stef added in the background. But then Officer Mirks's smile turned *sharp*.

'Are you being sarcastic to your commanding officer, Navigator Anev?' she said. 'Perhaps you aren't aware of the countless *brave* struggles Captain Green has overcome in our fight against the insurgents?'

You know when a teacher praises you too much, and you just want them to stop before everybody in the classroom hates you? It was getting a bit like that. Navigator Anev and Officer Mirks stared at each other. Stef's proper stubborn, and she's never been big on manners, but there was real steel in Mirks's glare.

'Yep, you're right,' said Navigator Anev, waving it away. 'My bad.'

'*My bad, SIR.*'

'. . . My bad, *sir*,' Stef said through gritted teeth.

'Better!' Officer Mirks said, her smile getting all soppy and adoring as she turned back towards me. Don't get me wrong, I *love* praise all day long, but this was too intense!

'So sorry about that, Captain Green,' said Mirks. 'Did you want the drones destroyed?'

'I – er, yep!' I said, and did that pointy order thing with my finger. 'Navigator, *engage!*'

At that, there was an awkward pause. Officers Mirks's smile grew sad again.

'I think you'll find that Tactical fires the weapons, *sir, Captain Green sir*,' Navigator Stef said drily, and I winced.

'Phh,' I exhaled. 'This is a lot.'

'I can give the order, sir,' said Mirks eagerly. 'Tactical, lock on to the first Viper drone and fire at will!'

There was an excited pause while I waited for fireworks and *CHOOM CHOOM CHOOM*s . . .

. . . but nothing happened.

'Tactical,' Mirks repeated. '*Fire at will.*'

That's when I glanced back to the Tactical Officer, and . . .

'Ah, nuts,' I murmured.

It was Luke. And he looked as baffled as I did.

'Kay, he was all grown up like me, Captain Kyan Green . . . but it was definitely Luke. He'd grown a long moustache, but the rest of him hadn't even changed that much; it almost looked as if it were *our* Luke wearing the comedy fake moustache I'd given him. He was standing over his console, which to be fair had about five hundred light-up buttons, and he looked petrified.

'Tactical?' Officer Mirks said, her smiling voice dangerously soft now. 'Would you please blast those drones out of the sky today?'

His face bright red, Luke slowly pressed a button . . .

'SWITCHING ALL OF SHIP'S POWER AND SYSTEMS OFFLINE—'

'Oops, not that,' Luke said nervously, and pressed the button. The lights – which had all gone a pale blue – went back to normal again. He pressed another button.

'SELF-DESTRUCT SEQUENCE INITIATED—'

'Nope, nope,' he said, and pressed the button again. Now the lights stopped flashing red and, again, went back to normal.

'Tactical Officer Smith,' Mirks said, and her smile was *seriously* frosty by now. 'Would you please tell me why—'

Right at that moment, a man's voice blared out of the badge on my chest.

'Captain Green,' the man said. His voice was abrupt and *tough*, but something about it was familiar. 'Captain Green, it's Spanners here. I've noticed we're not firing lasers. Are you testing my plan to capture one of the drones to see how they're tracking us, sir?'

'. . . Exactly!' I said, more to Officer Mirks than 'Spanners'. 'That's what Tactical Officer . . . uh, Luke was waiting for. We're going to capture a drone!'

'Hmm, interesting idea,' Officer Mirks said, but she didn't like that plan at all, I could tell. Her smile was still there, but it was clinging to her teeth by its fingertips, and worry lines made a McDonald's 'M' across her forehead.

'However, to capture the drone would require us to evade its strafing rounds,' she said. 'The vector required to get close enough and activate our tractor beam would be exceptionally difficult to maintain, wouldn't you agree?'

Well, I did not understand a word of that. I stared at Officer Mirks, trying desperately to keep my Captain's thoughtful face on. Then, thankfully, Navigator Stef couldn't help but make a dig.

'Wouldn't you agree, *sir*,' she muttered, and Officer Mirks whirled around, her smile curdled into a furious smirk.

'OK then, Navigator!' she said, her voice high and aggy. 'Seeing as you *clearly* know so much, why don't you turn around, and fly at that drone?'

Stef stared back at her coolly, for a long moment. Then she turned back to the controls.

'OK,' she replied, and pushed the thruster right up.

Now, I don't know what game she'd played that worked with those buttons, but it was *amazing*. She flew straight at the Viper drones, our massive starship flipping like a coin around the volleys of laser blasts fired at us by the darting drones. Just as we passed between them she straightened up, paused for a microsecond, then just as the drones fired again smacked the up-thrusters on, sending us plunging down so fast that my tummy did flips and everybody went 'Ooh!' – just as the drones' shots fired into one another.

'Woohoo!' I shouted, as everybody cheered, and slapped Navigator Stef on the back. 'Now ACTIVATE THE TRACTOR!'

There was a pause ... and a painful silence spread across the bridge. At first I thought it was because I'd forgotten to say 'tractor beam', sounding like an overexcited farmer instead. But then I heard Luke muttering curses and hammering buttons behind me, and I realised that, again, everybody was waiting for him.

'SWITCHING OFF ALL POWER AND—'

'*No, nope . . .*'

'SELF-DESTRUCT SEQU—'

'Not that . . .'

'WINDSCREEN WIPERS ACTIV—'

'Oh *come* on!'

'TRACTOR BEAM ENGAGED,' another voice said.

It was Officer Mirks. She had reached over and pressed the correct button at last. Now, as our tractor beam fired up, and the enemy drone was pulled along by an invisible force, she gazed at Luke with open dislike.

'I forgot to mention, Captain,' she said sweetly. 'What did you want me to do with the boy we found hiding below decks? He was disguised in a crew member's uniform. One belonging to a Dimitar Anev.'

13
Super Saturn

'He must've had his flipping earphone in like always,' Stef whispered furiously. 'But he didn't have glasses, did he, when we hopped into this universe. So his clothes would've changed, but not his face.'

'So where's he being kept?' I whispered back urgently. 'Where's Celestine? How do we even escape this universe when we can't just leave the spaceship?!'

'How should I know?' Stef whispered back. 'It's *your* bougie robot vacuum cleaner that sucked us up!'

'That wicked thing is nothing to do with me,' I hissed. 'But this place is huge! Look – *Engine Room, Holodeck, Astrometrics*. What even *is* Astrometrics?'

Me, Stef and Luke were sat around a tiny table at the

end of the small 'Briefing Room'. We had to be quiet – I mean, we'd just found out that Dimitar had been arrested as an imposter, this room was *right* next to the bridge, and by the time I'd finished asking for directions to it, everybody looked like we were suss. With stars streaming past the window at something called 'warp speed', Stef managed to make a hologram come out from the Briefing Room table, and we were now studying a map of the good ship *Vengeance*. I had never been more confused. Stef, on the other hand, was in her element.

'This is insane,' she breathed, and as worried as she was about Dimitar, I could still hear excitement in her voice. 'I mean, how does *Star Trek* get so much right?'

'RIGHT?!' Luke stared at her like she was crazy. 'What's "right" about this?! It was hard enough just to fire the stupid lasers! Why can't they just auto-fire when you're pointing at them, like shoot-'em-ups on the tablet?'

'Hmm, I think you'd end up in a lot of accidental fights then, bro,' I said, as kindly as I could.

'You'll be able to control it easy next time, Luke,' Stef said. 'If you're not such a plonker, anyway. Your buttons looked the same as the controls on the last *Star Trek DS9* game, Sisko's Revenge. That orange circle on the bottom right is *definitely* your torpedoes. There's arrow buttons around it – that's for you to select what you're going to target. And then there's the smaller blue button to the right of it – that's got to be laser cannons.'

'Right,' Luke said, looking happier. 'Thanks, Stef.'

'Yeah, you'll get there, Luke,' I said, and it was supposed to be encouraging. But when I looked up, both Stef and Luke were staring at me in furious amazement.

'You are a full piece of work, you know that?' Stef said. '*You* just sat there getting compliments off your girlfriend Officer Mirks!'

'Girlfriend?!'

'Yup,' Luke snorted. 'And what's with that *Captain Supergreen* voice when you're speaking to her?'

'What voice?!'

'Yah, hellew,' mimicked Luke in a deep, posh voice. 'Yah, ah'm the feymous Kahptain Sewpah Green.'

'That's not . . .' I began, outraged. 'That's not how I sound!'

'Ah thahnk aht ahs,' said Stef, and both she and Luke snickered. 'Anyway, Supergreen, we've got three things to worry about. How do we get *my* brother and *your* sister, and how do we get out of here?'

Luke nodded.

'There's also the mission,' he pointed out. 'Spider Ace

said the Infinite Race sends us to wherever we're needed the most. As messed up as it is that we got hoovered into this universe, there might be something important we have to do that Captain Supergreen can't do on his own.'

'What could that even be though?' I said.

Just then the door to the meeting room slid down, and Officer Mirks came in.

'Ah,' she said. 'It was about time for the officers' meeting. Ahead of the game as always, Captain.'

'Ahhh.' I said it poshly . . . before I caught Luke and Stef looking pointedly at me.

'Yep. Good.'

Loads of officers followed Officer Mirks into the room – humans and non-humans of all shapes and sizes. Seriously, there was a tiny green person with two heads, and what I *swear* was a giant talking goldfish with a tank jammed over its head. And still, they weren't what *really* made me stare.

Nope, the officer who *really* shocked me came in last. He was a gnarled, flea-bitten man with a gold tooth and eyepatch, a spanner-shaped badge on his uniform over-alls, and tattoos of engine parts *drawn across his face*. The man was older than the last time I'd seen him, and scarred with the wounds of a hundred battles. But still, I knew who it was.

'Oh my days,' Stef murmured. 'That's our *headteacher*!' And before we could stop him, Luke *stood up like it was assembly*.

'Good morning, Mr Wimpole!' he said. 'Good morning, everyone!'

'What is this, school?' 'Spanners' Wimpole growled back, 'Sit yer snuff-luffin' backside down, *Mr* Luke. We've got enough to be getting on with.'

'Luke!' I muttered. 'Sit down!'

That's when I realised that there were only three chairs. Where was everyone else supposed to sit? The other officers looked at me as though waiting for something, and I scanned the Briefing Room, in case there was another little room behind a curtain, like in our school hall, somewhere with stacks of chairs and gym equipment. Fortunately, Stef nudged me, and pointed to the screen in front of me, where a new option had appeared.

EXPAND MEETING TABLE, CAPTAIN? Y / N

I hit '**Y**' – and flinched as the end of the table *shot out*, chairs collapsing out from underneath each new place.

'Aye,' Spanners Wimpole said, sounding gruff and apologetic. 'The extending tables are still a bit quick. I can't figure out how Stringer's engineer kept the speed down.'

Stringer's engineer. Me, Luke and Stef exchanged significant looks, all of us thinking the same thing: this had been Stringer's ship!

'I bet that was some battle when you took Chief Stringer's flagship from him,' Officer Mirks said. 'Incredible strategy, a real David and Goliath tale! And now, after a long struggle, we have the chance to complete our mission.' She stepped forwards, tapping on a tablet she had in her hand, and as she did, a space map came up on the holographic screen in front of me. It showed a planet with rings around it. *Loads* of rings.

'We've found him, Captain,' she said confidently. 'The coordinates for Stringer's hideout were hidden on the Viper drones *you* captured. He's hiding out on an alien base, near a planet called "Super Saturn". The base he is hiding on is unstable and easy to destroy. With just a few torpedoes, the Stringer Chief won't torment the universe any longer.'

'*Brilliant!*' I said, and as all the officers around the table cheered, stamped their feet and banged the table, Officer Mirks beamed. This was more like it, the kind of big win I'd dreamed of, ever since Spider Ace had explained the destruction the Pure State could cause.

'Erm . . .' said Luke, suddenly, and the table fell quiet. 'Er . . . You said it's an alien base. Well . . . do the aliens on the base *know* that we're after Stringer?'

Officer Mirks's eyes froze a little . . . but then she smiled.

'We are fighting an interstellar battle for freedom, Tactical Officer Luke,' she said gently. 'I'm afraid we haven't always got time to talk to everyone. Now, do we have your orders, Captain?'

'Yeah!' I said. 'I mean . . . yes. Go for it! Engage?'

'Marvellous,' said Mirks. 'Excellent work, Captain, brilliantly handled. Now, our, ahem, *rustic* Chief Engineer, Spanners, wanted to update you about the damage we took in that fight.'

'Great,' I said, and tried not to shrink back, as 'Spanners' Wimpole staggered to his feet like an awakening zombie.

'Captain,' he growled, in a voice that could make fizzy pop flat. 'With the drone attacks today, yesterday and the day before, we've taken some hits. It's a good job we had a new stock o' nappies in the stores last week – am I right, ya big bunch o' snot-rags?'

There were uncomfortable murmurs from the assembled officers. I got the impression he called them 'snot-rags' a lot – kind of like how our Mr Wimpole repeats his jokes all the time, except much much harsher.

'Now,' he continued, 'I'm not gonna lie, we're in deep dodo-doo-doo. Our shields are at five per cent. One more big hit, and the first ship who finds us will wonder who left all those bits of metal and limbs floating through space.'

'How well can you repair the shields before we reach Super Saturn?' I asked.

'That's the thing,' Spanners said. 'I've had your sister working on them all morning, Captain, but if we want the firepower to destroy this base, then I'll need her on proton torpedoes. Nobody will be as quick as Engineer Tines on those nukes.'

'Nukes?' I exclaimed. 'We don't let her change the batteries on the remote!'

Still, I was relieved to hear she was OK, and I just thinking of a way to ask about Dimi without sounding suspicious when Officer Mirks told us first.

'There's also the question of the intruders, Captain,' she said, and for a moment her gaze fell uncomfortably on Luke. 'The stowaway child we found who stole Toilet Tech Anev's uniform.'

'Where is Dim— the prisoner now?' I asked.

'Well,' Officer Mirks said, 'he was so clearly an enemy assassin planted by Stringer that I presumed you wanted him thrown out of the airlock . . .'

'NO!'

Me, Stef *and* Luke shouted that, all at once. *Everyone* looked stunned. Officer Mirks looked suspicious.

'Er . . .' I continued, thinking furiously. 'I have a better idea, a real lesson we can teach Dimi when we get to Super Saturn. Listen to this plan, and tell me it's not the best way to show our enemies who's boss.'

And with my own crew staring at me like I was suss, I came up with a solution that hopefully left nobody thrown out of an airlock.

Some time later, we were all back on the bridge, as the good ship *Vengeance* pulled out of warp speed and the planet Super Saturn came into view. It was like nothing I've ever seen.

You know the planet Saturn, right? Well, imagine visiting its seven rings. At first, further away, they look almost solid, like a racetrack you could drive around in a go-kart. Then you get closer, and you see that the rings are actually formed of millions of icy rocks, some as small as beach balls, some as big as cars, all of them zipping around the planet in a massive orbit *thousands* of miles wide. Then imagine seeing all of that . . . but *waaaaay* bigger. Imagine there's not seven rings, but seven *thousand*, some so wide that from a distance they look like *one-thousand-lane motorways*, roads wide enough to drive a whole fleet of airplanes around and still have room for a drive-thru. Imagine that as you get closer, you see that these roads are made of the same icy rocks as on Saturn – but that while some are as small as beach balls, some are as big as *mountains*, all zipping around a planet so big that it might be a dim star . . . but from here looks more like a brown tennis ball, because these rings stretch for *millions* of miles.

That was Super Saturn, and as it came into view, everybody was stunned into silence.

Everybody, that is, except Officer Mirks. Officer Mirks was too busy with our prisoner.

'And now, evil stowaway,' she sneered to the prisoner, 'Captain Kyan Green – yes, *the* Kyan Green – is going to teach you a valuable lesson about your beloved Chief Stringer.'

I turned, and as perilous as the situation was, part of me really wanted to laugh as I faced the 'stowaway'. Staring back at me, looking very unimpressed, was Dimi – our Dimi. His wrists were cuffed, and he was wearing some kind of electronic gag that covered his mouth, but just from the look on his face I could guess what words he wanted to come out with.

'Well, Captain?' Officer Mirks chortled. 'Any words for our prisoner?'

'Er . . .' I said, taken by surprise. 'I hate you! No, nah, that's . . . hmm. Errr . . .'

'Approaching Stringer's base now, Captain,' Stef said quickly, just as Officer Mirks was starting to frown. Then she paused, and added, uncertainly, 'It *says* it's here anyway.'

We all stared at the rings speeding beneath us. I couldn't see anything that looked like a base, just a gap in the rings along which a small moon was speeding like a Scalextric car. Although . . .

'Navigator,' I said quietly. 'Go and take a closer look at that moon.'

With expert ease, Stef coasted just above the icy rings, until we reached the big missing lane. The moon was spinning as it approached us, its gravity gathering bits of ice from the rings around it like a hoover. Finally, it turned all the way around . . . and a host of flashing lights showed on the moon's surface. We'd found the alien base, Stringer's hideout.

'*Excellent* call, Captain,' Officer Mirks said with a smile. 'I'll check telemetry.' She hurried to another console, giving me the chance to quickly mouth *Sorry!* at Dimi.

'*Kyan! KYAN!*'

The whisper came from behind me. It was Luke, leaning over his workstation, and *still* whispering too loudly.

'*What are you doing?!*' I hissed, looking around for Officer Mirks. '*Lean back!*'

'*Yep,*' Luke whispered, *not* leaning back. 'It's just . . . *Are we the baddies?*'

'*What?!*'

'*The baddies. Do you think we're the baddies here?*'

'*Luke, lean BACK,*' I hissed. '*We are NOT the baddies! STRINGER's the baddie, why can't you see that?*'

Luke *still* didn't lean back.

'*But if he's the baddie, then how come we're the ones throwing people out of airlocks and about to blow up an alien base without talking to them?*'

I was really losing my temper with Luke now. He'd been there, all those times Stringer had attacked us: why couldn't he see how important it was to beat him?! But before I could speak, something strange happened. A strange logo appeared . . . almost like it was beaming through my eyeballs. It was a low-battery flashing icon, and it flashed three times. Below it, some words appeared.

Kinetic Energy Low

I blinked, and shook my head, and the logo disappeared. Luke was shaking his head too, and as we looked at each other I knew he'd seen the same thing.

'What was that?' I whispered. But before he could answer, Officer Mirk returned.

'It's confirmed. That alien moon base is Stringer's hiding place all right, Captain,' Officer Mirk said. 'Starboard weapons are ready and trained to engage the bogey. Tactical Officer confirm?'

She was looking at Luke of course.

'. . . Did you just say bogey?' said Luke.

Officer Mirks sighed, her smile now clenched between gritted teeth.

'I mean,' she said, 'it's definitely Chief Stringer. Are you ready to blast him, Tactical Officer Smith?'

Luke stared back at her.

'Wait, so . . . we're actually going to do that, then?' he asked quietly. 'Shouldn't we at least call the base first?'

'*Call the base*,' Officer Mirks repeated, her voice dripping with sarcasm. She turned to me, her voice soft and urgent.

'You've done it, Captain,' she said. 'After all the harm Chief Stringer has caused you, your family, the entire galaxy, you've chased him down and now you have him in your sights. Do you really want to give him another chance to escape, now when you're so close?'

She wasn't wrong. I'd been chased, cheated, shot at and run off the road by Mr Stringer in universe after universe. He'd tried to splat me with a magazine, had sent his army of bugs to eat me, and had tried to take away my home. Even worse than that, I now knew that he was a part of something even dreader than him, an evil empire called the Pure State, that had used Stringer in its efforts to dominate my universe, my home. How could I miss an opportunity like this?

'Tactical,' I said, and I liked the boom in my voice. 'Target Stringer's base, and fire.'

There was a long pause. I turned, and glared at Luke.

'Please, Luke,' I said at last.

And, with a look of deep unhappiness, he pressed the FIRE button.

'Thanks, Luke,' I began, as torpedoes floomed out, three glowing purple stars that arced across the viewport, and—

'*No,*' Luke said, and before anyone could stop him he fired our laser blasters straight afterwards, exploding the torpedoes!

'*What?!*' I roared. 'You idiot, why did you—'

'Captain!' Spanners Wimpole's voice crackled urgently through my badge. 'Those torpedoes exploded too close to us! Brace for impact!'

BOOM! The shockwave battered into our shields, sending the whole ship trembling – not the worst blast, but enough for . . .

'Shields and weapons down, Captain, shields and weapons down!'

As if things couldn't get *any* worse, Officer Mirks hurried forwards . . . and seized Luke's wrist.

'What is the meaning of THIS!' she said, and held it up.

Most days, there would've been no meaning at all. It was just Luke's arm. The trouble was, while the rest of him had clearly been transformed into his cosmic twin, this

184

was the arm of a young boy. That strange symbol appeared again in the corner of my vision, and my blood ran cold.

Kinetic Energy Low

'Another imposter!' Officer Mirks exclaimed. '*It's an invasion!*'

We were trapped, on this stranded ship, in this unfriendly universe, and our disguises were failing.

14
On the Run through the Ship

We all stared, petrified, at one another. Officer Mirks held the grown-up Luke's tiny-looking wrist.

'Honestly, when you don't expect it? A kid's arm on an adult is so creepy,' I murmured. Behind his gag, Dimi *mm-mm*'d in agreement.

'*Another* traitor in our midst!' Officer Mirks snarled. 'Surely now you have to let me throw him out of the airlock, Captain!'

'Whoa!' I said. 'Let's stop with the airlock for . . .'

I broke off then, for one very good reason. The battery symbol appeared in my vision again.

Kinetic Energy Low

I felt my arm go funny, glanced down . . . and shot it

behind my back as quick as I could! Like Luke, my Year 6 arm was attached to the muscly grown-up shoulder of Captain Kyan! The situation could not get any worse. Desperately I searched for an escape. It didn't look good. Green-uniformed security guards had gathered at each end of my console, making the display change as it had in the Briefing Room:

EXPAND MEETING TABLE, CAPTAIN? Y / N

'Captain,' Officer Mirks was saying, 'this saboteur is a dangerous criminal and traitor. If we don't set an example with the airlock now, his childlike co-conspirators in tweenage treason will—'

'What if it's a misunderstanding?' asked Stef. 'What if he's just a plonker who sometimes *self-destucts*?' She fixed Luke with a meaningful glance, then nodded to his console.

'Misunderstanding?' Officer Mirks sneered. 'This imposter has snuck on to our ship and murdered Tactical Officer Luke!'

Stef nodded to the console again, and suddenly her plan made sense.

'You're right,' I said. 'You're right! It's no good, especially not after he *pressed the self-destruct button earlier*.'

Luke caught my glance, and gave a start. *Press it!* I thought desperately at him. *Press it, and they'll be distracted into switching it off!*

Only problem? Apparently I'm not as subtle as I thought I was. Officer Mirks's frown deepened, and she began to gaze at me. She walked over to me, and before I could stop her she *grabbed* my hidden arm and –

'*YOU!*' she snarled. '*YOU'RE AN IMPOSTER TOO!*'

'SELF-DESTRUCT SEQUENCE INITIATED,' the ship's computer said, and Luke raced for the clear door. Officer Mirks ran to Luke's console to deactivate the self-destruct sequence, just as two Security Officers hurried forwards to arrest us all . . .

And I hit '**Y**' on my console. Immediately the table *fired out*, slamming into both green security guards! One tumbled into Stef, who took out *her* de-transformed arms and *waved* them in the other guard's face!

'BLEEEARGH!' she shouted.

'ARGH!' the security guard screamed, scrubbing at his face as though he'd caught a disease. 'ARGH! SHE GOT ME WITH THOSE HIDEOUS CHILD'S HANDS!'

'RUN!' Stef shouted, and the three of us ran after Luke, Dimi bounding along on his shackled feet. The door slid open to reveal Luke standing in a long, bright corridor, and as soon as we were through it, Stef turned back and began to tap desperately on the control panel next to it.

'KY!' she shouted, and pointed at the panel. 'LOOK IN HERE!'

'Eh?!' I said, looking into it. Something scanned my eyes, a light turned green, and the ship's computer said, '*Captain's Authorisation Granted, Bridge Secured.*'

'That might give us some time,' Stef gasped.

'MMMM MM MM MMM-MMM?!' Dimi said.

'I don't know. Ky, where are we going?' Stef said.

'We *have* to find Celestine, then get *off* this ship,' I said, 'just not through the airlock. We need to steal a shuttle. They must be being kept somewhere on a ship this size.'

'Great!' Stef snapped. 'Just when we had a simple mission for once.'

Luke didn't speak, which was just as well, because I was mad at him for messing all this up. Biting my tongue, I looked around for directions, and saw that the nearest holoscreen had them:

\\\\\\\\\

ENGINEERING / HOLODECK /
SHUTTLE BAY – FLOOR 1
TURBOLIFTS

← ← ← ← ← ← ← ← ←

'Shuttle Bay!' I shouted. 'It's on the same floor as Engineering – we can sneak Tines out and get out of here.'

'Let's get the Turbolift down then,' Stef said.

We ran down the corridor towards the Turbolifts, which was harder than it sounds with my balance being thrown out by one strong adult arm pumping alongside a scrawny kid's arm. Soon that battery logo appeared on my

eyeballs again, and my heart sank . . . until I saw that it was a *different* logo.

Kinetic Energy Recharging: 1%

'My glasses are recharging!' I yelled with relief, just as we reached the Turbolift.

Stef nodded, and was about to answer when the lift doors opened to reveal *another* member of crew standing there! For a moment we all stared at him, while he stared back.

'Be the Captain, Ky!' Stef whispered to me. She dug me in the ribs, and I blurted out:

'There's baddies on the bridge, sailor!'

'Sailor?!' Stef said.

'I need you to get back out there and start arresting people, ya hear?' I said.

'I . . . ah . . .' the crew member stammered. Then he got a determined look in his eye, and saluted. 'I'll do it, Captain,' he said, and as he ran off down the corridor, we shuffled gratefully into the empty lift, the doors closing behind us.

'ENGINEERING,' said Stef, and the lift began to drop down. I glared at Luke, whose mouth was tightened in a stubborn grimace, and I was just about to let him have it when something strange happened: my arm swelled back up into its adult size.

Kinetic Energy Recharging: 11%

'Now my glasses are recharging even quicker!' I said.

'So's mine,' Stef said, and both she and Luke held out their re-transforming arms. For a moment, she thought, biting her lip,

'Kinetic Energy Low . . .' she muttered, then looked up. 'I *think* the batteries went flat because we weren't moving enough.'

'*Moving* enough?'

'Exactly. Kinetic Energy is a motion energy.'

'What's that mean?' Luke asked.

'It's not really the time for a science lesson . . .' Then Stef saw my, Dimi's and Luke's baffled faces, and sighed. 'Right. Quickly. So there's loads of different types of energy, and it's *always* being turned into something else. Say a lump of coal, right, that's got all this energy called Potential Energy, like energy that's locked inside it. When you light the coal, it catches fire and that Potential Energy turns into Heat Energy, which is then turned into a load of other types of energy that make you feel it and all that. Does that make sense – energy changing into other types of energy?'

'Yeah,' Luke said. 'So when I put my tablet on I'm changing the energy in the battery into other types for the screen, the speakers, the—'

'The whole thing,' Stef said impatiently. 'Exactly. The energy you use while moving is called Kinetic Energy. I'm guessing these glasses somehow turn the Kinetic Energy into Mechanical Energy for them to work. Which means that to keep them working, we have to move around.'

It made sense. Suddenly I remembered something. I felt in my uniform pocket, and pulled out the folded Infinite Race Instructions. At the bottom, next to a *, was the Bonus Clue:

> *BONUS CLUE: Goggles are powered by Kinetic Energy. So stay in the jam jar and off the scotch pegs if you don't want your charm and flattery flat.

'Jam Jars and Scotch Pegs . . . Oh my gosh,' I said, 'That extra bit on the Instructions said *Jam Jars*. I bet that means *Cars* and *Legs*! That's what the bonus clue says: Stay in the CAR and off your LEGS if you don't want your . . . charm and flattery . . . *battery* flat!'

Just then the Turbolift came to a smooth stop.

'*Engineering*,' the Lift Computer said, and the doors slid open to reveal a wide, futuristic metallic and white room.

Unlike the bridge, Engineering was *not* built for comfort. There were no chairs, no carpet, and every free space was covered with light-up tubes, see-through cables, wiry metal frames and holographic consoles. At one side a huge viewscreen revealed the rings of Super Saturn below. At the other, a glowing tube hummed, blue lights scrolling down it again and again.

'*Star Trek*, man . . .' Stef said. 'I mean, was it right about *everything*? Look, that's the warp engine, that's the power conduits – I bet Spanners is the Chief Engineer and—'

'MMM!' said Dimi, and nodded his head frantically past us. 'MM *MM-MM*!'

I turned – and saw Spanners Wimpole headed straight for us!

'Do it again, Ky,' Stef muttered. '*Be the bighead.*'

'Captain,' Spanners said urgently, before I could scowl at Stef for the 'bighead' comment. 'It's a good job you're here, I—'

'Thank God *you're* here, Spanners,' I said in my smuggest Captain Supergreen voice. 'But I haven't got all day to dilly-dally. Squad goals.'

'Squad *wha*t?' Spanners said, looking baffled. 'What on earth are you saying, Captain?'

'I . . . uh . . . There are enemies on the bridge. I need to take Engineer Tines, and get to the Shuttle Bay for an emergency mission.'

'*Take* her?!' Spanners said. 'You can't! She's my best engineer!' And before I could come up with a reason that my sister *had* to go, that blasted message appeared in my eyes again.

Kinetic Energy Low: 0%

'Oh no,' I whispered. I felt my arms and legs begin to change again, right when Spanners was looking strangely at me. I had to move.

'We need ideas, Spanners,' I demanded. 'And we need them fast!'

And at that, I began to jump up and down.

'What on *earth* . . . ?' Spanners exclaimed.

'Sometimes it helps the ideas pop out my head!' I shouted. 'Come on, everybody!'

Stef and Luke began to hop up and down as well, as did Dimi. When, reluctantly, one or two of the other engineers began to join in, Spanners *almost* hopped . . . but then bellowed with frustration.

'I DON'T SEE HOW THIS IS HELPING, CAPTAIN!'

Kinetic Energy Low: 3%

'You're right, Spanners,' I said, and stopped hopping. 'I just really need to find Engineer Tines.'

'That's the thing of it, Captain,' Spanners exclaimed. 'She's disappeared!' As if noticing poor Dimi there for the first time, he turned on him and bared his teeth.

195

'Have you asked the *saboteur*?' he asked savagely. 'I don't believe you're just a kid, whoever you are. I liked Toilet Technician Dimi, and if I find you've harmed a hair on his or Celestine's head I'll wrap a warp-infuser array around your sabotaging skull!'

'Flipping heck, Spanners!' I said. 'Go easy, yeah?!' But then the message returned to my eyes again – these glasses were a *nightmare*.

Kinetic Energy Low: 1%

'WHAT DID YOU DO TO DIMI!' I shouted, waving my arms and dancing my feet until the warning sign stopped. 'TELL ME WHAT YOU DID, YOUNG MAN!'

'We've got to get out of here,' Stef said, star-jumping now and looking *extremely* tired.

'Spanners,' I said urgently. 'Let me tell you the truth about why we're here.' I lowered my voice to a whisper, tried to think of the right lie . . . but could only think of this instead:

'We're going on a secret mission to grab Stringer from his hideout,' I said finally. 'So we don't, uh, have to fire on the base.'

For one dread moment, Spanner stared at me. Finally, he frowned.

'Ya know what, Captain?' he said. 'It'd be nice not to go cannon-crazy for once. Be like old times.'

And, just like that, he stepped aside to let us past. And that's when our luck ran out.

'IMPOSTERS!' a voice shouted at us, and I turned. It was Officer Mirks, grinning with a blaster aimed right at us.

'RUN!' I shouted.

The chase was on. We sprinted around the thrumming engine, right for the door at the other side, blaster bolts flying over our shoulders. Reaching the corridor, I skidded around the corner and felt this *horrible* twinge in my back. Captain Kyan's old-man body seemed messed *up*!

'Oof!' I shouted, sounding *scarily* like my dad getting up off the sofa. Stef and Luke weren't faring much better. Luke was red in the face, while Stef, who was second-fastest in our five-a-side football team last year, seemed as achy as me, and Dimi was *still* in shackles and sweating buckets after bunny-hopping his way across the ship! Still we sprinted, through corridors, across maintenance bridges and under humming conduits. Finally, just as I was seriously flagging, we reached some huge, thick steel doors marked SHUTTLE BAY . . . and they wouldn't open.

'No!' I begged, pounding the door and tapping the control panel. 'Captain's Permission! Captain's Permission!' But it still wouldn't budge.

'It's a hangar door!' Stef said. 'Like in a garage! Somebody must've locked it from the inside!'

'Open the door!!!' we all yelled desperately, kicking and thumping the heavy metal. 'Whoever's in there, OPEN THE DOOR!'

The footsteps came closer, I heard the sounds of a blaster charging . . .

. . . and the door was *hefted* open by Celestine – not 'adult' Celestine, but the kid sister I know!

'Dimi!' she shouted as we ran inside, then took a closer look at the rest of us. 'Ouch! You guys age *badly*. Now come on, *quick*!'

The Shuttle Bay was *massive*; sleek, small spaceships docked in a line in front of titanic, grey hangar doors. The ceiling towered *epically* high above brown walls, and a concrete floor that looked smoother than a bowling lane.

'I got here and none of you were anywhere,' Celestine said as we ran. 'Mr Wimpole was here, but this Wimpole was *loco*. He wanted me to fix the ship!'

'Yeah, that's what I heard,' I said with a grin. It was a relief to see my sister OK.

'Then I started to change – I mean, like, *transform* back into me! These glasses are *rubbish*, Ky!'

'I think they're supposed to be good when you're moving,' I said.

'Whatevs,' Celestine said. 'Either way, I ran out of the Engineering room before anybody could spot me, and hid out here. I figured you guys would come here to escape, so I tried to find a shuttle for us to escape to, but only one was open.'

We kept running past the other shuttlecraft until we reached the one Celestine had found open. I could see why nobody had bothered to lock it too – compared to all the sleek and shiny flyers docked here, it was rusty, tattered, and *covered* with scorch marks. Even the name on its hub was burned out to show only E_R__A- Q_E_T. Strangely enough, I could've sworn that I knew this ship.

Still, there was no time to wonder. We raced up the rickety steel steps to a dark, dingy interior. There were no seats, just uncomfortable standing stools and the kind of handles you hold on the bus. Another, even smaller ship was docked right in the middle, and *again* I had this familiar feeling, like I knew this place, but couldn't quite place it. I did know one thing though: after my swanky Captain's Bridge, this rickety old ship was a *big* comedown. *We've made everything worse for our cosmic twins in this universe,* I thought, and again felt a sudden surge of anger towards Luke. Fighting the sense of desperation that came with it, I scoured the ship's controls, and something *horrible* occurred to me.

'Uh, how do we get the hangar bay doors open?'

'I know how,' Stef said, and I looked up with alarm because she didn't sound happy about it. She hurried to a tablet hanging from the wall by a cable, and as as she began to tap away at it, the ship's tinny computer spoke in response, and even *that* sounded familiar. Just where did I know this ship from?

'Preparing for take-off – Hangar Bay Doors Opening.'

'Yesss!' I said, as those massive doors in front of us opened with an enormous *WHIRRRRRR*. 'How did you know, Stef?'

But Stef's face was pale. She walked up to my control panel, and pointed a finger at the logo on it.

'Because we've been to this universe before,' she said. And the pieces fell into place.

EUROPA QUEST

We had been here before, in this exact universe, on this exact craft! We had found ourselves orbiting Europa, one of

Jupiter's moons, where Chief Stringer – the same Chief Stringer we'd just chased to Super Saturn – had been stealing water from the moon's inhabitants, the Erie aliens. But the spaceship we'd used to get there – this spaceship, the *Europa Quest* – it had turned out not to be a spaceship at all.

'We're on a submarine,' I said, my throat dry.

'A submarine?' Celestine asked, horrified. 'How are we going to escape in a submarine?'

The hangar doors slid open wider to reveal Super Saturn's rings stretching out majestically beneath them: close enough to see the boulders of every size and shape floating among a foggy haze of icy particles. In the distance ahead, I could see the alien moon base where Chief Stringer was hiding out. It was all so close . . . if we weren't in the wrong vehicle.

'There's bare guards out there . . .' Dimi called from the back of the submarine. 'We need to go!'

'Go where?!' I shouted. 'Go how?!' Then Officer Mirks's voice echoed *horribly* loud through the hangar bay.

'IMPOSTERS! YOU HAVE NO ESCAPE. WHEN WE GET IN THERE, WE'RE GOING TO THROW YOU OUT OF THE AIRLOCK LIKE WE SHOULD'VE DONE STRAIGHT AWAY!'

I scoured my controls, wishing that there was any option we could use . . . then finding one. There, in the middle of about 300 buttons, there was one marked HIGH-VELOCITY POWDERED ALUMINIUM JETTISON SWITCH. It was a turbo boost, a one-time option, that would rocket us out of this Shuttle Bay . . . but not do anything else after that. We would escape this universe. But what happened to Captain Kyan Green and the rest of our cosmic twins after that . . . I didn't know. I looked up and saw Stef staring at the button too. She looked nervous . . . but she nodded.

'Everyone, hold on to the bus handles,' I said, and I hit the button.

BOOOOOOOOSSSSSHHHHHHHH!!!!!!

We went from 0 to CRAZY FAST in no time, a super-charged boost that sent my feet flying, with my fingers clinging desperately to the bus handle above me. We burst out between the huge hangar-bay doors, and the controls, the ship, the beautiful rings of Super Saturn . . . all of it dissolved into strings as we escaped the *Vengeance*, and escaped this universe as well. Worries flooded through my mind. What would happen to our cosmic twins? Would they ever make the boost, with all those lethal asteroids hurtling along the rings, and with their own crew suspecting them of being murderous imposters? Would they even know why they were stranded outside the good ship *Vengeance*? And what about us? If Stringer somehow escaped this, what would it mean for the 'Pure State', those infesting strands of red that I pictured every time I closed my eyes? Worst of all, what would Spider Ace say when she found out what we'd –

WHOOMPH!

The landing was sudden, and came from the side, not below, like a massive hand had reached through the strings and snatched me away. The wind burst out of my lungs, and as I coughed back a breath, I felt myself slowly rotate . . . only to realise that I was sitting in a swively office chair, slap bang in the middle of the Multiverse Map.

'What . . .' Spider Ace said, and she was so mad she had to take a breath. 'Just WHAT WAS THAT ALL ABOUT?!'

15
The Split-Up

O ur Sector looked worse than ever. From every direction, red tendrils reached out from the darkness, some as thin as eye veins, others thick and sickeningly muscular; all of them suckering and squeezing at our diseased 'verses.

What hurt the most was that the universes most under attack were the ones we'd 'helped'. The Fungiverse toadstool was smothered with those red tendrils, a fungus with its very own mould. The Wheelie Bin, where we'd fought off the Giant Grinster, had a deep gash of red down one side of it, while the Hammer – which I guessed was the universe we'd just escaped – was flickering like a dying light bulb. And at the centre of them all, close enough that I could smell the its stench of decay like rotten meat, was our very own universe, the bubble shaped like a Sippy Cup. Draped with those leeching red tendrils, festering with a red sore spreading across one side. It wasn't just grim, it was disturbing; and in front of it all, Spider Ace stood bat-like, fury in her eyes.

'Just *what* has been going on?' she demanded for the second time.

'It was an accident,' I pleaded. 'My dad's stupid robot vacuum cleaner went AWOL . . .'

'You know your own cosmic twins might be able to remember some of this, don't you? Can you imagine how you'd feel if your adult arm suddenly shrank to a child's? Do you know how terrifying that would be?'

'It is quite freaky,' I admitted.

Spider Ace whirled around, and swiped at the fetid air. From nowhere, a list of figures, codes and percentages scrolled down. They made no sense to me, but she read them out like a shopping list.

'The famous Captain Kyan Green, an imposter. He and his friends, on the run. His ship, stranded and without power. I'll have to sneak Babyface Virus into the databases of both the *Vengeance* and the *Europa Quest*, and hope that both crews discover it before it's too late. What a pig's ear.

And all because you went into the Multiverse with glasses on, when you were TOLD not to go without a Level Five Racer.'

'It was an accident,' I insisted again. 'The stupid vacuum cleaner sucked us up. When we were in there we didn't know how to escape the universe! It's not exactly like we could jump out a window, is it? And then the glasses stopped working, and . . . but we figured out how to get them working again, and—'

'Then how in the *hell* did you get Captain Kyan Green in this situation?!'

I didn't know what to say. I glanced to Luke, whose fault this all was. But he was barely listening, staring instead at the scrolling numbers behind Spider Ace. *At a time like this*, I thought with disgust.

'The crew might work it out,' Dimi said, although even he didn't sound convinced. 'They might all . . . make friends.'

Spider Ace sighed. She looked tired.

'One thing I have learned from travelling the Multiverse is this,' she said. 'Evil is as much part of the fabric as neutrons and electrons. With the best will in the world, people manipulate, bully, steal and cheat. And right until they have way too much to lose to ever change, they convince themselves that they're on the good side, that they are the underdog who is just seeking out justice for themselves. I'm sorry, but with the Pure State affecting things as well? When we leave universes in a bad way, don't expect the people on their own to make it better.'

There was a long pause. A deep, sinking feeling twisted my stomach, a strong suspicion of what Spider Ace was about to do. The trouble was, I couldn't think of anything except:

'Please . . .' I said, and trailed off.

And then, of all people, *Luke* spoke up.

'Won't thinking that all of the universe is evil make it impossible to see any good?' he said simply.

I took a deep breath, more angry with him by the moment. After *all* these mistakes, *he* was the one criticising *Spider*. She was staring at him, her eyes like deep pools barely lit by our gloomy universe. Finally, I couldn't take it any more.

'Typical!' I spat. Luke looked up at me in shock, and saw the anger in my face. Then he looked down.

'Your world, your entire *universe* should be hugely grateful for what you've done,' Spider Ace said at last, and a panic gripped at my chest.

'No, Spider,' I croaked desperately, 'No, Spider *please—*'

'You have been an incredibly brave Racer, and I am proud to have known you. But until the situation changes, I can't risk you or this Sector.

'Spider, *please*—'

'I'm so sorry, Kyan,' Spider Ace said. 'Until you get some direction, I have to take the Infinite Race from you.'

We didn't tumble back into my bedroom. Instead, the rotten, red-infected bubbles around us faded away, and as I turned around to *beg* Spider Ace for one last chance, she was just . . . gone. The darkness eased out, and my bedroom faded in, until I was standing in the space where the Infinite Racetrack had been, my friends all standing in silence around me.

My friends . . . and *Luke*.

'You got your wish then,' I said, not wasting any time.

Luke flinched back as if he were stung.

'I don't know what you mean,' he said.

'I *mean*,' I spat it out, 'you've got your wish. We've lost the Infinite Race.'

He stared back at me.

'I'm not going to say sorry,' he said stubbornly. And that was it. I was proper mad.

'Do you remember . . .' I seethed, getting right in his

face. 'Do you remember when Chief Stringer tried to kill us? Do you remember when he laughed about it? We could've beaten him, finally properly beaten him. And instead, after everything he did, you let him go!'

'Destroyed him, you mean,' Luke said. 'We would've destroyed him. And everybody else on that base.'

'We weren't going to!' I yelled. 'We were just going to destroy his hiding places!'

'Oh cos that's better,' Luke began, but I was on a roll.

'Every mission we had, *you* made it harder. Now our other selves are stranded on a submarine, if they're even alive at all!'

'How is that one my fault?!' Luke said in amazement.

'It's your fault because . . . because . . . Bro, that man wanted to take our home away! He wanted us out just for some extra money – he didn't even care! Do you know what it's like to have somebody who could just wreck your life like that? I don't get why you don't just . . . just . . . grow up!'

'All right,' Luke said, but I could tell that he was hurt. His face went red and his eyes went watery, and he scoffed, in that way when you really care but don't want to admit it. 'Well, that's just dib, I didn't—'

'Ah, *nobody* says "dib", bro.'

'Well I don't CARE!' Luke shouted, and suddenly *I* was stepping back. 'I don't care about football or slang or even winning the next stupid race. I'm no good at any of it. I just want things to be like they were. I just want to be a kid. That's what we are, aren't we? I'm so *sick* of you apologising for me being a kid, or trying to bring me along or whatever. I don't like walking home, because it freaks me out walking alone, *because I'm a kid*! Why can't we walk back with your grandma, I like your grandma! She's your grandma!'

'Bro . . .' I began, taken aback.

'No! No, NOT bro! I didn't change, you changed. I want to go back to *not* letting Alex Bridges *shoplift* from George's

Shop just because you want to impress him. I want to go back to *not* wanting to destroy people, and caring only about some *stupid* Level that we don't even understand what it means, and hating bubblegum Freezie Pops because ... because I don't even know why with that one, it's so PATHETIC!'

Luke paused, breathing hard. I tried to come back at him, but couldn't think.

'I want to go back to it being OK to be good. I want to go back to being a kid. I want to go back to being your friend, and not your "bro".'

After that outburst there was silence. Luke turned, and walked out. Stef, Dimi and my sister stood there awkwardly.

'I mean, you are kinda killing that word, bro,' Dimi said at last.

I didn't know it was my worst day, not yet. I'd had two runner-ups before then. Second was when I got chicken pox for the *third* time, and I got *nuff* sick and had to spend half the day in this weird oaty bath while listening to Grandma tell people how unusual it was to get chicken pox three times like I was going to win a prize. And the worst day before this day had happened? Hands down, when I was *definite* we were going to lose our home, thanks to Mr Stringer.

But now I'd lost the Infinite Race. I'd had a massive row with my best mate. And then the clodhopping footsteps of my dad came up the hallway, he poked his head in, looked past me . . . and his mouth dropped open.

'Oh good God,' said Dad in a trembling voice, and pointed. 'You've broken Robot Pattinson.'

Then I knew it was my worst day.

16
The Worst Week

I get out of bed. It's morning but the skies are all dark, the clouds a strange tint of red. I go to the kitchen, and my family are all faced away at the kitchen table.

'Mum, Dad?'

When they turn, I scream . . .

Then I'd wake up.

Scratch that whole worst-day thing. It was the worst *week*. For the next seven days, every thought I had was clouded with panic about our world being infected by the Pure State while I was powerless to stop it. Every sleep was curdled by nightmares about those writhing red tendrils covering our universe, our world, our school, our family . . .

Not that being awake was any picnic either. My mum and dad grounded me for the week after breaking Robot Pattinson, which I think my mum *kinda* thought was over the top, but probably held my dad back from telling the police I'd committed murder. At school, my argument with Luke had poisoned our whole gang. Stef sat with him in one class on Monday, which I couldn't help but think of as her taking his side. Then, on Tuesday, Dimi joined me and Alex Bridges for a kickabout – but caught sight of Luke watching us, and shuffled off the pitch! Oh, and Alex . . .

Alex was . . . bad, and I don't mean bad-meaning-good. He was mean, for one; I mean *proper* mean. He said horrible stuff about people all day, teachers and other kids, stuff that I felt rubbish just for hearing. But also, for someone I'd always thought of as popular, he was *desperate* for me to laugh, and became offended when I didn't. He kept bringing in sweets and stuff, stuff I was sure was nicked from George's Shop, and trying to share them with me. He sent me links to these grim videos on my phone, and even the ones that weren't grim felt too old, like *wrong*.

By Wednesday, while I was hiding from Alex, I was *also* starting to worry about Luke. He vanished at break. I saw him sneaking back into school after hometime, and wondered if he was so scared to walk home that he was waiting for his dad there now. By Thursday, he looked tired, and pale, and I would probably have told a teacher, or at least Edie Scrap, if I didn't still have that horrible hole in my heart where a lifetime of possible adventures had once been; that gap on my shelves where the Infinite Race used to sit.

At last, the final bell came on Friday, but I struggled to look forward to the weekend, even as I was desperate to get out of school. I saw Alex, *still* looking for me to play football with him, and I straight *ran* to those school gates to get away from him . . .

. . . and my mum was there.

'Mum,' I said, and gave her a massive hug.

'Whoa, whoa!' she said, and hugged me back, looking at me strangely. 'Everything OK?'

I didn't answer. Some kid somewhere made a crack, that was probably about me, and still I didn't care. But when I let go, I saw that my mum looked upset.

'What's up?' I asked, 'What's happened?'

'It's George at the shop,' said Mum. 'He's taken ill. They're taking him to hospital now.'

*   *   *

The ambulance was already parked outside my favourite shop, its blue lights flashing quickly. A small crowd of people were there, my grandma at the front. She had a serious look in her eyes, but she managed a smile and squeezed my hand.

'Is he all right?' I said breathlessly. 'Grandma, is he OK?'

But instead of answering, she looked up. A couple of people called out –

'Go on, George.'

'Get better soon, George!'

A stretcher was being carried out. George was lying on it, wearing an oxygen mask. He looked very pale, very sick. But still, when the stretcher reached Grandma and me, he waved for the paramedics to stop.

'You need to get better, George,' Grandma said sternly, but he shook his head.

'Did I do all right, Loretta?' he asked weakly.

'I don't know what you mean . . .' Grandma began, but he shook his head desperately.

'Did I do all right?'

Grandma nodded, that weird, strict look still on her face. 'You did all right, George,' she said.

'All right?!' I protested, not really getting what this was about but not understanding why my grandma was being so harsh. 'You did great! He did great, Grandma, tell him! Best shop ever!'

George's eyes crinkled in a smile. But then that pained look creased his face, and he looked back to Grandma again.

'Would you tell him?'

'What?' Grandma said, surprised. 'No, George, there's . . . You're sick, don't go worrying about—'

'Please,' George begged. 'Else it doesn't mean . . .' But before he could say any more, the paramedics insisted, and George's stretcher was carried on and he was taken up to the ambulance. A face appeared in the shop door behind them all. It was Mr Stringer, and he looked *seriously* stressed.

'I'm going to get this all cleaned, George,' Mr Stringer called awkwardly after the stretcher. He gave a wild look around at the crowd, and his eyes caught mine. But rather than sneer, or look hateful, he just got that knocked-back panicky look again. I wanted to say something harsh to him, right when I knew it would hurt. But then I caught sight of a yellow windbreaker jacket standing in the crowd, and I whirled around to face the boy wearing it.

'Here to steal from George again?' I said, my voice shrill with rage. There was a silence: an awkward void of shock and confusion.

Alex Bridges, the most popular boy in school, the star footballer, the kid you can't just tell to bog off, stared back at me. An ugly look of denial twisted his face, but I didn't look away. I couldn't look away – not now. For a moment I thought he was going to step towards me. Then he seemed to notice the other people in the crowd, the narrowing eyes, the growing looks of suspicion.

'Bro, you'll be sorry you . . .' he said in disgust. But he never finished the sentence. Instead, he got on his bike, and cycled away.

'Come on, Ky,' Grandma said. 'Let's go to the Community Gardens.'

* * *

We sat at the bench for a while. Some younger kids were playing by the big tree, bragging about how they'd climbed higher than anyone ever had before. I looked over to say something to Grandma ... and I realised that she was playing Candy Crush on her phone.

'I thought we were here to talk?' I said, outraged, and with a laugh she put the phone down.

'What's wrong, Kyan? Something more than George is up, nuh?'

'Yeah,' I said gloomily. 'More like the whole world is just *bad*. It's like ... it's like evil is part of the fabric as much as electrons and neutrons.'

Grandma raised her eyebrows, shocked. Then, as if making up her mind, she set her face.

'When we first moved here,' she said, 'there were kids who didn't like us. They were horrible, and I didn't know why. Your Auntie Christine, she was tough with it, she battled back. But I didn't. I lost my confidence. I hated them, just quietly, on my own. But one of them, one of them wouldn't let me be.'

'Did you tell someone?' I said. 'Did you get him into trouble?'

Grandma shook her head. She let out a sigh and I could tell the memory still hurt.

'It wasn't so easy, Ky. Some of those kids, their parents were the people you were supposed to tell. And this wasn't just a one-day thing, this was years, this one boy setting out to ruin my day, every day he could. Then, finally, he moved away. This boy who'd *really* made my life miserable – he was almost a man by then, that's how long this had gone for – he moved away, and things got a bit better.'

I thought of my grandma, my brilliant grandma, being scared and feeling bad about herself. Suddenly I wanted to find the boy who'd made her feel that way myself, even though he'd be an old man now.

'Did you ever see him again?' I said, my anger bubbling. 'Did you ever get him back?'

There was an engine noise from the road outside. The ambulance slowly pulled away, passing the Community Gardens, and the kid up in the tree made binoculars with her hands like she was spying on it. Grandma watched the ambulance pass, and for a moment she got that strict look she always had with George. Her eyes narrowed, like she wouldn't be fussed if the doors opened and George's trolley went skittering out down to the busy road.

'I did find him,' she said, her voice hard. 'And when I

did, I was in a community that loved me, and *he* was the new one. Things had gone very wrong for him, prison and all sorts. He was on his uppers, and I could've ruined his life. He knew that too. And there's been days, even now there's days where I've wanted to.'

The ambulance paused at the junction. Its lights flashed silently, and it turned left towards the main road. I looked at my grandma again, and was relieved to see that her expression had softened.

'But after all those lollipops he used to give to my kids, then my grandkids,' she said softly, 'after all the times he helped with my shopping and said don't worry about the change when I only had a pound . . . maybe I made the right choice.'

It took a moment for the horrible truth to dawn on me. Somewhere far away the ambulance's siren sounded, but I couldn't see it any more. It carried George, the nice man at the shop, the man who my mum had asked to check on me walking to school, the man I'd known forever. I would never be able to think of him in the same way again.

A heavy load pressed on my chest. It was older, grown-up. It didn't feel nice, but I had it now.

And I knew how to save the Multiverse.

17
The Gang Return

Guys meet me at school ASAP we have to fix it!!!

we can't

We can!!!

No i mean we cant go school this late

fix what

EVERYTHING

Thats the most Kyan msg eva

Summer was properly over. The sun had set already, the air was cold, and Edie Scrap's heavy metal library looked more threatening than ever, its iron grille and rims casting long pointed shadows across the schoolyard. I saw Stef and Dimi cycling through the school gates towards me, and as dark as it was, I could see they weren't happy.

'Fam, my uncle's coming to check on us in two hours,' Dimi said as he skidded to a stop. 'And if we get caught running out *again* we'll have to spend every evening doing our homework in Mum's canteen.'

'I wouldn't say this if it wasn't really important,' I said. 'You know that . . . Do you . . . know if Luke's coming?'

'Luke?' Stef's face fell. 'Luke never uses GangChat, Ky. He's still just on GroupMe.'

A sinking feeling sunk my stomach like rocks. When had I even last checked my GroupMe feed?

'OK,' I said, my voice croaking a bit. 'I'll . . . I'll find him afterwards.'

We raced up the school drive like ninjas, *positive* we'd run into Mr Wimpole or, even worse, Mrs French. But nobody stopped us, and I dared to hope . . . until I saw the folding doors of Edie's library *open*, and heard the *tap-tap-tap* of a computer keyboard inside. Someone was in the library, *using* the Commodore 65 already.

'Who is it?' Dimi whispered. Shaking my head, I made a *shush* sign, crept forwards . . . and tripped up the steps –

CLANG CLANG CLANG!

'Dammit!' I swore, and looked back, wide-eyed. Stef and Dimi said nothing, but they both made a sarky *shush* sign back at me. The keyboard tapping had stopped, the library silent, and with no choice, I crept inside. A hazy green light dribbled from the Commodore 65's ancient monitor, illuminating the stacks of books, the messy whiteboard, the peeling drawers . . .

I'd reached the Commodore 65 when I heard a creak, and turned . . .

'YAAARRRGH!'

With a scream, a shadowed figure hurtled out from behind the books, waving a hardback straight for my head! I fell back with a cry, and flung my arm up, bracing myself for . . .

'Luke?!' said Stef, and I opened my eyes.

'What . . . what are you lot doing here?' Luke said, still wielding a flea-bitten hardback of *The BFG* like a baseball bat.

'La naiba, Luke, what are you doing here?!' Dimi said, and began to laugh. 'You had Ky *scared*, fam, that was hilarious.'

'I wasn't the only one,' I said crossly. 'And besides . . .'

That's when I trailed off. Because there, on the

Commodore 65 screen, were the three worlds we'd last visited: the Hammerverse, the Fungiverse, and the Wheelie Bin 'Verse, where we'd helped to smash up the Giant Grinster's Breakfast Table. Information was scrolling down one side the screen, blocky words and numbers that made no sense to me.

'You can *understand* all this?' I asked.

'That's the thing, Ky,' Luke said. '*I learned from Proton Wars!*'

'What?' I said. 'You mean that game you've wanted us to play this whole time?'

'Tch, "*game*"!' Dimi said. 'That thing's a torture device.'

Luke grabbed the Proton Wars book off the desk, and gave it to me. As I flicked through it, all those charts and maps and XP points . . . I saw that they were all ordered in the same way as the Commodore 65 was showing information about our universe right now.

'I told you the first time we saw the Multiverse Map on the Commodore 65 screen that I knew these figures, right?' he said. 'But it took me a while to realise *where I knew them from*. All the rules and charts and XP stuff in Proton Wars – the Commodore 65 uses the same stats!'

'Sick!' said Stef. 'That's like learning to do actual magic just from playing Dungeons and Dragons!'

'Sort of,' Luke said. 'It's *really* complicated, but I can find out what's happening in these different universes, even how to get there. I just wanted to find a way out of all . . . all the mess I made.'

'Luke . . .' I said. But he suddenly looked *really* down.

'You were right, Ky. I didn't want it to be true, but since I refused to fire on Stringer in the Hammerverse, things are worse everywhere. Everything we've done, from destroying the Giant Grinster's favourite glass, to locking up the String Ripper's Beast Army, it's all been twisted to make the Pure State even more powerful. It's like we took medicine that turned out to be poison, and according to the Commodore 65 there's only two ways out. The first is impossible, and the second is destroying Mr Stringer. I'm sorry, I should've listened to you.'

I stared at him, as he finished awkwardly and looked away. Then I shook my head.

'Nope,' I said, and he looked up in surprise. 'I was wrong. All this time I've been acting grown-up and tough, and you reminded me that we're still kids. All this time I've wanted to hurt Mr Stringer, and get my revenge on him, and you showed me that it wouldn't make things better, and might make things much, much worse. And all this time I've wanted you to do what I do, and like what I like, because we're best mates. But you didn't want to do them. And I am really sorry for not seeing that.'

There was a long pause. Luke stood there, his mouth pulled down, trying to set his face.

Finally, Stef added, 'I could possibly be a bit more chill when you make mistakes as well—'

'A bit?!' we all said at once, and laughed. But then Luke grew serious.

'I'm just no good at driving, Ky,' he said sadly. 'You've seen me, I'm awful. The thing was, I *wanted* to be really good, but I don't – I don't *like* it even. I don't really like football that much, and I hate being scared, and I'm scared all the time! I'm even scared to walk home on my own! I'm even scared to have a proper phone!'

'And still you've been walking back here and sitting in this dark room every night,' Dimi pointed out. He paused, then added, 'And, fam, I would not be seen *dead* in this creepy old death metal library at night.'

We all chuckled at that, me and Stef nodding as well.

'There is a *presence* here or something . . .'

'Flipping guy's crazy, innit, crazy brave Luke.'

'You don't have to be a driver, Luke,' I said. 'If you want to join in with the missions, you can – and if you don't, you don't. Let's face it, all the ones with animals I *suck* at.'

Everyone laughed again.

'Horses, bugs . . .'

'I mean, Ky, nature *hates* you—'

'You don't have to do *anything* you don't want to,' I continued. 'I'd still take whatever advice you'd give me. You're our *Navigator*.'

And that's when something *mental* happened. Right after I said *Navigator*, the Commodore 65 made a *ding!* sound, like our microwave going off but even *more* old-fashioned. The library began to rumble and shake. Stacked books tumbled to the floor, a loud mechanism sounded behind the wall opposite . . .

. . . and a tabletop *burst* out! It knocked through three stacks of books, slid out between us, and *jerked* to a halt.

'The Infinite Racetrack!' Dimi cried. 'We've got it back!'

It wasn't Spider Ace's track: it was *mine*, all seven pieces forming that big 'U' shape around the tabletop. To one side, the box lay open. Inside it were four rickety pairs of sunglasses, and a whole new message was printed across the Instruction Manual, that sheet of paper that didn't crease or tear:

Prepare for the Ride of Your Lives

Congratulations! You are now at Level

5

Level 5 Infinity Racers can regain the Infinite Racetrack they so foolishly lost by accepting their own limitations. As reward for reaching this level, the Racers are given permission to use Facemorphic Goggles.

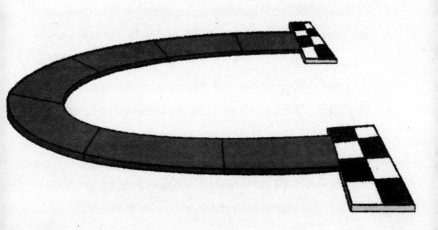

The major reward for Level 5 Racers, however, is the use of Navigator Luke Q. Smith. A Navigator can direct the Racers to whichever dimension they wish to travel, and can advise them on weather, war and circumstance.*

* Batteries not included, and they should never be taken for granted.

Luke stared at the Instructions for ages, completely speechless. I think all of us got why, cos we shut up till he looked up, his eyes shining. I felt *proper* proud of him, my best mate, who never backed away from the right thing, even when *his* best mate didn't have his back like he should.

'Is it right?' Stef asked. 'You can send us to a definite universe, we don't just have to guess?'

Luke nodded . . . but as he pointed at the screen showing the Wheelie Bin, Hammer and Fungiverse, his face grew worried again.

'I just can't work out *what* you'll do when you get there,' he sighed. 'There's only two ways to fight off the Empire I can think of. One, we destroy Mr Stringer. The other one? That's just—'

'Impossible,' I said. 'Yeah, I don't suppose it's the same impossible I was thinking of, is it?'

* * *

We spent the next half-hour planning. Finally, when we knew what we had to do in all three universes, Luke hefted up his bulging rucksack and sat it on the drawer top.

'Right,' he said. 'From what Spider's said, and what I've figured out from Proton Wars, everything we do has a wave effect. If we help people fix things in one dimension, their cosmic twins are more likely to want to fix things in the next dimension. Get that?'

We all nodded.

'So, I thought we should use that to work out an *order* of worlds to visit. If we go to the easiest universe first, we'll be more likely to succeed, which will hopefully create more Cosmic Connections with other 'verses. By the time we visit the hardest universe, we'll hopefully have a whole wave of Cosmic Connections behind us. Get that?'

'Well, the Fungiverse is the hardest,' Dimi said abruptly. '*Gotta* be. All those monsters, and we still don't know what was making the eco *system* wrong.'

'Wrong,' Stef said abruptly. 'And the way you say "ecosystem" makes me think you don't understand what it is. The hardest challenge we face is the Hammerverse. We're on the run from our own crew. We're stuck out in space *on a submarine*. And our ship – which we're not allowed on, did I mention that? – is floating without power, weapons or shields, right outside Stringer's base!'

'Yeah,' Luke said sheepishly. 'Again I'm sorry, I should've just—'

'I thought all the weepy talk was over with?' Stef snapped, and Luke, grinning, zipped his lips.

'Besides,' I said, 'what about the Wheelie Bin 'Verse? The Grinster's an *actual* giant, with bug spray that fires *actual* bugs, massive killer ones. The last time we were there, we wrote a rude word in milk all across his table-cloth, and he doesn't just *think* of us as the *pests*, the *nits*, the *bed bugs* . . . In that universe, that's kinda what we *are*!'

They all stared at me, taking this in.

'Yup, that sounds like the hardest one,' Dimi admitted.

'Right,' said Luke. 'That's the one we'll hit last then. I think the Hammerverse will be *almost* as impossible as that one, and that the Fungiverse will be . . . just a little bit *less* impossible. So we should go Fungiverse first.'

'Great!' I said. But then Luke gave me an awkward look.

'There is *another* problem. I've been watching what's happened in the other 'verses the last few days, and it seems like you'd be using different vehicles than before.'

'So no Springfeet?' I said hopefully. 'Great! Just so long

as it's not them again . . . Oh, and maybe not flying, cos I haven't done that and—'

'You're still on the Springfeet,' Luke said apologetically. 'But apparently you're . . . *flying* on them somehow.'

'Great!' I said sarcastically. 'What do the Springfeet use to fly, then, some kind of twig?'

Luke's face grew even *more* apologetic.

'I think it's more of a seed . . .' he began.

'Eesh,' Dimi groaned. 'What about the Hammerverse? What vehicle do we need for that?'

'In the Hammerverse we're all still stuck in the *Europa Quest* submarine, but I *think* I've figured out a way to collect you *in the strings*. So all you'll have to do is jump off your Springfoot as if you were coming home. I'll be sure to get everything ready before, and I'll sort of pick you up.'

'That's good!' I said, brightening. 'And what about the Wheelie Bin 'Verse? What's our vehicle there?'

'We can look at that later,' Luke said, and shot a nervous glance to his rucksack. I wanted to ask just *what* there was to be nervous about, when another, more worrying question occurred to me.

'Wait, Luke,' I said. 'Once we complete our mission in the Hammerverse, how do we get out of that dimension? We *still* can't just shoot ourselves out into space.'

Luke grinned. Now he *did* look pleased with himself.

'I might've found a rule for Level Six Infinity Racers in that Proton Wars book. It was a note, right at the back. It seems like it was given as a suggestion, look.'

And he opened the book on to the back page.

I've added a mod to the latest Infinite Racetrack so that exiting is easier than before. Now, simply by clapping your hands three times, you will exit the universe and return home. Had thought would fit for Level 6s, but happy to follow your lede. E.A.

'Amazing!' Stef exclaimed. 'We just had to clap our hands three times to leave a universe all this time! I wonder who *E.A.* is?'

'I couldn't find it anywhere else in the book,' Luke said. 'But there's literally *tonnes* on the Commodore 65 and in Proton Wars that I haven't even seen yet. Maybe it'll come up.'

He turned back to the Commodore 65 and checked the changing stats on the screen.

'You need to go if this plan's going to work,' he said. 'Is everybody ready?'

'I was born ready,' said Dimi in his grittiest voice.

'You were born reedy,' Stef quipped, and they were still arguing when Luke finished typing.

RUN: Enter to: 'Fungiverse'

He hit ENTER, and stood back. At once, the Commodore 65 began to vibrate, its processor humming louder than ever. It began to shake ... and then, so did the entire library.

'You're sure this is right?' I called over the noise.

'It's supposed to help the Racetrack guide us to the right universe,' Luke called back. 'But I don't know if it's—'

Just then, the Fungiverse's giant toadstool bubble appeared above us, slimy, very stinky – and rotten with those thin, crawling tendrils that showed the Pure State's control. I felt the spatter of mud across my face, turned, and saw that the Infinite Racetrack had turned into a swollen, bulging brown river.

'It worked!' Luke cheered. 'Now we just need the bugs!'

'Bugs?' I said. 'Bugs from where?!'

But Luke had even thought of that. He unzipped his rucksack, and took out a bug jar. Hopping about inside were three small midges.

'OK!' he shouted, and unscrewed the lid as he walked closer. 'I'll do this carefully—'

And on 'carefully', he tripped. The jar tumbled from his hands, the bugs flew out and grew, transforming into chirpy Springfeet. The Springfeet hurtled towards me, Dimi and Stef, hoovering us up like powerful magnets. My face smacked into that horrible bristly back, I whirled head over heels into the track, and as the world folded into mud and dirt around me, I caught one last glimpse of Luke, waving his panicky arms.

'Whoops!' he said. 'Sorry, I . . .'

Then I was gone. It was so good to have my best mate back again.

18
The Fungiverse 2.0

' And if you go one *prokaryote* away from that
... branch and only that branch, then you'll spend
your free time washing Grubmunsters till autumn: do you
understand, Ky-Ky?'

I blinked. I was back in the Fungiverse, sitting on
my cosmic twin Ky-Ky's Springfoot, Something Wrong,
again. This time was different though. I was in a group
of kids, a *big* group, stretching far back behind me, and
this time I was wearing a heavy backpack. On the front
of each shoulder strap was a cord, but before I could
work out what these cords did, my Almost-Gran-Gran
loomed over me, a frown chiselled into her windswept
face.

'*Do you understand, Ky-Ky?*' she repeated, in a voice you didn't ignore. 'You *stay in the group!*'

I blinked and nodded.

'Yes, Grand— uhhh, Gran-Gran,' I said. Behind her, I saw Dimi and Stef grinning from their Springfeet. Almost-Luke-Luke was there too, but he didn't look at me. *This Fungiverse-Luke is still mad at me here*, I thought, and felt crummy.

Then I looked around us . . . and felt crummier still.

We were outside the tree once again, in a higher area I hadn't seen before. But where the Fungiverse before had been this oasis of giant flowers and nature, now it was . . . *dying*. Every branch was stripped of leaves, every flower was destroyed. Even the mighty tree our Mycelium had been built beneath was failing, its wood rotten and crumbling. Ahead of us the ground fell away sharply to reveal more trees below. The first trees were stripped back like an elephant's graveyard, and even the skies seemed to be laced with doom; strangled by dark clouds and ripped bloody with howling winds. I'd been sent here to find balance, by stopping the String Ripper from hunting our Springfeet to extinction. How had I made things so much worse?

Then Almost-Grandma leaned in, her voice softer and more urgent, and gave me the answer.

'I know I've asked you this so many times, Ky-Ky, but ... there is definitely *nothing* you remember about your last encounter with the String Ripper that might explain where all of his beasties have gone?

My heart sank further. Spider Ace had been right; I'd used technology that was so advanced, my cosmic twin Ky-Ky had blanked it out – Edwin's lever, the Bugnotiser, everything.

'Gran-Gran ...' I started to confess, but Stef coughed loudly, shaking her head. *It'll make things worse!* she mouthed, and she was right. What if I tried to explain Infinity Racers and blew my Gran-Gran's head up?

'Not to worry, Ky-Ky,' Gran-Gran said eventually. 'Hopefully your parents and the others will get the Springfeet numbers down enough to control them without the Beast Army.'

Springfeet numbers! This had all been done by Springfeet?

'I never knew the Springfeet were bad,' I whispered.

'They're not bad, Ky-Ky,' Almost-Gran-Gran chided me. 'That's what I've been saying all this time. The Springfeet build the Mycelium. All the tunnels, this entire forest uses to travel and communicate and connect, they wouldn't exist without them. That's why we care for them, why it was a worry that the String Ripper was hunting them to extinction . . . but everything has to be balanced. If some Springfeet aren't eaten by the String Ripper's maggots and mosquitoes and spiders, they spread out of control. There is no good or bad . . . at least not in the creatures, anyway.'

Smiling sadly, she walked away and climbed up to her Springfoot at the front of the group. As she raised a fist to her forehead, everybody fell silent.

'So,' she said, sighing. 'It's time for the Great Escape. It is a long flight, and I wish you'd been through more training, but . . . you'll be fine. It's a straight flight to our new home. All you have to do, when you get to the front of the queue, is kick out your Springfoot's . . . sprung foot. The foot will open your helicopter seed as it launches you into the air.'

'How do we turn?' said a small boy ahead in the queue. Almost-Gran-Gran smiled at him.

'There are two cords on your shoulder straps, and these are for turning left and right.'

'Which one's which?' asked Dimi. I think we all stared at him for a moment, until finally he nodded. 'Yep, stupid question, fair one.'

'If you lean gently forwards, you'll speed up, and if you lean back, you'll slow down,' Gran-Gran continued.

'Leaning forwards too much will make you drop, but leaning back won't make you climb unless you're in an updraught. But remember: *you only have to fly straight.* The wind is straight behind us, our destination straight ahead. So no tricks. I want us all safe, for as long as possible, in our new home, of Woodverhampton. OK-kay?'

'OK-kay!' we all shouted.

Gran-Gran turned, until her Springfoot was facing out over the cliff, Almost-Luke following behind.

'I will lead,' she said. 'After I leave, Luke-Luke here will call each rider person forwards, and tell you when you can kick off. He will bring up the rear.'

With a kick of her feet, her Springfoot SNAPPED up, and a big helicopter seed unfolded out of her rucksack like a wooden parachute. We all craned up to watch, and just as she began to drop down again, the propellers on the helicopter seed began to turn ... and she flew away into the stormy skies.

'NEXT!' Almost-Luke-Luke called, and the next kid went up. He was clearly terrified, but Almost-Luke-Luke spoke comfortingly to him.

'KICK!' he shouted, and the boy must've listened as his Springfoot SNAPPED up. His helicopter seed spun out, and he glided safely on towards Woodverhampton.

The line went down *fast*, one kid leaping out at a time, then two. Before I knew it, I was on the cliff edge, just able to see a line of helicopter seeds spinning through the air ahead. I took a deep breath, nervous . . . and then Almost-Luke gave me a nudge.

'It's OK,' he said, though he still wasn't smiling. 'Your Gran-Gran let me have a test flight yesterday.'

'Luke . . .' I began, but his eyes were cold and I shut up.

'KICK!' he shouted, and I kicked out the safety bar, sending the Springfoot soaring through the air.

I would say it was a strange way to fly . . . but this was the first time I'd ever flown. The helicopter seed tumbled out the moment I soared up, and I could see why Almost-Luke hadn't been worried, because as soon as they turned I hovered through the air. Soon I was fighting back a smile . . . then gave up the fight and started to laugh. I was *flying*. And this world was *incredible*.

Each tree was a city, busy even at night with fireflies and low-voiced night-birds. The mist had cleared, and looking up I could see the line of whirligigs making the Great Escape, and I realised: we were barely moving along four trees, but this was a whole other country to us. A million stars seemed to light up the sky above and below me . . . then I looked up and realised that I was beneath the canopy,

243

that those 'stars' were these endless fireflies, lighting up all at once, before fading into darkness, then lighting up again. I wondered who decided when they all lit up . . . but I don't think anybody did. It was like they had some bond we couldn't see, just as the trees were connected by the Mycelial Network that I'd hated so much . . . and just as we were connected with our other selves across the Multiverse. Basically, I became very soppy. Then the mist cleared, and I was snapped from my daydream by a very nasty shock.

Down below, sitting by a campfire on a tree branch the width of a motorway, was the String Ripper. I flinched in panic, kicking my legs and nearly pulling my shoulder straps to turn away, even though he was surely too far away to attack. Then, just as I was calming down, an even more unpleasant idea occured to me.

If we were going to get his Beast Army out of the cavern and attacking the Springfeet swarm, would we need the String Ripper?

I closed my eyes, and took a deep breath. Then, pulling at my right cord, I leaned far forwards, and began to descend.

Only I *really* didn't plan for how quickly I'd swoop down. I tilted right, too sharp, and began to tear through clusters of leaves. Panicking, I swerved-leaned forwards –

and plunged even faster through the twigs, flinching backwards just as the leaves cleared and a thick, knotted branch rushed out at me! If it wasn't for Something Wrong, I'd be splattered. Instead that brilliant bug flurried its little feet, running along the branch and bouncing me around into an untidy heap. At last we came to a stop, Something Wrong chirruping happily, me flat on its bristly back, all the wind knocked out of me. By the time I raised my head again . . .

. . . the String Ripper was standing over me, armed with a club.

He ROARED in my face, and ROARED again. I got the worst smells, of week-old burps and raw meat. But he didn't attack. Not yet.

'Come to finish the String Ripper off?' he snarled with an evil glare. *Not evil*, I corrected myself, *just angry*.

'I'm not finishing you off,' I said. 'Why are you giving up just because things are a bit hard?'

That got to him. He jumped to his feet, and beat his chest at me.

'The STRING Ripper doesn't give up! The STRING Ripper was *cheated*, out of all the things that are *rightfully* his.'

There was the flutter of leaves above, and he raced back to the end of the branch, holding his stick up threateningly. I breathed a big sigh of relief – it was Stef and Dimi, although the graceful way they floated down to land near me made me *seriously* glad they hadn't seen *my* dodgy landing.

'You all right, Ky?' said Dimi. 'Has he hurt you?'

'Should we knock him off this branch?' said Stef icily.

The String Ripper danced up and down beating his chest, before pulling a load of muscle-flashing moves that *kinda* looked halfway between terrifying and ridiculous.

'So your chummies are here to finish me off as well,' he sneered when he finished. 'What a shameful smattering of cowards.'

'A coward is somebody who bullies a whole town, then goes off crying when the town fights back,' I said sharply. 'You weren't *supposed* to be attacking our tunnels, were you?'

The String Ripper glared at me sullenly . . . then he said something I never thought I'd ever hear a Stringer say in any universe.

'Sorry.'

For a long moment I was too stunned to talk. I never once imagined it, and I *never* imagined that he'd say it like a little kid.

'Er . . . *well*,' I said, 'I guess I'm sort of sorry too. Are you going to help us then?'

'Help with what?' the String Ripper replied suspiciously. 'I won't move to Woodverhampton. I'll WAIT for your beloved Springfeet to come and eat me, like a proper hero.'

'*Hero?!*' I said. Then I stopped myself from laughing. Maybe he *needed* to feel heroic. 'You know what a hero would do? A hero would get his army back, and use it to stop the threat that's going to destroy this whole wood otherwise.'

The String Ripper glared at me. But he was interested.

'My beasties have gone,' he said. 'They've disappeared.'

'What if I knew how to find them?' I said, 'What if I could help you get them back? Your army would tear through those devouring Springfeet. You'd have saved the entire town.'

A glint appeared in the String Ripper's eyes. I didn't like that glint, but at the same time I didn't know what else we could do.

'Where would we have to go?'

'To the chasm where we last . . . met,' I said. 'Can you get us there?'

The String Ripper scoffed, and poked moodily at his campfire.

'The String Ripper could make it to there 'fore spuddling comes to dimpsey, sprat.' I *think* he was bragging.

'Should you even have a campfire on a tree?' said Dimi.

'This isn't a fire, sprat,' the String Ripper sneered. 'Do you think the String Ripper is stupid? My buggy-wugs make two liquids. Mix the two liquids together, and it makes a warm light.'

Just then, moonlight clipped through the branches above, bathing us in blue. The String Ripper turned, and stared across the busy, bustling wood. Then, *completely* ridiculous, he tensed his muscles up in a bodybuilding pose. Stef grinned at me, and I fought back a laugh. When the String Ripper had finished, he turned back with a nod.

'OK,' he bellowed. 'The String Ripper will help you.'

'The Stef says thanks,' quipped Stef, and that was it. We cracked up.

19
Joining Forces with the String Ripper

'Fold-ey,
Rold-ey,
POLD-EY, ROLDEY-ROLLLLLLL!!!!
Fa,
La la,
LA FADELLYLADELLY FAAAAAAA!
These are a few,
Of my favourite words,
That is why,
I sing like a BIIIIIIIIIIIIRD!!!!!!!'

'Does he ever shut up?' Dimi muttered to me. 'And what's
with the lame-o songs? I know we're not allowed to bring
tech here, but can I at least give him a playlist?'

'You want him to learn about rap?' I said, my eyebrows
raised, and with a grumble, Dimi trudged on. I wasn't

going to complain about the String Ripper's singing, not while it drowned out the sound of Springfeet devouring everything down below.

We'd been walking along branches a mile long, bouncing from leaf to leaf, and, when we needed to, helicoptering across branches. It had been amazing, if *exhausting*, at first ... and then we had reached close to the ground. That's when I'd heard the sound, a never-ending sound of a million gobs chewing and chundering. It was the sound of the Springfeet infestation.

'Tarry a look, sprats,' the String Ripper said.

At first I thought it was a carpet, then my eyes sharpened to the dark, and I saw the carpet *moving*. Every possible millimetre of ground from the tree we were standing on to my Almost-Home was *covered* with Springfeet. They were devouring *everything*, stripping all the vegetation back like a plague. I swallowed, and felt more ashamed than ever.

'We thought we were so smart,' Stef said sombrely, and I nodded in agreement. Then, as though the whole scene couldn't get any creepier, the String Ripper began to make this *horrendous* buzz-saw sound.

'What's he doing?!' Dimi shouted over it. 'He's nuts, Ky, I think we should shove him off the tree and make a run for it before he tries to eat us for—'

He was interrupted by another loud buzz-saw, floating through the air towards us. I looked out ... and we stumbled backwards as quickly as we could, as a *massive* flying beast landed on the branch.

'Oh ... my ... gosh ...' I whispered, trying to back away as much as I could. The String Ripper grinned wickedly, and leaped on to the monster's back.

'Sprats,' he boomed. 'Meet CeeCee Da Cicada! CeeCee is *desperate* to see her fifth husband alive and well. Not many of her kind get past their first marriage, so I value her cunning beyond any of my flying beasties.'

The cicada, this giant bug with *massive* buzzing wings and gimlet red eyes, stared back at us, and I am *sure* she looked hungry. If bugs could grin ... CeeCee grinned.

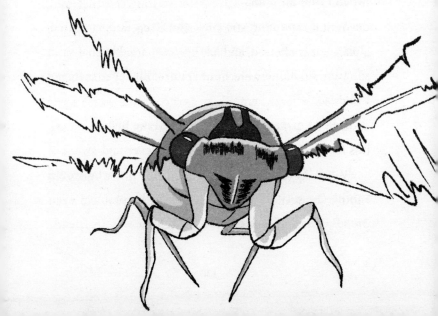

'Don't be shy, sprats.' The String Ripper chuckled. 'Say hello.'

'A'right!' squeaked Dimi. Me and Stef didn't even manage that.

'Now,' the String Ripper boomed. 'Over there, behind that clump of bunzlebushes and scrubworts, is the training pit where you cowardly snipes snuffled my bastallions. How do you release them?'

'There's two branches sticking out there,' I said, 'both pointing down. You'll have to lift the top one up and—'

'NO!' the String Ripper bellowed. 'I'm not taking CeeCee there. Some strange siren song is snuffling any beastie that dares approach.'

'But . . . I switched the Bugnotiser *off*,' I said, confused, 'when I shut the door.'

'Well it is on now, yon cow!' the String Ripper roared. 'Too many o' my beasties have been snozzled by that siren song and stood there like hunkypunks till they're snatched by birds.'

It didn't make sense. If I'd switched the Bugnotiser off, had somebody come back to lift the lever and switch it back on? If so . . . it had to be Edwin. But why would another Infinity Racer *want* to make the problem even worse? Edwin seemed cool. I'd thought he was my friend.

'Not answering, eh, sprat?' the String Ripper said eventually. 'Fine. I'll *guide* you there, so *you* can save my beasties!'

'How?!' Dimi scoffed, and gestured to his whirligig. 'These are *gliders*, Chief. They don't fly.'

'*Don't fly?!*' the String Ripper scoffed back. 'What do you know? I've seen your other sprats do it. They go up somehow, then come down.'

An idea occurred to me. I leaned forwards, shuffling Something Wrong to the branch's edge, looked over . . . and felt a breeze of warm air, flowing upwards.

'The updraught,' I said to the others. 'We just have to catch the updraught. Feel that warm air? We just have to make big circles, and keep following them till we circle upwards. I've done it before on a horse.'

'That . . . does make sense,' Stef admitted. The three of us went to the edge of the branch, waited to feel the warm draught of air, then . . .

'OK,' I said. 'Three, two, one . . .'

We leaped up, and I felt the breeze catch me. And it was like my whirligig wanted to throw me off!

'No!' I yelped, and rolled off Something Wrong's back . . . then clung on, just pulling myself back to safety. In the corner of my eye I saw Stef having the same trouble –

somehow she was lying on her *back*, clinging to Springer, her Springfoot, in a crab position. At last I felt a hand grab mine, and *pull*, moving me to the middle of the updraught where I *finally* stabilised. It was Dimi.

'Done this before, did you, fam?' he grinned, and soared away, over to Stef. He was so *infuriatingly* good at this, moving *with* every gust that would've toppled me, surfing up and down the breezes, where I tensed every time. Soon he had Stef in the centre of the updraught, and after we'd all been encouraging him before this, we were now following him to keep up with that one, massive, invisible hand moving us up like a slippy lifting platform in a platform game.

'Now, turn right!' he shouted. We all banked right behind him, and began to rise more as we circled around. I saw the String Ripper below, buzzing straight ahead on CeeCee Da Cicada, not having to worry about catching *any* draughts, up or down. But it wasn't long before Dimi *stood up*, before nodding confidently.

'We'll make it now!' he called back to me, pointing to where the waterfall plunged down into the base of the tree. 'Let's surf to the edge of the draught and drop off. Maybe we can even make the String Ripper see dust, innit.'

'OK,' I said through gritted teeth. I followed Dimi and

Stef's lead, leaning over until *just* before the point where the updraught started to shake me uncontrollably. Then, after taking a deep breath, I made my move . . . and leaned *right*, plunging out of the updraught and *swooping* down. There was a horrible moment where I was *sure* I would fall to my death . . . then the helicopter seed began to spin like mad, and I glided down *way* more gracefully than you'd guess from my gurning face and sweaty back.

The speed was *intense*. Every time I feel like I've experienced every kind of fast there is, something comes and surprises me. On these whirligigs, it was more the *long* acceleration and *longer* braking that was terrifying at first . . . then thrilling. Dimi had got the height just right, and as we kept diving down away from the last tree and towards the next, I felt the wind pulling tears from my eyes, and for the first time here I *enjoyed* it. Soon I was overtaking Dimi and Stef, laughing as I swooped, and as we raced up behind the String Ripper, I even felt goodwill towards *him*.

That's when I felt the shadow of another whirligig above me . . . and looked up to see Edwin grinning down at me.

'Great job, Ky!' he called with a laugh. 'I knew you wouldn't run away before you'd had chance to finish him off!'

'*What?!*' the String Ripper snapped, whirling to me with murder in his eyes.

'What? No!' I said hastily. 'Edwin, we're . . . we're trying to release the bugs.'

'*Finish him off?!*' the String Ripper bellowed again.

'No, String Ripper, we're honestly not—'

'You've *got* to!' said Edwin. 'He's your nemesis, Kyan. That's what you do to nemeses, you *destroy them.*'

'*Treachery!*' the String Ripper roared. '*Wickeds and murderings!*'

'No, Ripper, please!' I protested. 'We're going to help you.' I turned and shouted up to Edwin, 'We're going to help him! It's the only way to stop the Springfeet destroying everything! We've got to work together.'

As though he hadn't heard me, Edwin laughed, his eyes *hard* behind the smile. I shouted for him again, but now he darted down, clipping the String Ripper on the shoulder, *almost* knocking him off.

'MURDERINGS!' the String Ripper screeched. 'LIARS AND SPRATS!'

'No!' I yelled, but it was no good. One more clip like that, and the String Ripper would fall to his doom. There was only one thing for it. He might be older, quicker, better on his whirligig . . . but I'd have to stop Edwin.

I leaned *right* back, almost bringing us to a halt, and Edwin shot down past me. With him directly below, I staggered to my feet on Something Wrong's bristly back, standing in a surfing crouch, and putting *all* my weight down on my front foot, until we were leaning right down and the wind whipped at my face. Just as we shot past Edwin's spinning helicopter seed, I leaped down to my butt and yanked my left shoulder cord hard. It was *just* enough. We tilted sharply left, until we were practically horizontal, and Something Wrong's flurrying legs kicked into Edwin's whirligig, snapping one propeller clean off.

'What?!' Edwin said, looking up in shock, before he *jerked* right.

'Sorry, Edwin!' I shouted. 'We need his help!'

Edwin didn't answer. For one moment his Springfoot steadied, and I was *sure* he'd attack me.

'I'll see you soon,' he snarled, but before he could explain that further, he'd jerked right again . . . and with a loud CRACK he *vanished* into nothing.

Breathing out shakily, I saw the String Ripper buzz up alongside me, absolute shock on his face.

'You saved me!' the String Ripper exclaimed, then looked around. 'He must have fallen down!'

I nodded, and pointed forwards. We'd made it: the

chasm where I had activated the Bugnotiser and trapped the String Ripper's entire army in a hidden cave. But already I could see a problem.

'If we go down there, that Bugnotiser might stop *our* Springfeet from moving,' I said. 'What if we can't reach the door or something? We'd have to leave our Springfeet, and our cosmic twins wouldn't remember that the door was even there!'

'We'll have to speed up then,' Dimi shouted back. 'Break it down!'

'Not the door!' Stef shouted. 'That was made of solid metal, remember? But maybe, if we're lucky, the dirt above it will be just that – dirt.'

I swallowed. It was a *mad* idea, and we all knew it. The only one who seemed happy at all was the String Ripper.

'We will splat into smashing splatheroons!' he screamed, laughing insanely. 'The ultimate hero's death!'

'As least *he's* happy,' Dimi grumbled. But he leaned forwards with the rest of us, and we bulleted towards the space above the hidden door. Together we sped up, up, up: four human cannons and the nutty bug-lover who was *supposed* to be my Cosmic Nemesis. The bridges flew past me, the ground rocketed towards me, a gale screamed through my ears.

And at the last minute I ducked down and shut my eyes
tight . . .

BOOF! We smashed through the dirt cliff at the same
time, and it collapsed. Edwin's door fell below us, his
Bugnotiser tailing off like the batteries needed changing,
and we kept cannoning through the cave *packed* with –

SCREEEEEEE!

The screech was so harsh I clapped my hands over my
ears. Hundreds, no, *thousands* of gigantic bugs were scurrying towards me, a flurry of gnashing teeth and snatching
claws all hungry for my blood. I'd helped free all the
bugs in the Bug Pit – but these monsters were *ravenous*,
I realised, and I was their first meal. The String Ripper
followed me in, and as I turned to look at him, I saw that
glint in his eyes, and dismay clung at my throat. *He's tricked
me!* I thought. *I've freed his army, now his army's going to
eat me.*

But then I heard a whistle, and heard the *click* of his
two liquids mixing. There was a bright light in the dark,
and all of the String Ripper's monsters turned away from
me towards him.

'Here!' he shouted, and the light turned away from me,
bobbing away into the dark. And, like a tap turned on, the
String Ripper's beasties *poured* out of the cave.

259

I'd made the first step, had trusted him. Now the String Ripper had returned the favour.

By the time I followed the String Ripper out, seeing my shell-shocked friends, the pit was practically emptied of mosquitoes, maggots and murderous spiders. We bounced up after them, but they were too fast, and by the time we reached the top of the chasm, I could hear the terrible screams and snarls of beasties *ripping* through Springfeet, devouring them across bushes and grass.

'I can barely look,' said Dimi.

'That's just . . . what's supposed to happen,' I said finally. 'Things are out of balance now. When the numbers are down, we'll have to help protect the Springfeet again.' Still, it was hard to watch.

That's when Luke spoke in my ear. Not *Almost*-Luke . . . *our* Luke.

'Kyan?' he whispered. 'Kyan, can you hear me?'

'Luke!' I exclaimed. 'How are you speaking to me?'

'It's through the Commodore 65,' Luke said. 'I didn't want to talk before in case I distracted you, but I'm reading a massive boost of cosmic energy spreading out from the Fungiverse. Has the mission succeeded?'

I smiled, and closed my eyes. 'Yep,' I said. 'Yes it did.'

'Brilliant!' Luke cheered. 'But it's just in time; we have

to get to the Hammerverse straight away – before our crew is *destroyed*.'

Stef and Dimi glanced back to me.

'*We'd better go*,' I said.

Stef nodded, and clapped three times. It was strange; one moment she was there. Then she blinked, like she'd been reset. Then she smiled at me like things were back to normal.

'It's crazy how the String Ripper's Beast Army could all get stuck behind the one root like that by accident!' she said over the screeches and chomps and screams. And hoping against hope that I'd helped to fix my terrible mistake here, I clapped three times before I had to reply.

20
Defending the Good
Ship *Revenge*

Without a vehicle to fall into, I fluttered across dimensions like beach litter, tumbling through strangely shaped strings and past mysterious worlds, falling faster and more violently than I ever had before. Panic clenched at my jaw, a strangled cry escaped my throat . . . then a futuristic engine roared towards me. Suddenly a bright light shone at me, so bright that I shielded my eyes and –

WHOMPH!

I landed, face down on the cold, hard metal of a cheap, rusty ship.

'Kyan!' Luke said, and hurried to help me up. 'It worked! I was worried I'd entered the wrong commands, but the Commodore 65 plucked all of you from the strings!'

'Good job, Luke!' I said, then winced as my achy adult body stood up. 'Ugh – I forgot how much this hurts.'

'THE FLOOR, OR AGE?' a menacing voice hissed behind me. But with my head still foggy, and with Luke hurrying away to help Celestine, Stef and Dimi, I barely noticed it, and instead staggered painfully to the viewscreen – where my heart sank.

We were still stuck in the *Europa Quest*, the spaceship that isn't a spaceship but a submarine. After our nitro-boosting escape from Officer Mirks and our own crew, the *Quest* had crash-landed on one of the mountain-sized asteroids that helped to form Super Saturn's second ring. Our cosmic twins had been busy making repairs, with bits of metal and even gaffer tape. But clearly they hadn't yet found a way to move the ship.

'Well, I'm glad they found a way to untie me,' said Dimi, walking up beside me with a grin. His grown-up self looked annoyingly like an action hero, with a smart haircut and a chiselled jaw. 'But things look rough, fam.'

He wasn't wrong. To our right, orbiting along an empty lane between Super Saturn's rings, was the moon base that held my Cosmic Nemesis Chief Stringer. To our left, past this inner ring of giant slow-moving mountains, and one more, outer ring of rapid, warhead-sized rocks, the good ship *Vengeance* loomed over us like a gigantic sleeping, er, robot vacuum cleaner.

'At least their ship's still out of action too,' Stef muttered. The *Vengeance* power had been mullered the last time we were here, when Luke shot our own torpedo too close to the ship.

'Yeah,' Dimi replied, 'but we'll be in trouble when Wimpole does fix it.'

None of us had any words to say to that. All the adrenaline from helping the Fungiverse was seeping away, leaving us tired in the face of what looked like an impossible situation. Only Luke looked from face to face, his smile faltering as he took in our gutted expressions. Finally, he nudged me, and pointed ahead, where light from a distant star glistened through the millions of miles of rocks and dust and ice.

'At least the view that way is nice,' he said hopefully.

'UNDOUBTEDLY,' a snarling voice behind me rasped, and I whirled around in fear.

Splayed across the *outside* of our rear viewscreen was a space monster. Her sinewy limbs were stuck to the glass like a sticky wrestler. Her teeth were *inhumanly* long and sharp, her mouth taking up almost her entire head, leaving no room for eyes or ears or a nose. Wriggly worms slithered

up and down her, swelling and shrinking as if helping her to breathe in space, and as she slid slowly across the glass, she let out a slow, terrifying scream that tore through my eardrums

'HOW'S MY FAVOURITE CREW THEN?' she said. And we *cheered*.

'Stacey!' we cried.

We'd first met Stacey the alien on Jupiter's moon Europa, deep in the fathomless ocean below its icy crust. With her jagged jaws, horror-movie rasp and the *massive* megalodon she rode, we'd assumed she was the enemy. But that had turned out to be completely unfair – Chief Stringer, the rotten Stringer of *this* universe, was in fact stealing Europa's water, and Stacey was just trying to protect her homeland. After we'd helped Stacey to foil Stringer's plot, she had helped us to escape his furious wrath.

'It is *well* good to see you!' Dimitar said with a grin. 'What are you doing here?'

'I WILL EXPLAIN IN A MINUTE,' Stacey said. 'WHAT IS WRONG WITH LUKE?'

I turned, to see that Luke had hung back, his cheeks red and his eyes cast down.

'No . . .' Luke said. 'No, honestly. It's great to see you. It's just . . . I'm the reason we didn't take out Chief Stringer's base.'

'YOU THOUGHT I WOULD BE ANGRY YOU DIDN'T BLOW UP MY COUSIN'S HOME?'

It took a moment for me to get what she was saying. I looked out to the pale grey moon orbiting near us, the round ball I'd wanted to blow up, and my mouth felt suddenly dry.

'Wait . . . that moon over there?' I said, stunned. 'That's your *cousin's* base, not Chief Stringer's?'

'Stacey . . .' Stef said. 'I'm sorry, we didn't, we never would've . . .'

Stacey chuckled, (which sounded like a demon's evil laugh), and shook her head.

'NO POINT IN APOLOGISING FOR WHAT MIGHT HAVE BEEN. CHIEF STRINGER HAS BEEN IMPRISONED BY MY COUSIN FOR SOME TIME.'

'I can't believe we nearly destroyed your *cousin's* moon, Stacey!' I said. 'Why didn't they tell us when we got here?'

'THEY TRIED TO CONTACT YOUR SHIP MANY TIMES, BUT YOUR SHIP HAS REFUSED ALL COMMUNICATIONS.'

'*Refused?*' Luke exclaimed. 'Why?'

'Somebody didn't *want* us to know,' I said thoughtfully.

'Somebody *wanted* us to attack Stacey's cousin's home, thinking it was Chief Stringer's base. But who?'

Just then, the ship's radio crackled, so loudly that we jumped. Then, distorted and filled with static, a high, strained voice came through the ship's speakers.

'Imposters on *Europa Quest*. This is Captain Mirks of the good ship *Vengeance*. My Chief Engineer, Spanners Wimpole, is about to restore power to the ship. Unless you surrender immediately, we will destroy you *and* Chief Stringer.'

'What can we do?' Dimi hissed.

'There's nothing for it,' I said. 'We have to surrender. Stef, can you radio back?'

Stef was already on the tablet, but she was frowning, her face growing increasingly desperate.

'It's not letting me. Our signal's being rejected – somebody on the *Vengeance* doesn't want us to surrender. Somebody wants us destroyed!'

But that's when Stacey stood up – *literally* stood up – on our viewscreen.

'I CAN HANDLE THIS,' she said.

Standing tall above us, she turned and faced the distant *Vengeance*, putting one hand on her chest. I hadn't seen the Erie do this before, so I didn't know that it turned her voice into a broadcast signal that could travel through space. It's a pity, because I *definitely* would've stopped her.

'WE COME IN PEAAAACE!'

It was an almighty scream, one that ripped through my eardrums like a murder threat and even moved our ship, sending us sliding across the icy surface of the asteroid before easing to a halt. Stacey looked up to the Vengeance, held out her hand, and gave a friendly thumbs up – except she was *two* fingers out.

'WHOA!' we all shouted.

'That's a middle finger, Stacey!' exclaimed Stef, 'not a thumb! You just gave Captain Mirks the middle finger!'

The radio crackled again, and we heard terrified screams in the background, the sound of a crew racing to battle stations.

'We won't surrender to your threats and foul gestures, savage alien,' warned Officer Mirks. 'Spanners Wimpole has finished repairs, and our ship has power once more. Our weapons are back online. Prepare to be destroyed.'

The speaker went dead. A thin, red, war-coloured pulse of light shone from the band running horizontally across the *Vengeance*'s wide hull, the same as Robot Pattinson's charging light. Waves of green and blue energy began to vibrate along the bottom of the ship, revealing lethal-looking cannons that were pointed directly at us.

They were charging up their weapons.

'Uh, Kyan?' said Dimi. 'Shouldn't we be leggin' it?'

'I can't,' I protested. 'This is a submarine, remember! I can barely wobble.'

The controls for the *Europa Quest* are pretty simple – a joystick rotates you around, a throttle blasts you forwards and backwards, and four STRAFE buttons fire you directly left, right, up and down like sidestep buttons in a shoot-'em-up. They're pretty responsive too – so long as you're UNDERWATER. Out here in space though? I waggled the stick, hammered the STRAFE buttons … and we did nothing but lean about. I pushed the throttle forwards to full power, and we hardly left the ground.

'See?' I said.

'Wait a minute,' Stef said thoughtfully. 'Stacey, your Scream Blast moved this ship. The only thing keeping us stuck here is this asteroid's gravity. If you aim that Scream Blast *down*, at the same time as Kyan fires the throttle, do you think we'd get enough movement to clear this rock?'

Stacey thought for a moment.

'IT MIGHT WORK,' she hissed.

'Then do it now!' Dimi yelped, 'They're about to—'

CHOOMCHOOMCHOOM!

It happened at once. Three huge bolts of green energy fired from the *Vengeance* at the same time as Stacey flipped around and *SCREAAAAMED* into the asteroid beneath our ship, and at the same time as I *JAMMED* the throttle up as hard as I could. We launched upwards, just clearing the rock as the energy bolts SMASHED into it. The asteroid was vaporised into dust behind us, and the blast shockwave whipped us forwards at a furious speed.

'Yes!' I whooped, before Dimi let out another terrified scream.

'TURN!' he shrieked, and gestured madly at two huge rocks straight ahead of us. I gritted my teeth, jammed the joystick to the right ... and the *Quest* rolled 90 degrees, slicing sideways between the two juggernauts. I breathed a sigh of relief. We couldn't slow down or speed up, but I could tilt and turn!

It was a good job too, because the *Vengeance* was just getting started. The mighty battleship slowly rotated to follow our path, those enormous cannons pounding massive bolts of energy that raked behind us, each one closer than the last. Desperately I swerved up, strafed down, rolled right and strafed left. Rocks exploded all around us, ice dust and shards peppering our hull, the blast

waves hurtling us ever faster. This was getting more dangerous by the moment . . . and I was running out of ideas.

'Wait,' Celestine said suddenly. 'This was *Stringer's* ship
before it was ours, right? Can we ask him if there's any
other way to contact the *Vengeance*?'

'We *tried* talking, sis,' I said impatiently. 'Officer Mirks
doesn't wanna know—'

'Not Mirks,' she said, cutting me off again. 'Spanners
Wimpole, the Chief Engineer. The last time we were here,
when I was in Engineering? He was really complaining
about Officer Mirks and, um, you.'

'Me?!'

'Yeah,' said Tines apologetically. 'Sorry, Ky, but he was
saying he thought Captain "Super" Green had changed
since Officer Mirks had joined the crew. If we give him a
good reason to follow your orders, not hers, he might
listen.'

I thought about this. After our adventures that summer,
I'd promised to listen to my sister's ideas, and this one
sounded promising. Dodging more blaster fire, I rolled away
behind two more asteroids, before looping back to tuck the
Quest behind the safety of an extra big asteroid on the very
inside of that ring. Safe for the moment, I turned to Stacey.

'Did you hear that, Stace?' I said. 'Can you contact your

cousin's moon base and tell them we need to speak to their prisoner Kenneth Stringer?'

Stacey nodded.

Turning to face the nearby moon, she held one hand to her chest and SCREAMED in an Erie language I couldn't understand. After a moment another scream vibrated through the ship like an energy wave.

'*ARGHARGHARGHAAAAAAARGH!!!!!*'

'I'd hate to be at their family dinners,' Dimi muttered, and Stef punched him on the arm.

'CHIEF STRINGER IS BEING BROUGHT IN NOW,' Stacey said. After a moment, the ship's radio crackled, and that smug voice I still hated sneered through it.

'Well if it isn't Kyan Green,' gloated Chief Stringer. 'Come to apologise?'

'Nobody's apologising to anyone, ya stinking bag of—' I began hotly . . . then Luke tapped my shoulder.

'C'mon, Ky,' he murmured. 'You've got this. We need him, and he needs us.'

I stared back and, finally, nodded. With a long breath out, I pushed the button again.

'All right, *Chief Stringer*,' I said. 'We need to contact the *Vengeance's* Chief Engineer without anybody knowing. You had the *Vengeance* before us. Is there any back door?'

'A back door?' Chief Stringer sneered. 'Why on earth would the famous Captain Supergreen need to sneak through the back door of the ship he himself stole?'

I sighed through gritted teeth.

'Because—' I began, then Luke shouted over me!

'*BECAUSE OF YOU, YA BIFFA-SNIFFER!*'

'I thought we were playing it cool?' I whispered. 'And what's a biffa-sniffer?'

'We are here, *Kenneth*,' Luke seethed, 'because Officer Mirks wanted to blow you out of the sky, and I wouldn't do it! Now, to stop her from blasting you anyway, we need to secretly contact the Chief Engineer. You can help us do it, or we can all get blasted so bad the first ship who finds us will wonder who left all those bits of metal and limbs floating through space!'

There was a long pause.

'Wait a minute, did you say "*Officer Mirks*"?' Chief Stringer said at last. 'As in, high voice, high eyebrows, compliments you all the time?'

Everybody shot me a glance and I felt my face getting warm.

'That's the one,' Stef said with a grin.

'But *she* was on *my* team!' the Chief whined.

'Wait, what?!'

'She wasn't *Officer* Mirks then, she was Councillor Mirks,' he continued. 'I don't know where she came from, but she was *sharp*. When I met her, I was just a small, almost-honest businessman, looking to drain the water from a few backward planets, and supply it to our beloved Emperor for a modest profit. Then Councillor Mirks appeared. She was my *biggest* fan, even while she encouraged me to cut *more* corners, take *bigger* risks . . . and break *more* rules. If Officer Mirks is why you're stuck out on that ship, then I'll help.'

'So how do we contact Engineering?' Luke asked.

'It's the one design flaw of my beautiful *Vengeance*,' Chief Stringer said. 'It's all-powerful . . . unless a small ship can make it close enough without being blasted. Then, the phaser cannons can't get you, and if you can make it beneath the belly of the ship, all the ship's communications can be picked up.'

'Can we do that?' Stef said to me.

I sighed, and looked out of the viewscreen. Straight ahead was the first ring of slow-moving juggernauts, some of which could splat us with their gravity alone. Then, further ahead, there was the outer ring, thousands upon thousands of hurtling rocks, any one of which could puncture through both sides of our hull before I even knew I'd made a false turn. Finally, even further in the distance, there was the distant *Vengeance*, sat cold and mighty, every one of its cannons waiting for us with an itchy trigger finger attached.

It's all too much, I thought. But I didn't say that.

'Stef?' I said uncertainly. 'You should take the blasters.'

'Already on it,' Stef growled, and hit the red ACTIVATE BLASTERS button that caused a rusty cannon to swivel out the front of our ship.

'Dimi?' I continued. 'We'll need a speed boost at some point.'

'Toilet Technician Dimi reporting for duty,' Dimi growled, and marched to a sign marked *WARNING! FLUSHING BOTH TOILETS WITHIN TEN SECONDS MAY CAUSE DANGEROUS ACCELERATION.*

'Good,' I said. 'And, Luke? You'll need to hop into the *Europa Flyer* and get ready to fire its missile, just in case.'

'Tines should do it,' Luke said promptly. 'She's probably a better shot anyway. And if I get a chance to transport off this ship, I should. This universe's Luke will be more help than I can be, and I need to get back to the Commodore 65 to set up our next jump.'

Of course – in all the excitement I'd completely forgotten that we still had the Giant Grinster's kitchen to fix! *It's all too much*, I thought again, and a sudden wave of exhaustion smothered me. I closed my eyes, and prepared to tell everyone that it was over, that we wouldn't be able to do this. *It's all too much.*

That's when I heard Celestine.

'Why can't you just clap your hands three times to go home now?' she was asking Luke.

'Erm – nah,' Luke said politely. 'I should be off the ship. Back in the Fungiverse, my cosmic twin figured out that his friends weren't his *real* friends, and it . . . wasn't pretty.'

'Ugh.' Celestine shivered. 'When you put it like that . . . Did *you* feel anything?'

Luke paused before answering.

'Yeah. For a while I felt the same way.'

I opened my eyes again then. Suddenly my tiredness had turned to anger. This was no time to give up. I had mistakes to fix. We had universes to save. And, thanks to the extra-big asteroid curving away along the path of Super Saturn's rings, we had barely any time before our hiding place was gone.

'We can do it,' I said, and the gang all looked at me. 'We can make it.'

There was a pause, like they were just believing that themselves. Then the radio crackled.

'Excellent,' Chief Stringer boomed. 'Now, seeing as I've helped you, how about you free me from this dump? You know, these savage beasts scream for no reason and they—'

SLAM!

Luke had pounded the RADIO button off.

'Shall we go then?' he said, and I grinned.

'You ready, Stace?' I said.

'I WAS BORN READY.'

And with a grin, I turned away from our hiding place and went straight for the *Vengeance*.

And *straight* away things went wrong. A thundering stream of phaser fire cannoned towards me, faster than I could've expected. Flinching, I slammed the joystick over so hard we somehow managed to barrel roll and headed *straight* for a massive asteroid! Too late, I tried turning sharply around it, but just as I thought we would clear the icy rock, I felt the sudden draw of the asteroid's gravity yank us in like a lasso.

'No!' I gasped, pulling back on the joystick with a sick panic, hammering the UP STRAFE button at the same time. 'Not . . . going . . . to . . . happen . . .'

It was my best mistake *yet*. Practically grazing the huge asteroid, we whirled all the way around it for three seconds of terror, before being *flung* off it like a slingshot straight for the *Vengeance*. Confused, one of the *Vengeance*'s cannons whirled around after me – and blasted another cannon to smithereens!

'YESSSS!' my friends hollered. Grinning at our luck, I swerved left and right, catching the gravity of every big asteroid I passed and letting it sling me faster and faster towards the *Vengeance*. Before long we'd reached the inside edge of Super Saturn's outer ring, where the smaller rocks raced past like youngsters rushing for the dinner queue

'Blasters ready?' I asked. Stef didn't have to reply.

CHOOM CHOOM CHOOM! She fired that cannon as rapidly and accurately as anybody could, clearing a path through the outer ring. Before long all around us was a cloud of dust, red beams and explosions as Stef scored hit after hit. Occasionally one or two rocks would make it past her deadly blaster fire, causing me to strafe desperately left and right, to twirl and barrel roll to safety. Then, just as we got near the edge of the ring, disaster struck.

CLICK CLICK CLICK CLICK.

'I'm out!' Stef shouted. 'It's not working!'

'Oh no,' I croaked. Without Stef blasting them away, the dust cleared to reveal a whole cluster of rocks hurtling towards us like a moving wall. All my adrenaline turned into fear, and I knew. There was no way I could dodge all that.

That's when I heard a toilet flush. I turned, looking to the toilets at the back of the *Quest*, as Dimi hurried out of one cubicle and raced around to the other ... before pausing.

'Awww, man,' he moaned. 'Who left a present in this one?'

'DIMI, HIT THE FLUSH!' we all screamed, and he did.

'*Warning,*' the ship's computer said. '*Acceleration at high levels—*'

And we rocketed forwards, so fast my teeth chattered and my mouth danced around like claymation. The last of Super Saturn's rocky rings hurtled harmlessly behind us, we hurtled out into clear space, and there we were, *racing* for the good ship *Vengeance* against all odds! The mighty battleship blasted every round from every cannon it had, but the 'design flaw' Chief Stringer had been on about was clear from here: we were too close for them to hit. Phasers blasted pointlessly, missing us by miles, and as we coasted along at a steady speed, I sat back and grinned with delight as the giant robot vacuum cleaner-shaped hull *whoosh*ed overhead. Sticking out at the very centre of the *Vengeance* was the giant viewscreen of the Engineering level, and as we hurtled towards it, I saw Spanners Wimpole working furiously at a console behind it.

'Celestine,' I said. 'Lock on to the *Vengeance.*'

'Done it!' Celestine said, and as every monitor behind Spanners turned a sudden warning amber, he stopped, looked up . . . and saw us, both Stef's blaster and Celestine's *Europa Flyer* torpedo aimed straight for him.

'Good morning, Mr Wimpole,' said Luke. 'Good morning, *everyone*!'

Spanners Wimpole scowled, and tapped his console. Chief Stringer had been right. When he spoke, we heard him.

'The imposters are here, Captain Mirks. They're beneath the ship. Be advised they can hear me, but you can't hear them.'

'Beneath the ship?!' Mirks bellowed. 'Then DESTROY them!' Spanners typed at his console, and a series of smaller blasters all swivelled out around us . . .

'Wait!' said Luke. 'We had the chance to destroy you, Mr Wimpole. And we didn't. So *please* . . . listen to us.'

There was a long pause, then Spanners nodded.

'We're not imposters,' Luke continued. 'We went through a horrible case of Babyface Virus.'

'Babyface Virus,' Spanners said doubtfully. He tapped away at his console and I saw pictures and files flickering across the monitor behind him. Spider Ace had done it, I realised with relief, she'd added 'Babyface Virus' to the ship's computer.

'Babyface Virus,' Luke repeated. 'And it was the worst timing, because it was just when we discovered that Officer Mirks was the real imposter.'

'You said before,' I added, 'that it would be nice not to go cannon-crazy for once. How long's it been since we tried *not* to destroy things?'

'Engineer Wimpole, what are you waiting for?' Mirks shouted through the radio. 'Destroy them! Destroy them all!!!'

'I bet it was just about when Officer Mirks joined the ship,' I continued, 'when I . . . uh . . . started to lose my way a bit, is that right? Think back.'

Spanners shrugged. 'I mean, you always had a big head—'

'Not too far back. . .'

'But yeah. Since she got involved, with all her Empire liaison rubbish, that was when we got rough trying to beat Stringer.'

'You know what though, Chief?' Tines said. 'We've already beaten Stringer. He is imprisoned on that moon by the Erie. The best way we could lose now is to keep firing after the battle's over.'

Spanners stared at us, not answering. I thought of what Luke had said, about all of our Cosmic Connections working together, about lots of other Kyans and Lukes and even Wimpoles pushing each other to change. Could this be the moment when they made a difference?

'OK,' he finally said. 'Luke, you can teleport over here. The rest of you can dock, and we'll talk.'

I looked at Luke. He grinned.

'We did it, Ky! Time to go and prepare the next hop,' he said. I grinned, tired but buzzing from this victory. Suddenly his idea that we were riding a wave and that we'd be stronger by the final universe made sense.

'OK,' he said. 'Er . . . beam me up, Spanners!'

There was a pause, then, in a haze of blue light, Luke . . . was gone!

'*Star Trek*, man,' Stef said in admiration. 'It's right about *everything*.'

'We have Tactical Officer Smith here, Captain,' Spanners said. 'Now, if you dock here, I'll make sure you're unharmed . . .'

Just then, I saw another officer hurry up to Wimpole and whisper in his ear. Wimpole looked confused for a moment . . . then he looked at us.

'What?' I said. 'What is it?'

'It's Officer Mirks,' Spanners Wimpole said, sounding *freaked out*. 'She's disappeared.'

I stared back at him, not sure what to say. After a moment, Luke's voice spoke into my ear.

'I've made it home, you guys,' he urged, and I realised this was *our* Luke back in *our* universe, 'and it looks like good news. There's Cosmic Connections blasting out all across our Sector. *But* – and I know I keep saying this – we have to move fast. I've checked out the Grinster's house, and it's worse than it could ever be.'

I looked out of the viewscreen, at the good ship *Vengeance*. That name needed changing, I decided. And maybe somebody would have to go have a word with the 'Emperor' of this universe. But that was for another day. For now, I clapped my hands three times, and as the universe exploded in a *poof!* of strings, I wondered if this clapping thing would *ever* not look lame.

21
The Designer

Strings clumped together into atoms. Atoms grouped up into molecules. Molecules joined together into blurred shapes ... some of them making that plasticky trundling sound toy cars make, others buzzing alarmingly through the mists towards me.

'Right,' Luke said in my ear, 'I think I know how to do this ...'

'That doesn't fill me with confidence,' Stef said.

'Is ... is there a fly in here?' I said uncertainly. And just as everything came into focus ...

My wheels hit grey tiles at ear-popping speed.

I was cannoning along the Giant Grinster's kitchen floor. My car was another bubble car, 'cept it was *souped up*, with these big wheels that moved up and down with the terrain, making its whole frame bounce like some moon-buggy SUV. It was helpful, *especially* when a ditch came out of nowhere.

'Argh!'

I slammed the brakes way too late, launched across the ditch, and landed on the other side before coming to a juddering stop.

'What was that?!' I squeaked, looking back. The ditch was perfectly straight, and went on far into the distance.

'Squad Leader Loretta to Bubble Truck Kyan,' my Almost-Grandma barked through the radio; more and more I was thinking of her as General Loretta. 'Why'm I reading that you've stopped after grout joint A3?'

'Of course! A grout joint!' I said. 'My dad got me to grout our bathroom after he tiled it, filling all the gaps between the tiles with this white paste . . .'

That's when I realised I was alone. Wherever my friends had hopped to, it wasn't here.

'Whatcha playing at, young buck?' General Loretta bellowed. I guessed that the radio range was still rubbish in these cars. 'Get back to Oven Base now!'

Taking a breath, I pushed down on the accelerator again, and my bubble truck smoothly sped away, clearing the next joint with ease. It wasn't difficult to locate the 'Oven Base' – I could already feel the heat radiating from a gigantic rattling oven just ahead, past spatters of rancid grease and boulder-sized food crumbs. Red landing lights blinked in the dark space beneath it, and teams of busy engineers worked furiously on all kinds of bubble cars, bubble trucks and even hornet drones. I slowed as I passed them, the heat getting more unbearable by the moment, until I saw General Loretta sitting on a strange, curved glass bench that I recognised from somewhere. Course, she's my *Almost*-Grandma, so she was *still* wearing a jumper even in this heat.

'What took you so long?' General Loretta demanded, then stuck a cigar in her mouth and began to chew it. 'We're in a war here, Green!'

'War?' I said, and looked back out to the kitchen.

And my stomach *dropped*.

The Giant Grinster's kitchen was a burned-down, smashed-up, scorch-marked war zone. The blue walls were peppered with bullet holes, the ground littered with bomb craters. The air buzzed with hornet drones, swooping down on bubble trucks, smashing their stingers through the splintering table leg . . . even ripping through *other* hornet drones.

'It's *carnage!*' I gasped.

'Welcome to reality, greenhorn,' General Loretta growled.

'But my friends,' I said. 'Where are they? Are they OK in this?'

'None of us are OK,' General Loretta snapped. 'That's why yer gonna intercept a message to the Grinster from the *Designer himself.*'

'The Designer?'

'The Designer, Green, the Designer! That murderous

soul who first built this house on our town. The Designer who supplied our clodhopping Grinster friend with all these hornet drones, sticky pads and every other instrument of death we're up against. And he's walking up the front path as we speak, which only gives you five minutes.'

'Five minutes,' I mused. 'Slow walker, eh?' That's when I remembered how slow the Giant Grinster moved in this 'verse.

Luckily, I think Kyan in this 'verse always needed a lot of explaining, because rather than ask why I was forgetting all these obvious things, General Loretta just shook her head with a tired look, then hurried away to a big piece of kitchen towel. It was covering a strange shape as tall as she was, held tight by a thick elastic band.

'Our scientists have been working on a top secret recording device,' she said, taking a knife from her waistband. 'We call it the B2T – the Big-To-Tiny Translator.'

'No problem, General,' I said confidently, trying to make up for my foolishness so far. 'Do you want me to put it in my pocket, or—'

That's when General Loretta cut the elastic band, and the kitchen towel dropped to reveal a *massive*, karaoke-looking microphone.

'Oh!' I said in shock.

'Yup.' General Loretta chuckled, thinking I was impressed. 'They've got it smaller than ever. The B2T records Giant conversation and speeds it up to a speed we can understand. Course, those big old clumpfoots still take forever to speak, so you'll have to find a good hiding place.'

With great difficulty, she hefted the microphone up on to her shoulder. I couldn't get out and help her, else I would be sent back home, so I just sat and watched, feeling awkward, as she staggered over to me, and lay it heavily on the back of my bubble SUV. She took ages, and once she was finished she returned to that curved glass bench and sat back on it heavily.

'Please, don't get up,' she said to me with a sarcastic scowl. I looked away awkwardly . . . and then, suddenly, I twigged just what that curved glass bench actually was.

'That's the handle of the glass we broke!' I said. 'The Grinster's favourite cup!'

General Loretta grinned, looking more like *my* grandma than ever.

'Recon Team found it after your last mission. I was gonna see if my engineers could make anything of it, but I'm starting to like it where it is.'

'Is the rest of the cup still on the table?' I asked, and as she nodded, her grin widened . . . then dropped back into a scowl.

'Quit beating your gums, Green, and let's talk about your microphone. It can broadcast all the way back to this base, so I'll hear everything those mouth-breathers say – at least until I have to go to Fridge Base and direct the Big Raid. I still won't hear you though – so after I tell you to leave, you're to return to Oven Base and wait until the battle's over, roger?'

'Who's Roger?' I asked, which apparently wasn't a good question because she gave me yet another tired look. Then, surprisingly, her face softened.

'I know you're disappointed not to be selected for the air strike team with your friends,' she said, 'but this is important as well. Go to it, soldier.'

I hadn't been selected . . . Feeling more self-conscious of this universe's hopeless Kyan than ever, I left Oven Base and headed across the kitchen floor, towards the distant door. Only as I left did her words settle in. My friends are on the air strike team. Up there, in all that carnage, that's where they are.

Now, I've been in some hair-raising situations before. But nothing – *nothing* – has caused me so much terror as driving through an ongoing battle. The drums of guns and bombs pounded through my skull and shook the ground as I sped up, my wheels bouncing over the uneven tiles across that dirty kitchen floor. The heat wasn't just coming from the oven now, it was *everywhere*, a smell of smoke hanging bitter in the air. As I drove, everything grew louder, hotter, scarier, until just as I veered around a towering chair leg, something *whistled* past me, too fast and way too close. A horrible panic gripped my bones, and for an awful moment I was paralysed by the dread feeling that *you're not going to make it, you're not going to make it.*

'No,' I grunted through locked teeth, and turned a sharp, skittering left through a pond of steaming tea, driving down into a grout-joint ditch. It wasn't much cover, but it helped, and as I raced straight to the peeling white kitchen door, that terror began to ease up, until . . .

'NO!' I shouted, then stopped and slammed the steering wheel with frustration. I'd reached the door, but stuck to the bottom of it was a thick, brush draught excluder, too thick to drive through. 'How can I even get through that?!'

'Private Green!' General Loretta shouted through the radio. 'What in tarnation you lollygagging about now?!! Get through the skirting-board hole!'

'What does that even *mean*?!' I snapped back. Luckily

the range of these radios was no better than before, and after looking around, I saw . . . *ahem* . . . a small hole in the skirting board. It was jagged, like it had been *chewed* out, with big shards of wood long enough to skewer me and still have room for peppers, and I was just wondering what might've made it, when the loud buzz of a hornet drone zipped above me, and my radio crackled static for a brief moment.

'Pilot Stef to Flight Commander Dimi. Another hornet down!'

'Stef?' I shouted. 'Stef! Stef!'

'Ky? Kyan? Is that you? How good are these drones?!'

'Stef!' I shouted again, and reversed out as quick as I could, but her voice was already disappearing into static. This was what General Loretta had meant about 'air strike', I realised. While Kyan had been picked to drive around in this bumper car, my friends – or at least Stef and Dimi – had been selected to fly one of the converted hornet drones we'd been capturing. Feeling more left out and hopeless than ever, I drove on through the hole in the skirting, all alone.

Almost alone.

Behind the skirting board was a gap between the walls that seemed to go on forever, so dark that my headlights came on. I saw bricks, that fluffy yellow insulation stuff, and a small hole through the opposite wall, and I was about to drive straight through it when I heard a . . .

shuffle

and I paused. I looked down the black space running between two walls . . . and my blood turned to ice.

There, to my right, was a large, furry, rat-shaped shadow.

With a shuffle, the shape shifted again. It was massive; how had it even got in here? Slowly I pressed the accelerator, and cringed. My engine was quiet, but the tyres crunched noisily over dirt and grit and wood chippings. *Come on*, I urged, and sped up a little . . . and drove over a thin shard of wood.

Snap.

The rat didn't move in slo-mo like the Grinster did. It turned around with terrifying speed, its thick, stalk-like whispers curling up against the bricks. It looked horrific – its mouth pulled back in a sort of snarl, those sharp teeth and black eyes drinking me up. I didn't hesitate, jammed my foot down, and felt the *SNAP* of jaws right behind me even as I sped through the opposite hole and out across a shiny, slippery hallway floor.

BONNGGGGG!

It was the most epic-sounding doorbell in history, and it made my teeth chatter. There was a welcome mat sat like a thick brown forest ahead and the front door towering beyond that. As I looked back I realised with relief that the rat had stopped chasing me. And then I realised why.

'*JUUUUUST AAAAAA MIIIIIIINNNNUUUUUTE!*'

Before I had time to react, two gigantic rubber Crocs came *booming* towards me! It was the Grinster's clodhopping feet, and as I swerved desperately between them, the doorbell rang again – *BONNGGGG!* – and the Grinster hurried in slow motion to answer it. Desperately hoping that I might find a hiding place, I raced right around the welcome mat, and let out a cry of relief when I saw a rucksack beneath a coat hook. It was the size of – I mean, just assume everything's big, right? – so I darted beneath the bag strap like it was a deep cave, pulled a *mint* handbrake turn, and waited in the shadows as the front door opened.

And opened . . .

And opened . . .

'*HELLLLLLLLLLLOOOOOOOOOOTHEEEEEERRRRRE . . .*'

OK, I'll admit it – I messed up right then. I was waiting for the door to open for *sooo* long . . . then suddenly I wondered if my Big 2 Tiny Translator was even on! I turned around in my seat, clambered up and reached over, my hands all over the mic end, when suddenly *Mr Stringer's normalised voice* blared out of it so loudly I jerked back and smacked my head on the windscreen, just in time to hear . . .

'Hello there – *crackle crackle crackle.*'

I had missed the name of this mysterious 'Designer', and already the Grinster's voice was booming its next sentence above me.

'HOOOOWWW AAAARRRE YOOOUUUUUUU . . .'

Still fuming about my first mistake, I rolled silently forwards to catch sight of the Designer, but his face was cast in shadow high above. But one thing I noticed was weird. The Grinster's body was as noisy as crisps – his breathing coming in gusts, his knuckles and joints making *cracks* and *pops* like twigs snapping. I could even hear the thud of his eyelids blinking, and the *swivel-swivel-swivel* of his eyeballs far above, even as his voice boomed over the top of it all. Man, humans are *noisy* when you're microscopic.

But this mysterious figure, the Grinster's mysterious 'Designer'? This figure was completely *silent*. As I got closer, I couldn't make out any breathing, any joints, even his eyeballs moving. There was something really odd, something really uncomfortably silent and still about him. It made me so uneasy that I dared to pull forwards to get a better look at him. It was a mistake. The moment I was out from under the strap, the Designer's head swivelled unnaturally *quickly*, and he looked. Right. Down. At. Me.

I did not move, my foot on the brake, my breath held. The long shadows of the Grinster's backpack still covered me, and I was *surely* too small for this giant Designer to actually see, but his silhouetted eyes were fixed on me like laser beams. This horrible sensation crawled over my skin, this feeling that he *knew* I was there, that he didn't just know it was Kyan Green, but even *which* Kyan Green it was. The B2T Translator suddenly blared the Grinster's last words:

'How *are* you?'

And with a gasping exhalation of breath, I reversed, right back beneath the bag strap, trembling. Almost as soon as I did, the mysterious Designer began to speak, a strange, warbling tone that I couldn't understand at all . . . at least, not until it came through my headphones as a cold, controlled, *correct* voice.

'I am fine, Mr Stringer,' he said, 'but I have many situations to resolve in many places. Now, to be clear about *this* situation. You are unsatisfied with the Happy Corporation, is that correct?'

The Grinster paused, and *umm*'d and *ah*'d . . . which

took another minute. In fact, just assume that every part of this conversation felt like it took years.

'Ah, no, no-no-no, not unhappy, not at all! I just . . . well, the bug spray you provided, for one. It . . . it seems to be causing a lot of damage?'

'The Happy Corporation does not cause damage, Mr Stringer,' the Designer said. There was an underlying threat to the way he said it, and I know the Grinster picked up on it, because I began to hear his heart beat, louder and faster. Something about this Designer was very, *very* wrong.

'Well, no, not damage,' the Grinster said nervously. 'It-it-it-it's just that the problem wasn't so bad before, and now—'

'Our scientists have come across many instances of homes with a similar . . . *infestation* to yours,' the Designer said, 'and our patented bug spray has never failed to clear them. The problem must be with you.'

The Grinster stared at him, for a *long* pause.

'The hornet drones . . . they smashed my plates, and my grandmother's favourite glass got hit, and – OK I think that was the Tinies, but still—'

'*If* you think that I'm lying . . .' the Designer said sharply.

'Lying's a strong word—'

'. . . then there is one small test you can take. To deactivate all of the hornet drones at once, you simply need to say a special command and all of the drones will cease hunting, and will at once return to the tabletop awaiting further order. This command is "PESTS ERADICATED".

A blast of static came through my radio right then, one that shocked me into yelping out loud. But then I realised it was the sound of cheering.

'Pests eradicated!' General Loretta called through my radio. 'You got us a Deactivation Code! Excellent work, soldier, we'll take a megaphone to the Fridge Roof Base and shout it out there. Once those drones drop off to sleep, this bombing raid's gonna be a cinch! Now get on back to the safety of Oven Base – THAT IS AN ORDER!'

The radio trumped, and the sounds of cheering stopped straight away. Part of me felt like cheering myself – after all that worry, I'd completed my mission here more quickly than I could've hoped! But the other part knew that this wasn't my *real* mission, that we weren't trying to destroy the Grinster, or his kitchen, or even his evil hornet drones. And as *this* part kept on listening, a sharp blade of anxiety began to twist across my gut.

'If you speak this code, "PESTS ERADICATED", the Designer continued in that same, soft, cold voice, 'your hornet drones will stop doing anything, Mr Stringer. Your kitchen, and all your favourite cups and plates, will be defenceless. If the Tinies still commit their wanton acts of destruction, you will at last know what I know already: that the Happy Corporation is only trying to make your life more peaceful, more ordered, and that your enemies are, always will be, the pests. Then you will contact me for a more drastic option.'

'M-more drastic?' the Grinster asked, and his heart was beating furiously now.

'We destroy your house.'

'What?' I said, and moments later the Grinster said the same thing.

'What? D-destroy my home?'

'Of course, we would build you a new one,' the Designer said. 'Even bigger, and for no charge at all. You see, Kenneth, the vermin you describe are rabid. And there is only one thing you can do with rabid vermin. Destroy their nest.'

There was silence, for so long that I dared inch forwards again, only a little, just to see that the Designer was still there. I saw his suit trousers, his hand hanging by his side. It was completely still, like the rest of him, but there was something *on* it – something as small as me. It crawled across his knuckles, all the way to the tip of his index finger, and just as quickly as he'd swung around to stare at me, the Designer flicked his finger, and the thing flew through the air and out of sight.

'OK . . .' said the Grinster. 'OK, thank you.'

The Designer made a noise, something between a laugh and a cough. He turned to leave, and then he paused.

'You are not aware of this, Mr Stringer, but the Happy Corporation is in fact part of a larger, far more powerful organisation known as Pure State. Do you know why it is so named?'

'I . . .' the Grinster began, then broke off, unsure.

The Designer let out a small, cold laugh, and continued. 'But of course, how could you! You see, the term Pure State actually comes from Quantum Physics. It is a type of science that is far beyond yourself, but, to put it in terms that you can understand, a Pure State is a system that is completely ordered. If you make a measurement on a system that is Pure, you can be certain that your measurement will be entirely, absolutely accurate. In essence, you can predict everything – even elements as vague and spurious as happiness – and because you can predict everything, you can also control everything. It is a precious thing to behold, a Pure State. And should something so dangerous as disorder threaten it ... well, that disorder must be destroyed. Otherwise everything becomes dangerously unpredictable. Even happiness.'

The Grinster stared at him then, his mouth open for so long that I heard bubbles of saliva pop beneath his distant tongue. At last, without another word, the Designer turned, and left.

As the Grinster closed the door, my mind raced furiously. If the Grinster – or my grandma – used the deactivation code, then the hornets would stop blowing up the kitchen. Which *would* be good, except that if the kitchen was still destroyed, the Grinster would destroy the whole house, *and* our homes beneath it.

'It's a trap,' I said aloud. 'I've got to stop that bombing raid.'

And I barely had a *minute*. The Grinster turned back and slowly walked towards the kitchen door. I raced up behind him, praying he didn't catch a glimpse of movement near his feet and start breakdancing around the room trying to squash me. He slowly reached out, and I sped across the floor between his Crocs, aiming straight for the growing gap in the opening door, *pounding* my radio as I did.

'Grandma!' I shouted. 'Stef! Anybody, anybody, can

you read me? It's urgent – can you read me?! Do not use the code, I repeat, *do not use the code! IT'S A TRAP—*'

That's when another car *rammed* into the side of me so hard that my bubble truck rolled. The world exploded, my organs were flung around my body, glass cracked and the floor smashed above and below me and above again . . . before I rammed into the thick straw stalks of the welcome mat and slammed to a halt. My wheels crashed back down, and with my head *pounding*, with my breakfast halfway up my throat, I let out a groan . . . and saw a bubble truck at *least* twice the size of mine come to a stop right in front of me.

'I told you I'd see you soon,' sneered Edwin through my crackling radio. 'I owe you some beats.'

22
A Race Across the Grinster's House

I stared through a cracked windscreen at the Level Ten Infinity Racer I'd once trusted. His bubble truck rolled slowly towards me, dwarfing mine.

'Please,' I said. 'Edwin, I thought you were . . .'

'Your friend?' sneered Edwin. 'I could've been your friend, Kyan Green. You could've joined us.'

'And sell out everyone I cared about?' I said, looking desperately for an escape route. 'That's what you did in your universe, wasn't it? You were losing, so you gave everything up to the Pure State.'

Edwin smirked again . . . but even from here I could see anger in his eyes.

'I didn't sell anybody out,' he said. 'Your beloved "Spider

Ace" promised me revenge. But she's too weak to understand how far I would go to get it. Like *THIS* far—'

Edwin *floored* it, and that truck had a *monster* engine,
because it went from 0 to 100 in seconds, giving me no
time to react. Just in time, I swung the steering wheel a
hard left, and slammed the accelerator down, smoke
billowing from my spinning wheels as they skittered and
slipped on the shiny wooden floor. Edwin *whoomphed*
past me, laughing, and by the time I looked in my rear-
view, he'd already pulled a U-ey and was chasing me again.

He was a *crazy*-good driver. You know when you're up
against someone, in football or a fight or a game, and in
seconds you *know* you'll lose? Well that was me then. I dough-
nutted all the way around the Grinster's massive rucksack,
exploding through a dustball as I straightened up. I bombed
it beneath a shoe rack, spiders scuttling out of my way, and
roosted clumps of shoe dirt straight for him on the turn. I
darted under a door to a plush-looking living room, tapped
the brakes and turned sharp back into the hallway again.

None of it mattered; Edwin matched me turn for turn,
and was *always* right behind. Twice he shunted me from
the side, smashing me almost out of control before pulling
away with a loud, unhinged laugh. My hands trembled,
my body ached, but Edwin wasn't tested at *all*. With every

sideswipe, every painful collision, I saw his manic, grinning face, and knew that he wasn't even trying, that he was just toying with me.

And then I saw it, sharp to my right; the hole in the skirting. Instantly I hit the brakes, again sending Edwin careening past me, again with him laughing like it was nothing. Nuff props to whoever built these bubble trucks too, because the turn was *90 degrees sharp*, but I made it, and straightened up aiming *right* at the hole. But again, Edwin had made it too, was *right* behind me, edging sparks out of my back alloys, swinging out and *slamming* back into me, forcing frightened sobs from my throat with every collision. The skirting hole tore towards me, but in my terror I *knew* that I couldn't escape, that even after we raced through the mousehole he would –

CRUNCH!

I didn't notice it for a second. I raced through the hole, my eyes blinded with tears of panic, racing across the darkened gap between walls with my wheels bouncing on snapping sticks and sawdust . . . and then, just as I reached the hole in the skirting opposite, I heard it: the sweet sound of nothing. No tyres racing behind me. No maniacal laughter. Nothing at all. And as dumb as this was, I stopped and looked back.

Edwin's truck was wedged into the small mousehole, each side trapped in the chewed-up wood. He revved his engine, *over-revved* it, but the ground was just mulch, and his wheels spun uselessly. His smirk had curdled into Joker-rage, and as his eyes met mine, he forced a laugh that became a screaming, arm-flailing toddler tantrum.

'Eesh!' I said. 'You know, there's something really messed up about somebody who never stops smiling.'

'We'll get you, Kyan,' he snarled. 'You have no idea how powerful we are. You think you've been caught in the Designer's eye? You have barely existed for him now, and when he turns to face you, you and your pathetic friends, and your pathetic family, you'll wish you were . . .'

But before he could finish, a scrabbling sound came from the dark gap between the walls.

Shuffle.

We both stared. There it was again, louder this time.

Shuffle.

Then again, quicker, closer, until it became the racing of claws, until bits of yellow insulation began to *poof* up into the air, until I could hear the rapid, grunting breaths of a deadly creature. I looked back to Edwin. His face was pale.

'You should get out,' I said, then hit the accelerator and sped out of there, just in time to feel the mouse *whoosh* behind me. There was another CRUNCH, I heard Edwin scream . . .

. . . and I was out, driving across the kitchen tiles, amazed to be still in one piece.

But *still* with a disaster to stop.

The battle was fiercer than ever. The air was thick with hornet drones, swooping and stabbing at booming tanks, at speeding bubble-butts, and at each other. And stood beside the dinner table, watching all this devastation unfold, was the Grinster.

He looked stooped, this Stringer. He was big enough to trample me into dust, but he didn't look powerful. He looked beaten. He looked sad.

And, with a deep, loooong breath, he spoke.

'*PESTSSS ERRRAAAADDDICAAAATTEDDDD!*'

'Oh no,' I said. The change was immediate. As soon as the Grinster finished shouting the code phrase, a strange, hollow silence fell on the battlefield. The buzzing of hornet drones stopped almost completely, and one by one, the Grinster's drones began to fly back to the table.

'General Loretta!' I shouted into the radio. 'Stef! Dimi! Tines! Can anybody hear me?! Don't attack the drones, it's a trap!'

There was no answer. Another idea occurred to me, someone I hadn't tried contacting yet.

'Luke?' I said, and tapped my ear. 'Luke, can you hear me?' But there was no answer. Even though our Luke had been able to contact us through the strings before, he was silent now.

A glint of movement on the fridge caught my eye, and I looked up. A steady stream of vehicles was driving vertically up its shiny white wall; missile launchers, tanks and jeeps packed with bazooka-holding soldiers. I followed their path to the top of the fridge, up to a blinking red landing light similar to the one in Oven Base. High above me, hornet drones were slowly hovering to the fridge top, each one with a Tiny on its back.

This was 'Fridge Base', where General Loretta had said she was going to organise the final offensive. And from the gathering forces, it was going to be an *almighty* attack.

'Kyan Green to General Loretta,' I said again, sounding more desperate than ever. 'Can you read me? You *have* to call off the attack!'

There was *almost* nothing again . . . except more static came through the radio, and I heard snippets of my Almost-Grandma.

'Get the . . . second wave . . . destroy every drone before . . .'

'General Grandma!' I shouted, and raced towards the fridge. 'I mean – Almost-Loretta! Do you read me? You have to call off the attack!'

'Stef . . . imi . . . stine . . . lead th . . . attack . . .'

'Call it off, call it off!' I shouted, but it was no good. No way could I make it all the way up there before our side had destroyed the Grinster's drones, maybe even attacked the Grinster himself. We were about to fall for the Designer's trap, and give him a reason to destroy us all.

That's when I had a crazy idea.

I didn't even know how I would pull it off alone.

I also couldn't see any other option.

I pulled the handbrake and cracked a rapid U-turn, racing forwards across the tiles straight for the Oven. It wasn't a straightforward drive, I was bouncing horrendously on the lippy edges, swerving and skidding around grease slicks and old mashed potato, but I managed good time and was soon bombing beneath the roasting oven and up to the landing lights of the shadowy Oven Base. The base had been abandoned for the final attack, but what I needed was still there: the Grinster's nana's cup handle.

The only problem was, I had no idea how to load it into the truck without getting out. And if I got out, I'd go home.

'What are *you* doing here?' a voice asked. I turned, and saw my Almost-Bestie, wearing engineer's overalls and holding a wrench,

'Almost-Luke!' I said, then corrected myself quick. 'I mean, Luke! Mate, am I *glad* to see you – I need your help!'

But Almost-Luke didn't smile.

'What help?' he said. 'You worked out a new way to blow things up?'

So the argument I'd had with Luke back home, the argument Almost-Ky-Ky had with Almost Luke-Luke in the Fungiverse, it was still playing out in this 'verse too. I just had to hope that all the Cosmic Connections Spider Ace had told me about would have some kind of effect, that somehow this Luke would be more open to listening thanks to the apologies I'd made in other 'verses.

'I'm sorry,' I said, guessing wildly at what I was sorry for. 'I didn't listen to you, but you're right. We can wreck this whole kitchen, we might even destroy the Grinster himself . . . but it won't help. The only way we can win is by making peace. That's why I want to fix his favourite cup.'

Almost-Luke looked at the curved glass bench on the floor. He looked back at me. Then, without warning, he turned and ran away.

'Luke!' I shouted. 'C'mon, mate, just listen—'

'Just give us a sec, ya great galoob!' he yelled, and I shut up. He reached an old-school computer that looked *kinda* similar to the Commodore 65, and began to tap furiously at it. With the sound of juddering machinery, a big winch fixed to the underside of the oven began to whirr its way over to me. These big straps were attached to the winch, and when they were above the Grinster's glass handle, Luke tapped another key, and the straps lowered down. Almost-Luke then raced back and, with effort, tied the straps around the glass handle.

'Don't get up, will you, Ky?' he said grumpily.

'Sorry,' I said guiltily. 'I . . .'

But Luke was racing back, tapping expertly at the computer as it lifted the glass handle and dropped into the back of my bubble truck. It must've weighed a *lot*, because my whole bubble truck lowered down under the weight. Still, he was so smooth with the winch that by the time he'd untied the loop and sent the winch gliding away, there wasn't a single scratch on the handle.

'You're really good at that,' I said, impressed. He didn't say anything, just strapped the handle down next to the microphone, but when he got in the passenger side he *did* look pleased.

'All right,' he said. 'Where to now?'

I drove forwards . . . very . . . slowly, the heavy weight on the back of my bubble truck *badly* slowing my acceleration. For one horrible moment I wondered if we'd ever get going, then the truck's engine – wheezing like our family car by now – *finally* picked up speed. Still, as we left the cover of the oven and aimed for the closest table leg, I began to worry.

'I can't slow down!' I said, swerving between a pizza crust and a missing tile. 'Otherwise we won't make it up the table leg.'

But Almost-Luke was already ahead of me. He reached into his overalls pocket and took out a folded piece of paper. As he opened it up, I saw it was a sketched map of the Grinster's kitchen.

'Right,' he said. 'There's two cracked tiles coming ahead, so turn right two tiles, then go left, and there's a clear path between both the gravy pond and the jam trap.'

'Did *you* make that map?' I said, impressed.

'I thought you said it'd be a waste of time?' he asked sarcastically, and I winced again. This universe's Kyan had more bridges to build than I'd had! But again he looked pleased, and as I skirted the cracked tiles, turning left, to aim between both a pool of gravy and a mountainous dollop of jam, he began to give more orders like a rally-car co-driver.

'There's chips straight ahead, you'll need easy right then easy left. Two tile lips are after that, but they're only small, so if you ease off you'll keep to the surface. Then speed up through the rice, it's dry, not sticky, so you'll coast over it.'

'My grandma would *never* eat in this dutty kitchen,' I muttered to myself without thinking, but it must've been true for this universe as well, because Luke grinned.

'General Loretta?' he said. 'You know it, she finds this floor *plop*.'

I didn't like to ask if *he'd* made up that slang word, but Luke's navigating was on point, and by the time he guided me to the table leg we were *speeding* ahead. Just when I was wondering how to get up there, he was giving instructions for this as well.

'This is Table Leg C, so the ramp up is on the inside. The tiles are all flat here, so you can drive in a big circle all the way round, and you'll see it in front of you.'

He was right. Driving in a wide arc to keep my speed up, I circled around the spindly wooden leg, and saw a takeaway flier as long as an airport runway. It was leaning up against the leg, making a perfect ramp to drive up. It wasn't a moment too soon either. I saw the Grinster's Crocs stomping slowly across the floor towards the table, and heard something else: the buzzing of hornet drones. General Loretta was starting the attack!

'Here goes,' I said through gritted teeth, and floored it, ramping up the table leg and driving *vertically* upwards!

It felt *horrible*. Luke let out a gurgle as we were both pinned back into our seats. But as hard as it was to believe, the tyres *still* gripped the leg, and I pelted up it very ill indeed. We'd be *under* the tabletop: how were we supposed to get around that?!

I don't know if he guessed what I was thinking or not, but Luke gave me the answer again.

'OK, OK,' he said in a nauseous voice. 'Time for upside-down driving . . .'

Stef would be able to tell you why it worked, but to me right then it was magic. We hit the shaded back of the tabletop at speed . . . and still my tyres clung to the wood. We were driving upside down! I didn't dare turn, and I *definitely* didn't slow down. Well, not till we reached the curved edge of the table, and it tailed off so abruptly that I lost my nerve and took my foot off the accelerator . . .

'Don't-slow-down-you-muppet-else-we'll-fall!' Luke shouted in one, and I pushed my foot down again, our wheels bouncing *horrifically* before we finally curved up and around, the right way up on the tabletop.

'OH!' I shouted, and both me and my Almost-Best Mate started to laugh hysterically. We'd made it back on to the Grinster's table!

And we were too late.

The Grinster's table had become a desolate place. Broken shards of dishes, sauce bottles and teacups littered the filthy, burn-marked top, the place where dinner went to die. Far ahead, lined up into two rows, about twenty deactivated hornet drones awaited further orders, their metal eyes shiny black and unblinking. Beyond them, stood like some old relic from a decayed civilisation, was the Grinster's nana's favourite glass. Miraculously, it hadn't been damaged by the furious fighting – except for a missing handle, that is. But like I said, we were too late to fix it. Because flying towards us in a deadly strike formation, my friends rode the hornet drones I'd helped to capture. Strapped to each drone was a deadly-looking missile.

'We can't make it,' I said. 'By the time we even reach the glass, our side will have blown up all the hornet drones. And the Grinster will have his whole home demolished, just to get rid of us.

And that's when Luke leaned forward.

'Buck up then,' he said, 'and drive.'

I slammed my foot down, my tired bubble truck groaning now. There was a sun roof above me – something I hadn't even noticed until now – and Luke took a pair of binoculars out of his pocket and stood on his seat. Barely a moment had passed before he started calling down directions.

'You've got a crumb forest up ahead, so careful, then sharp right – *right*! Slippy milk coming up so – that's it, now left, *LEFT . . . I SAID LEFT!* – nice one, now jump ahead, take the butter-knife ramp up, it'll get you over the broken teacup, then triple caution, right, four over, big jump-off camber—'

'*What are you saying?!*' I squawked, and now he looked apologetic.

'It's this language I'm working on to navigate you with—'

'*But I don't speak that language yet!*'

'Fair point,' Luke admitted, then shouted, '*jump ahead!*'

We hit the back of a teaspoon and went *flying* up, landing in a pile of sugar, which played *havoc* with my steering, like somebody was kicking the wheels left and right. Things were suddenly going wrong. I made it out of the sugar, only to skid through a whole *slick* of tomato ketchup. That's when Luke had a *genius* idea.

'Sharp right, Kyan, sharp right! Ramp up the upside-down plate and along the bread NOW!'

I slammed my wheel down right, raced up the plate and went airborne again, landing on soft white bread. He'd picked the *perfect* slice – it was just going stale – enough that we didn't drop, but still soft enough for all the sugar and red sauce to smear across it, cleaning my tyres. With the grip on my wheels returned, I turned off the bread and back to the table. There was just a straight line between us and the Grinster's glass!

'YEAH!' I shouted. 'You did it, Luke, you did it!'

But we weren't out of danger yet. Between us and the Grinster's glass, two rows of glass-eyed killing machines still stood there, waiting for their next order. Even worse, I looked up and saw my friends swooping down, ready to drop those bombs across the Grinster's dinner table. Dimi, who was leading the attack, raised his arm as though preparing to make the order to *fire*.

'We've got to do something!' I gasped, and again Almost-Luke was on it.

'The olives!' he bellowed. I looked around frantically – and saw a broken bowl with olives inside . . . and those little toothpick cocktail-stick things resting on the side. Course, those little toothpicks were taller than a tree to us, but there was a broken shard of one that was just the size of Almost-Luke's arm, and as we got closer he opened the door, reached out . . . and snatched it up like a javelin!

'Now go for the napkins!' he shouted. I got what he wanted to do straight away. Veering around the bowl, I sped forwards on the straight, aiming for a piece of kitchen towel that lay battle-burned and smoking right ahead. Luke reached out with the toothpick shard, and as I prayed for good luck he pointed it forwards and . . .

RRRIPPPP!

A huge white sheet tore off the towel, and was pinned to the cocktail stick like a flag!

'YES, LUKE!' I shouted, then muttered, 'Please, Stef – please, Tines – please, Dimi – just see us, see—'

'PEACE!' Luke screamed. 'WE NEED PEACE!'

It happened just as Dimi was about to drop his arm. Celestine saw the white flag and her eyes widened. She turned right, straight in front of Dimi, causing him to pull back up as Stef saw us and did the same.

'Air strike team!' General Loretta bellowed through the radio. 'Why are you pulling back? I repeat, WHY ARE YOU PULLING BACK?!'

We'd prevented the attack!

Now we just had to deliver the message.

With Luke gripping determinedly on to our makeshift white flag, I sped us forwards between the two rows of hornet drones. We were so close, but as a shadow fell on us I looked up again and saw that so was somebody else.

It was the Giant Grinster. And, caught between the rows of hornet drones, I knew, if he wanted to squish us both right then and there, there was nothing we could do.

'The cup!' Almost-Luke shouted. Biting down on my desperate wish to turn, to run, to survive and fight another Stringer on another day, I sped up, racing through the rows of drones straight for the Grinster's favourite cup.

The shadow became darker. The broken glass came closer. And, pulling up the handbrake, I spun the bubble truck around, and came to a shuddering halt right in front of it.

'That's it,' I said, breathing hard, 'That's all we can do.'

It took another moment for me to dare look up, at that hairy face, with its tea-stained teeth and *clackalacka* nostrils. Almost-Luke jumped out of the bubble truck and untied the glass handle of the Grinster's favourite cup, all the while dancing about, and waving our white flag of truce so hard that he nearly toppled over. For what seemed like eternity, nothing happened.

Then, painfully slow, the Grinster reached down with a finger that could crush me like a bug, and . . .

. . . and he picked up the shiny white handle of his favourite cup.

There was silence; nothing but the thunder of the Grinster's breath. Then, as I looked up, I saw a huge drop of water plummeting towards us.

SPLASH!

His voice was so thick with tears, I couldn't understand what the Grinster said next. Not until the B2T Translator kicked in and repeated it in Mr Stringer's normal voice.

'My grandmother's teacup . . . thank you.'

And with that, the Grinster's shadow turned away from the table. Me and Luke turned to each other . . . and grinned, both sighing big with relief at once. I held out my fist . . .

. . . and froze, at the sudden sound of buzzing.

I turned in my seat, and saw it. Behind us, one by one, the deactivated hornet drones were waking up. This close, I could hear orders being relayed through them, and I heard that cold Designer's voice speak.

'Destroy them,' he said. 'Destroy them all—'

WHACK! The rolled-up magazine squelched all twenty of them at once, just as another teardrop sploshed nearby. The Grinster sat back in a nearby chair, what to us was a mile away, and I don't know how he could've ever seen my face . . .

. . . but I nodded thanks all the same, and so did he. The war between the Tinies and the Giant Grinster was over. Almost-Luke looked at me, and held out a fist to bump.

'You wanna get out of the truck?' he asked.

'Yeah,' I said.

The Grinster's kitchen table dissolved the moment I stepped out. And yep, I could've clapped my hands, but I really didn't know what Almost-Luke would see, and it felt like a whole driving-partners thing, stepping out at the same time. The universe dissolved into strings that could've looked like wheelie bins – if you were thinking of trash, anyway. I plunged through thousands of worlds, but for the first time I didn't look around: I just hung my tired head, closed my eyes, and as I braced myself for an uncomfortable landing in Edie Scrap's mobile library, I grinned.

We'd done it. We'd won the day.

Only . . . I didn't land. I opened my eyes, and realised that I wasn't falling either. All was dark around me, filled with grim clouds. There was a figure standing out there, and as my eyes adjusted I saw with shock that it was Luke . . . *our* Luke.

'Luke!' I shouted, but he didn't answer. A thin red dot appeared in the distance, then another. As more appeared, they grew closer, until I saw that they weren't dots, but . . .

red tentacles. They were flying through the strings towards me, speeding up, and although I began to move frantically, I couldn't get away. They slipped around me one by one, squeezing tight even as they pulled me along. Something was between all those tentacles . . . a shape, massive and terrifying. It was a face, a cold and furious face, its mouth grinning but its eyes as dead as skull sockets. Dragged through the strings towards it, I saw Stef and Dimi and Celestine drop into space nearby, and tried to yell out . . .

. . . except I couldn't. One of those tentacles was wrapped around my mouth, squeezing tighter and tighter. I bit down hard, and the tentacle released . . . before wrapping around my eyes, harder than before. I yelled out with pain, and could feel myself being pulled towards that face, those jaws . . .

'Shut your eyes!' a familiar voice shouted.

And just as I was about to say that my eyes were *being* shut, a bright blue light filled the air, and even through the tentacle blindfold it felt *blinding*. There was the sound of a motorbike zipping through the air, a horrible screeching sound, *all* the tentacles flinched back, and I felt myself dropping . . . *fast*. Shielding the light with my hand, I *just* caught sight of a silhouette racing through the strings ahead of me. The silhouette had a quiff, a leather jacket, and was riding a bike with plasma for wheels. She was holding some kind of glowing weapon, *literally* like a mythic blaster – and as she fired it, blue flames burst out, and the face screeched again. The light became truly blinding now, I covered my eyes screaming with pain and fright and I fell . . . fell . . . fell . . .

I plunged butt-first into a chair and gasped, coughing and winded. A moment later Dimi and Stef, Celestine and Luke, all landed in chairs around me. They were all safe, all my friends.

'What was that?!' I said heavily. 'And who helped us?'

'Don't be daft, boy,' Spider Ace said. 'You didn't think I'd leave you to face the Designer alone, did ya?!'

23
The End

'Kyan! Kyan, come on!'

I struggled to my feet, completely exhausted but refusing to give up. The colours on the screen in front of me dissolved to nothingness, and Celestine turned to face me, a look of grim determination on her face.

'I'm going to win this time,' she said with a glare. 'Nobody can get in my way.'

'Pffft, leave off,' my dad said, springing off his feet like a boxer. 'This is a Padraig song all the way.'

'A Padraig song,' Mum said drily, picking up her controller. 'Yeah, the first time I met your dad I thought – he should be a K-Pop backing dancer.'

'What song is it?' Grandma called from the kitchen. 'I

hope you're not doing disco without me?'

'No!' we all called back. (She says that before every song, either disco or soca or reggaeton.) The clock began to count down as we all argued: *You're in my way!* and *Spread out, spread out!* Then, just as my dad did a couple of practice steps that made me *know* he wouldn't win this one, his phone rang, *and* my mum's phone rang, and all of us groaned.

'Pause it, pause it!' Mum said, and wandered to the kitchen, as Dad made big exaggerated *sorry* mimes and went to their room. Me and Celestine looked at each other.

'Back to Proton Wars?' she said, and I nodded.

We squeezed past the boxes of Halloween decorations – Halloween's not for ages, but Dad found a new car boot sale, innit – and to my room. I hadn't reached the door before I could already hear Luke talking.

'So, if you go to each Protonsphere – that's like a universe – you can earn XP individually by doing little tasks, sort of like Side Quests. But the real time you can boost XP, I mean like *multiplying* it, is when you find a similar problem in each universe and solve them together. But you have to be careful – if another player is actually setting up *another* problem and your solution makes them worse, you could really quickly *lose* XP—'

'Is it my turn on Just Dance?' Dimi said quickly the moment I opened the door. He looked *very* tired.

''Fraid not, mate,' I said, holding back a grin. 'Mum and Dad had work calls.'

Dimi looked like he wanted to cry, but I'll give him credit, he didn't – we'd been promising to play this with Luke for ages. I was actually starting to enjoy it, and the tips it gave for Infinite Racing made a weird sense, although I knew I wouldn't ever have the patience to understand it like Luke. He handed me the dice now, and as I moved my spaceship across a huge starry board that looked very like the Map of the Multiverse, I turned to Stef and Dimi.

'I still can't believe you two aren't grounded!'

'Me neither,' said Stef. 'We got back so late my mum was home from work, but she just said how proud she was that we'd been selected for some maths team and made us hot chocolates!'

I shook my head in disbelief.

'That whole evening was *mad*, even by Infinity Race standards. I was sure we were going to be eaten at the end – and after we'd fixed all the problems in that universe. *Did* we beat the Pure State then? And who *is* that Designer anyway?'

'He's a lot of things,' a voice said. 'He's oh-so mighty, and he's powerful. But like you showed yesterday, nobody's power is absolute.'

We all stared at the other end of the table. Sitting there, like she'd been there the whole time, was Spider Ace. I'd never seen her like this before – she was *smiling*!

'Well done,' she said. 'You did it, you really did it. You saved your universe again.'

'All thanks to the magic of Cosmic Connections!' Dimi said. And just like that, Spider's smile dropped.

'It's not magic, it's science!' she snapped. 'I don't go calling your haircut a dead ferret, do I, just because it takes an expert to spot the difference?'

'Ouch,' I said, but Dimi laughed full-on, and I could've sworn I saw a twinkle in Spider's eyes.

'You went into a situation,' she continued, 'where the only way to stop the Happy Empire from infesting your universe and all the others around it was to do the opposite of everything that made sense to you . . . and to me. You worked together, each and every one of you finding a role that wasn't ever given to you, but that you knew would be the best for your team. And when the problems of the universe seemed insurmountable, a load too heavy to bear, you had the humility, the bravery, to seek help from those you have learned through bitter experience to hate. You should be proud.'

Spider Ace paused, and her mouth turned down at the corners, as she added, 'You also solved a mystery that has troubled me for a long time: the whereabouts of an Infinity Racer. Even if the answer was unpleasant to hear.'

I couldn't help it. I leaned forwards and asked, 'Who is he then? Who is the Designer?'

'I'll be telling you a lot more about the Designer, and Pure State, about *everything* very soon,' Spider Ace replied. 'Believe me, my experience with young Edwin has taught me not to reveal just what I think you need to know. Edwin was a brilliant Racer, but he didn't have friends like you, Kyan. Now, and perhaps because I failed to be clear about the true consequences of his actions, he has let vengeance twist him in ways more gruesome than he would ever have expected.'

I thought of that strange, never-ending smile on Edwin's face. I couldn't help it – it made me shudder.

'They're still after us,' I said. 'They still want to take over everything.'

'They do,' Spider Ace said. 'There are dark clouds ahead for all of us, Kyan Green. An enemy so big, yet so unknown, has you firmly in its sights now. And yet . . . in its quest for total control, the Designer is utterly misguided about the true strength of a Cosmic Connection. When I, somewhat brilliantly, plasma-biked into the strings and freed you from the Designer's pet, I didn't have to search far for an energy source to drive me. The force of Cosmic Connections you had helped to create, for a moment, made this most monstrous army of foes seem small and petty. You understood, in a way that the Designer never could, that we all, everybody, brings something to this Multiverse.'

We all stared for a long moment. Then I leaned forwards.

'You've got to admit though, my bubble-truck driving was the best, right?'

At once everybody groaned.

'Talk about ruin the moment!'

'Big headed Ky, innit.'

'And he blatantly never saw my hornet drone flying . . .'

For a moment, Spider was still there, looking around at us with a strange, quiet smile on her face. The next moment she was gone.

We spent an hour between the two games, Proton Wars and Just Dance. Stef was thrashing everyone at Proton

Wars, creating her own empire, while Mum, Celestine *and* Grandma got megastar on this song by some old group called Earth, Wind & Fire. I was just about to rescue my dad – who was sweating more than humans *should* sweat by now – when the doorbell rang.

'Ask who it is,' I said to Celestine, but she just glared back at me.

'Your turn,' she said.

I don't know what's up with that kid, she used to be so sweet.

With a big sigh I went to the front door.

'Who is it?'

'Mr . . . it's Kenneth,' the voice came through the door.

'Who's Kenneth?'

'Mr Stringer!'

'Oh,' I said, and opened the door. He was standing outside, still looking odd in his shop polo-neck shirt, looking down at all the old pizza and chicken-shop fliers that had dropped out of the letterbox on to the front step. He was fighting the urge to moan, and sweeping them up is *meant* to be my chore, so there was an awkward silence all round.

'I'll get my mum,' I began, but he shook his head.

'Actually,' he said, and coughed. 'Actually it was you I came to see. I thought you'd like to know that George is on the mend.'

'Oh,' I said. I had thought about George, a lot. I just hadn't known what to think – but hearing that made a weight lift from my head that I hadn't even known was there. I think Mr Stringer took my silence as something else though, because his face twisted into this awkward, unhappy expression. At last, he spoke again.

'After you saw me at George's Shop, and didn't say

about . . . you know, our arguments, when I could've lost my job, I never said . . . *ahem* . . . thank you.'

'Yeah . . .'

'So . . . *ahem* . . . thank you. Thank you.'

I stared at him. I'd literally never heard those words coming from any Stringer's mouth in the Multiverse. And, true, it looked like it hurt him to say it. But he'd said it anyway.

For a mad moment I thought about asking if he wanted to play Just Dance with us. But I'm not ready for that yet, and from the hurried way he picked up the fliers while muttering 'Bloody mess', I don't think he is either. He disappeared away around the corner, and I was about to shut the door, when my phone vibrated: a message.

U snitched.

It was from Alex Bridges. I stared down at it, and felt the shadow of thick storm clouds in the sky above.

Cos there was a storm coming. I'd stood up against a renegade Level Ten Racer, against a power-mad Pure State Empire . . . and the most popular kid in school. They were all terrifying enemies, and still . . .

'Did you ask who it was?' Mum shouted, way too late as always. 'Hurry up, Ky, Dimi took your go for that K-Pop song and your dad's put his back out. We need you for "Waka Waka (This Time for Africa)"'

'Wait, no – here first, Ky!' Luke shouted. 'Stef's sweeping across the quadrant, she's going for Mars itself!'

And still, I didn't think they had a squad anything like mine.

Acknowledgements

First off, I've visited a load of schools courtesy of indie bookshops this year, and although this probably sounds dead ignorant I'd never twigged just how big a role those bookshops play in an area. Thank you so much to you all, for the hard work you do along with the teachers and school / local librarians. Credit also to the tonnes of smart and engaged students I met too. Don't believe the hype – the kids are all right.

As before, huge thanks to Davinia Andrew-Lynch of Curtis Brown Agency, for your brilliant repping. After all this time patiently repeating that plans and clear pitches *can* be useful and *aren't* selling short my precious artistic integrity, it's honestly sinking in, I promise. I'll say the same to my editor Eleanor Willis as well – you really helped me see the heart of this story; thanks for making me tidy it.

Thanks again to everyone at Bloomsbury. David Wilkerson and the Design team especially – that sounds like an art-house band, but I can't tell you how many kids have gone 'wow' at your work this year. Grace, Evelyn and Jearl, without youse I wouldn't ever have visited those schools or done all those videos on Instagram or TikTok, which was something I was dreading and turned out to be *mega*. Thanks to all the proofing team, Jessica et al., for cleaning my bad grammar without once making the kids sound phoney. And MASSIVE good luck to editor Hannah Sandford in your freelance work – you changed my life taking a punt on me, Hannah, hand on heart.

As ever, my family and friends build most my life and half my characters. Mum, Dad, Corinna, Elan, Alex, David, Jean, Danny, Eoin, Ash (Shiftwork!) and Jackie B., Claire, Ikey Mo, Krystal, Paul, Raj, Neal, Dave, Hugo, Nat, Jan, Chris and Lanna – thanks for everything, and I'm sorry if I've ever been bolshie or argumentative with any of you. All right, most of you. All right, all of you.

Also have to say thanks to my workmates Nigel, Jack, Jamie C., Lee, Jamie J. and Guido – for the 'gram videos, the Cockney education, and for finding that website that claims I'm worth $16 million. Thanks also to David, Valerie and Mark at Vitruvius for the work and being understanding about all the days visiting schools – I really appreciate it.

And then there's the sprogs.

I'm writing this after bellowing at you all morning about chores. Leo, you've kicked *right* off about learning your poem, then gone and done it perfectly. Roobz, you lost your screen time, called me 'Yucky Dad', and then earned that screen back by sweeping the kitchen floor like a pro and cracking me right up while you did it. And Arf, your mate's round and you keep calling me 'Bob the Builder', and you *know* I'm mentally adding extra jobs to *your* list every time you do. You make me so proud, all three of you. Thank you (don't say, 'You're welcome'). Also got to mention the godkids – Conn, Cal, and Chas – for *more* replies to questions about slang / school / emojis, and for generally being excellent. Thanks also to Ginny and Sam and Sonny and Lottie, 's'amazing what confidence kids give you when they like something you wrote.

It's a bit random too . . . but I have to say thanks to whoever at the games company Codemasters made the driving game *Micro Machines* for the Mega Drive back in the day. It had this ace driver in it called 'Spider', and one of the tracks was on a breakfast table and ... basically, your imaginations were brilliant.

And as always, as forever, love ya, D. *'Nuff.*

About the Author

Colm Field gets called 'Colin' a lot. He doesn't help himself by mumbling his words a lot of the time, except in his job as a builder, when he winds up shouting instead. He lives in London with his three kids and his partner. Colm is happiest when he's excitedly writing a new story on his rusty old phone and his favourite mode of transport is walking, so obviously his debut children's novel was about high-speed multiverse-hopping on everything but feet.

About the Illustrator

David Wilkerson is a Black American illustrator who was born in Denver and is currently based in Maryland. He believes that there is healing in storytelling, and that it is the job of creatives to contribute to that cause. His career began in the animation industry and he has worked as a designer on various projects for clients such as Hulu and Cartoon Network.